Legends of the Sanctuary Tree
Book Two

In the

Light

Of the

Moon

To Teresa
I wish you
joy!

Amanda
10-20-12

AMANDA MORGAN

Sketches by Lynne Wenick

Burnt Sage
Quality Publishers
P.O. Box 1504
Boring OR
97009

IN THE LIGHT OF THE MOON

Published in the United States of America by:

Burnt Sage Publications
P.O. Box 1504
Boring OR 97009

Cover design by Gary Randall / Precision Artists
Burnt Sage Logo & Back Cover design by Mike Province
Cover and interior images © 2012 by Lynne Wenick

www.amandamorganbooks.com

ISBN: 978-1-47016-099-9

For my daughters
~
The Lights of my life.

Acknowledgements

Just as an archaeological project moves slowly and methodically from the present to the past to chronicle changes in man's lifeways, so too does this series of tales. Each ensuing novel digs deeper into the past of characters introduced in the previous story.

Just as life moves, not always slowly or methodically, from the present to the future, so too do our individual lives change. To those who have gone since I began the first novel in this series, know that I miss you. I pray that wherever your starwalk takes you there will be gods to welcome you with love, laughter, and peace.

As always, I am humbly grateful for the unwavering support and encouragement of my daughters Linda, Laura, and Lisa; my Beth, my Don, and my grandchildren. Their questions and counsel are invaluable.

My sister, Lynne's, illustrations are again a welcome, heartfelt, addition to the story and I thank her for her input. To Gary for taking her beautiful painting and turning it into a gorgeous cover, to Jeremy for his help in marketing and to Mike Province for his techno-advice, I am indebted to all of you.

As before, I sincerely appreciate the feedback of the several friends upon whom I have prevailed to read and edit the manuscript.

You have my heart, I've loved you for always.

Come take my hand, we'll share all our days

In sunshine we'll dance through meadows of flowers.

In dark times we'll laugh in the light of the moon

~Benjamin Adam~

PROLOGUE

The black band of asphalt crossed and crossed again the white ribbon of tumbling water to form a vivid, dynamic braid connecting the small towns in the Cascade foothills to the Columbia River forty miles to the southeast. Jill turned left off State Highway 97 just where the exuberant little Methow River met the staid and mighty Columbia. She saw, with only casual interest, the small car that had followed her for the past few miles had also turned onto the narrow road that snaked northwest through the deep green valley.

She sonorously addressed the image in the rear-view mirror. "Fellow traveler. On this desolate and boring stretch of thoust journey ye knoweth not that ye followeth the famed (and I dare say quite fabulous) Archaeologist Jill Reade, who do returneth to her digs after accepting—after she hath accepteth—a small, but significant, archaeological challenge. *Digs*. Get it? Yuk yuk yuk. Never mind. By the end of the coming summer, said famed personage shall knoweth all. Well...about some things anywayth."

She passed the large sign that tallied the number of deer killed on the road so far this year and set the cruise control at five miles below the speed limit. "It's a *ceiling* not a *floor*!" her Aunt Tiersie had always said when she caught her going over the limit. Never mind ceilings and floors, Jill had often heard stories of how quickly a deer would jump in front of a car. "Chase you down and *make* you hit 'em!" the locals often said. Still, she didn't want to be responsible for adding to the rising count no matter the blame.

She checked her mirror. She'd passed through the tiny communities of Methow and Carlton but was still a few miles from the larger settlement of Twisp. The other car stayed behind her, not tailgating but not passing when given the chance either. She passed a green mile-marker that told her she hadn't made much progress towards home. She was tempted to hurry and could make strong arguments for doing so. She ticked off a few on her fingers.

One, she'd driven this road many times without mishap; two, visibility was excellent—broad daylight with the afternoon sun not yet lengthening the shadows of the surrounding hills; three, the deer were having their afternoon naps—it would be a couple of hours before they started moving between the river and the apple orchards that nudged the verges of the road; and, most importantely, she was bursting with excitement—could hardly wait to tell her husband, Lane, that Professor Martin had agreed to send a crew to help excavate the old homestead at Wolf Creek as soon as the ground thawed.

Another mile marker, another sixty-five seconds. Brother! Was the clock even working in Lane's trusty old Suburban? She'd opted to take this rig because it climbed the dirt road that led to her father-in-law's cabin much easier than did her little car but it was showing signs of age and now she was second-guessing that earlier decision.

Wham! The stag had bounded over the guardrail from below the road and landed smack in the lane ahead. She couldn't have avoided him. She jerked to the shoulder, jumped from the rig, ran to the guardrail and threw up.

The car that had followed so patiently eased to a stop behind the Suburban. The driver walked casually to the front and inspected the crumpled grill while he waited for her to compose herself. He held out a yellowed business card and offered his assistance.

Jill, distracted and rattled, shook her head and murmured a thanks then focused on punching the cell phone buttons that would connect her to the local Washington State Patrolman—a lifelong valley resident and close friend of Lane's—and quickly grew impatient with his questions; Was she hurt? Was the car drivable? Was it off the road? Was the deer dead? Was *it* off the road?

"Good *grief,* Andy. Can you just be on your way and ask questions when you get here?!"

"I *am* on my way, Jill. This is actually a *mobile* phone. Technology has advanced to the point that even *we* now have the capacity to receive calls, talk to people, and keep both hands on the steering wheel, all at the same time. Sumpthin, huh?"

Jill squeaked into the phone, "Jill's evil twin, Pill, speaking. Must hang up. Jill must phone husband now. Good bye."

Before she could punch in Lane's number the dark stranger cleared his throat behind her. "Excuse me, Miss. Would you like to look at that deer?"

"Me? No! Good *Heavens,* no!"

"I think you'd ought to. It landed right at the edge of that bench, just where it drops to the water.

You can get down there easily enough. Just stay back away from the bank when we get there."

He wasn't demanding. If he'd been so her warning bells would have clanged like St. Mary's on a Sunday morning and she'd have hit *Redial* without another thought. He seemed to simply assume she would follow where he led.

"The fact that you 'think I'd ought to' is no compelling reason for me to go clambering around below the road, following you to look at a dead deer, and fall off a cliff into the river. It *is* dead, is it not?"

"It is dead. Your reaction to killing it indicates you are a sensitive woman. My people always say a prayer after killing one of God's creatures, especially the deer. We believe they carry the souls of our loved ones until they can move on to their appointed place in the...hereafter. Perhaps you would like to pray for the soul this stag was carrying before your friend the state patrolman arrives."

"How did you...?" Jill tried to recall her exact conversation with Andy but couldn't remember saying anything specific. "Oh never mind. 'Lead on, McDuff'. We have a minute before he gets here."

Jill punched in the number for Lane's cell phone and let it ring until the message came on. "Hey, Hon. I've just hit a deer. No, I didn't. A deer just hit me. I'm okay, the 'Burb is drivable, I think. Andy is on his way.

"I schlepped the supplies up to your dad's cabin with no mishaps. Everyone is well up there. Then I almost made it home. Halfway nearly. I'm just upriver from the Leighton place. I'm going to scramble down the bank to look at a dead deer now. Go figure. I love you. I'll phone with an update after Andy gets here. Great news from Professor Martin, by the way."

The stranger squatted near the head of the buck and, gripping the antlers, reverently moved the head into a more natural position. Jill gazed at the still beautiful creature. Had he jumped a moment earlier she might have been able to miss him. On the other hand, a half-second later and he would have been in her lap. "Thank you, God, for that," she breathed and closed her eyes in a slow blink.

"Jill?"

"Down here, Andy!"

"What are you doing down there?" asked her friend as he stepped across the guardrail and started down the bank. "Was it not dead?"

"It was...is, but this man said I had to pray for it."

"What man?"

Jill looked around. "Check his car. He's parked behind the 'Burb. He was behind me when I hit it and said I had to come pray for it! He can't be gone 'cause he was right here just a prayer ago!"

"Yours is the only rig up there, Jill. I parked the cruiser behind the 'Burb."

Andy had been working his way down the bank using the tall willows and sarvisberry clumps to steady his descent just as Jill had done. He rested a hand on her shoulder. "You okay?"

"Of course I'm okay. I'm certainly not hallucinating, if that's what you mean."

Andy smiled but didn't belabor the point. "What I mean is, two back legs are tucked under his body, one front leg is bent back alongside his ribcage; where is this guy's other front leg? What'd you do, Jill, chase down a three-legged deer?" he teased.

"Don't joke, Andy. I'm just sick about this. I can still see that poor deer flying through the air. Of course he had four legs. I'm, as certain of that as I am that there was a coppery-colored smallish car behind me with a dark-skinned driver who made me come down here to pray for it—the deer not his car. 'God's creature', he called it. Maybe he just wanted the venison. Maybe he was an animal-rights activist and was going to kill me for killing the deer and you got here too fast," she added flippantly.

"It wasn't too fast if that was his plan," said the trooper soberly as he tried to move the large stag. "Can you give me a hand here? Not squeamish, are you?"

"Yes. Matter of fact, I am. I like to get my meat at a super market that doesn't harm animals in the farm-to-table process."

Despite her qualms and her friend's derision she grabbed a hoof and together they tugged at the carcass. The sandy riverbank began to slide beneath their feet and both jumped forward to firmer ground. They turned to look behind them at the broken bank and rushing water. Ends of wooden planks and pieces of animal hide protruded from the fresh earth.

"Yel-lo, yel-lo, yel-lo!" mused the trooper. "Looks like when this guy landed he drove that leg clean through the top of an old bear den or something. That's why we couldn't see it."

"You couldn't *see* it because it's subterranean."

"I didn't mean the den, Smarty Pants. I meant that's why we couldn't see this guy's foreleg."

Jill knelt on the edge of the bank and leaned over to examine the boards. "This isn't a bear's den, Andy." She was assertive now, the dead deer forgotten.

"That wood has been sawn. And look at this edge of hide; it's rotten but this long side is too straight to have simply rotted where it was dragged and eaten by another critter.

"Wait!" she blurted as her friend reached towards a piece of wood. "Don't yank them out. I'd like to scratch around to see what else is there."

"I'd like you to get away from the edge of that bank. You fall over and Lane'll strip *my* hide—straight and true! Besides, it's just detritus left by poachers or the road builders."

"Too deep for the first and too far from the road for the second, I'd think. Our faster-than-normal spring run-off eroded the bank. By this time next spring all of this would have been in the Columbia if we hadn't found it. That man and his deer brought us to an archaeological site, Andy. Maybe his ancestors hid here. Hey... maybe it was one of Chief Joseph's hideouts."

"He didn't come this far west and you just cut it out. You're making the hair on the back of my neck stand up and whistle *Outer Limits*. Either you're crazy or this is weird. Cops don't like weird. Crazy we handle every day. Tell me about that other driver."

Jill closed her eyes and concentrated on the image of the man who'd urged her to scramble down the road bank.

"He was darkish...Native maybe...probably. Something he said...something about...Oh, I can't remember. Anyway, light buff-colored shirt, suede or such high-quality micro-fiber that it looked like real buckskin...faded neckerchief that was probably bright and multi-colored when it was new...silkish, not cotton, certainly. Earthy I'd say if I had to use just one word for him."

Andy cocked his head. "What about the car? Make? License number? State, even? You're a trained observer, Jill. Help me out, here."

"I don't even know that it had a license plate. And I've already told you...smallish, oldish, brownish ...copper-colored more like...white sport stripe on the hood...thinnish stripe and maybe a bit crooked...not a broad stripe that goes all the way up and back along the top like you see sometimes....

Actually, now this *is* weird, I looked in my mirror once and saw a chestnut horse with a white blaze right on the road behind me. I did a double take and it was really only that little car, but *that* was creepy. After I hit the deer I was busy throwing up so didn't pay attention to him or his car. He'd been behind me since before the turnoff but I couldn't say how much before or why he didn't pass when he could have.

"Here. He gave me his card." Jill took the worn yellowed paper from the pocket of her blazer and handed it to the patrolman.

"No phone number," he said examining the card. "Did you read this?"

"No. I told you. I was busy. Why?"

"It says *Ben Smith. Machinery Building and Repairs. Eden. Wolf Creek.*

"Hey! You okay?"

Jill could only stare at her friend and move her head from side to side in a slow negative gesture.

"No. No I'm not," she said quietly. "Ben Smith lived on Wolf Creek a long time ago. It was his ghost who haunted Belle's Creek Station until last spring."

ONE

Wrinkles came early to the faces of the Meadow People. Chief Sun and his Brothers of the Air—Rain and Wind—made certain it was so. Sun and the Great God of All blessed her people with the lines so they could easily recognize them when they arrived in the afterlife. Walk Ahead said that was so, but he also asserted that people, too, could use the lines to identify the families of the Meadow People and of Others. He studied the faces of visitors with great intensity and often won bets he'd placed on their heritage. How that man loved to place bets!

Gray Willow fingered the deep creases that began at the corners of her eyes and spread outward to her hairline. She traced the fine lines that covered her face like the bark of the ancient trees at the water's edge. She ached at the memory the gesture brought. Upon waking each morning, Walk Before would lightly stroke her face and thank the gods for her in his prayers. It was only one of the many things she would miss about her husband.

She had tawny skin and large round eyes that were the color of Beaver's coat. For more than two winters she had carried her daughter, Walk Before's daughter, on her back, wrapped snuggly in the cradleboard. The cradleboard had a slab of bark affixed to the top that covered the baby's head and much of her face to protect it from the assault of their great chiefs, Sun and Rain, so the child's dark forehead eventually took on a slightly flattened shape. Because of this distinctive shape, Gray Willow knew she would be able to identify the child she sought.

They had come in the darkest hour of the night, those riders bent on destruction. Three men of her family had died in the melee; one of those, her beloved husband. Three babies were taken, one of them her daughter.

The other mothers, grieve though they did, had more children, had husbands to fetch them babies again. But Grey Willow, with no more husband, no daughter to raise in the ways of her people, no child to support her in her later years, was compelled to go in search of her child, taking with her only the pieces of her broken heart.

She knew with a certainty that she would never again see her home on the river her people called Ka-la-poo-ya. That river, wide and frightening, meandered deep and swift through the expansive valley so she had not crossed it on her trek. She reasoned that the thieves who stole her child would avoid it as well, choosing instead a path closer to the foothills; a path that crossed many smaller streams eagerly rushing to join the larger Ka-la-poo-ya as she flowed towards Cold Maker; a path that provided birds and fish for trail food and trees for cover.

The trail of the raiders took her upstream, climbing gradually towards the hills where steep narrow canyons cradled the headwaters of her home river. She had heard about these hills and the strange lands beyond—lands that were beyond the reach of Cold Maker.

She'd often sat outside the glow of the firelight and listened to travelers entertain the men of her family with tales of a land where Chief Sun allowed Chief Rain to visit only during the dark moons. They told of Others who dug their homes into the ground to protect themselves from the heat and light and wind.

She had smiled in derision at that. Chief Rain laughed at holes her sisters dug into their land. He filled them in before any one of them could burn the location into her memory with the hope of finding it again later. And imagine the digging stick she would have to make to remove enough of the sticky soil to dig an underground room as big as the one Walk Before had built for her out of grasses and bark.

The raiders' trail turned again towards Cold Maker and her home river joined one that was even larger and more frightening. Then the scent faded and vanished. Still she searched—sometimes nearer to death than to her prey, sometimes sheltered by those who encouraged her to linger. But a good meal or a long sleep was the only gift she would accept before resuming her search.

She trudged the ridgelines protected by the cloak of Darkness until nearly time for a new Chief Sun to awaken. Then she crept to the creek bottoms, drank her fill, ate what green browse or soft roots she might find there, and retreated again to the ridges. Here she sang her prayer song in a silence that matched the depths of her despair then hid among the trees to sleep until Chief Sun died his next death.

She had reached the large plain where the valley river met with a still greater one. The delta was filled with the lodges of many different peoples and Grey Willow slipped among them watching for her daughter, listening for a familiar cry. Answers to a few well-placed questions directed her up the river towards where Chief Sun awakened each day and for many nights now she had followed a river broad and still.

The wide, worn path told her this was an important trade route and, though the going was easier here, she stepped with greater care. The understory had changed. Gone were the thorny berry thickets and the clumps of bracken. Plants here were less lush and leafy; drier with woody stems and smaller leaves. Less greenery meant less cover so now she must spend more time choosing a well-protected sleeping spot.

On this day Gray Willow woke to the blackness of early night. She rested where she'd wakened, cursed herself for a fool—a *tired* fool and soon to be a tired *hungry* fool—for sleeping through the time when there was light enough to see her way to a creek. It would be impossible to find a path through the scrub until the stars and the moon had attained their full brilliance. Never mind, she would close her mind to the hunger and thirst, grumble at herself for oversleeping, and pray for her daughter's safety.

The footfalls were quiet but she heard them all the same—several men breathing heavily with the weight of a burden. She made out the shapes of two men supporting a third struggling towards her through the darkness. They passed so near she was certain they would step on her and she held her breath—closed her eyes lest they reflect the pale light of the rising moon. The invalid gave a sharp cry of pain and would have fallen had the men not tightened their holds.

Gray Willow's eyes flew open and she gasped in surprise. The men were so focused on their burden her sound went unnoticed. She regained her self-control and watched the men gently lower the woman then sweep the ground with bare hands, making a place for her to rest. Gray Willow had grown to womanhood believing Others had no feelings for their women, but these two Other men were certainly taking care of this woman. She watched as the younger of the men knelt and spoke soothingly to the woman. The older man, an elder brother perhaps, watched the path behind for the danger that drove them through the darkness. Again the woman gasped in pain and Gray Willow could no longer stay still.

She rose from her place at the trunk of the tree and moved towards the three travelers. The men raised their lances, gesturing at the apparition that seemed to be floating towards them from the heart of the tree. Gray Willow ignored the fearful thrusts and brave posturing to kneel beside the laboring woman.

She placed her left ear against the enlarged belly and listened for sounds of distress from the womb. She shrugged the buffalo bladder from her shoulder and shoved it towards the older man, motioning for him to fetch water. She took from her medicine bag the leaves of a berry plant and rolled and squished a leaf between her sinewy fingers to release some of its juice then pressed it to the mouth of the woman. She watched her chew then swallow the whole leaf.

Gray Willow raised a shoulder in an imperceptible shrug. She had learned to make a tea with the leaves but reckoned wisely that, under these circumstances, if tea was good the leaf itself was just as good. Besides, the men were nervous. They would neither make a fire to heat water for tea nor wait for the leaves to steep in the icy water from the river.

Gray Willow knew the men would not understand her words so directed them in silence. They would do her bidding without question so long as they were frightened. Should she speak or otherwise betray her humanity they would be more likely to kill her than to tolerate the assertiveness of so strange an apparition. Their fear of what lay behind them was different from their mistrust of her only in that she was here before them. And she was just as certain as they that what was behind them would soon be here as well.

She pointed at the one she thought of as Husband. He jumped as if struck by her walking stick. She directed him to the feet of his wife and showed him where to massage the bottom of first one then the other.

Elder Brother took so long to bring water she had begun to think he might have bolted to save himself, but he did return, bringing the buffalo bladder full of good, cool drinking water. She showed him how to help Husband massage the feet of Wife then turned again to the woman.

Gray Willow dripped water onto the lips of the woman to slake her thirst then stepped back into the darkness. Here, beside her tree, she performed a much-shortened version of her cleansing ritual and stepped softly through the rhythm of her prayer. Finished, she paused to raise her eyes to the night sky and arch her eyebrows. Tonight's prayer had turned into one of acceptance rather than of petition.

Birthing this Other's child was not what she would have chosen to do. These people or their kin had killed her husband and stolen her child—the only two things in the world that had mattered to her. Was it fair of her gods to ask her to help bring one more of them into the world? Fair to ask Gray Willow to delay her quest for her own child in order to help this woman? She had seen birthings take days and days. It could mean facing even more danger than she had faced to now. Who knew what followed these three through the forest? Yet her training as a Healer and her belief in a loving Great God of All would not let her walk across the moonlit scrubland and leave them to their fate. Perhaps it was this Great God of All who had caused her to oversleep such a short time ago.

When she returned to the people on the ground the two men started as if seeing a ghost they believed had been exorcised. She again pressed her ear to the woman's belly and listened to the sounds within. She wanted to raise the woman into a squatting position to ease the path of the child but the woman was weak and her legs would not support her.

She motioned the men to carry the woman into a patch of moonlight and when they had done so, she motioned them away into the darkness. Alone with the woman she used the cool water to wash the Life Portal and was suddenly doused with Life Water. Only because she reached out so quickly was she able to catch the boy baby who shot from the woman as if he understood the urgency of the situation.

Gray Willow washed the tiny face with a dab of the cold water and, without cleaning him, tucked him inside his mother's skirt. She drew a green willow twig from her medicine pouch and used her teeth to peel off a narrow strand of bark. She tied knots with the woody string in two places along the Mother Cord then briefly kneaded the abdomen of Wife.

She checked on the boy to make sure he was breathing then motioned the men back to the scene. She was glad to see they had not been idle but had used their cloaks to fashion a sling they could drape over their necks and shoulders so the tired woman and her child could ride between them. They helped the woman stand and Gray Willow steadied her while the men took a place on either side. As soon as the woman had sunk into the sling, the men moved forward into the moonlit night. Gray Willow delayed long enough to raise her eyes Heavenward in the most uncertain of thanksgivings then set off in pursuit of the four.

She was hard pressed to keep pace with the men, even burdened as they were. Seeing a patch of bright moonlight ahead Gray Willow nearly sprinted to catch them. She tugged at the sling and when they turned to her she gestured to the ground. She thought they would ignore her but they did as she directed.

They gently lowered the mother then Husband moved cautiously ahead while Elder Brother retraced their steps back along the path. Though both stepped lightly and quickly, Gray Willow's ears picked up the cadence of their step step step pause, step step step pause.

She checked her patients. The baby seemed to be sleeping comfortably, resting there on his mother's abdomen. She was puzzled by the still-full feeling of the womb; concerned that the afterbirth had not been expelled. She resisted the urge to tug at it and, as before, relied on the Great God of All to guide her hand. She stood and the men were at her side. Without hesitation they lifted the sling and strode quickly onward.

So fast was the pace that several times she thought of dropping where she was and facing alone the danger that drove them so hard. Twice she saw one of the men look back at her then quicken his step.

She was light-headed and near to fainting when she realized she could discern a pale band on the horizon that heralded another awakening of Chief

Sun. Surely, they would be nearing the end of their trek?

She was so intent on muttering her morning prayer that she nearly stepped into the back of Elder Brother who had stopped, his head cocked as if listening. They waited silently for the briefest of moments when the man twittered like a bird.

His call was immediately answered by a similar sound and they plunged through a grove of willows to the shore of the great river. Here a large canoe with many paddlers was bobbing with the current and the two men hustled the woman, with her baby, on board the craft. The paddlers were shoving off when the woman cried out and stretched her hand to Gray Willow.

Before she could raise her voice in protest, Gray Willow was dragged into the midst of writhing bodies. She watched the paddlers' massive shoulders strain against the rushing current to get the canoe away from the shoreline as fast as possible. She held her breath and squatted as if a stone on the bottom of the overcrowded boat, fearful that a bump into one paddler would cause others to pitch overboard.

A coarse patty, something that smelled like smoke and fish, was pressed into her hand. She didn't even try to remember when she'd last eaten and normally would have wolfed down the offering with gratitude. Now however, while acting as a Healer it was imperative that she fast, denying all demands of self until her immediate services were no longer needed.

The movement of the canoe changed subtly from rollicking turbulence to a rhythmic roll and Gray Willow could see that they had reached a deeper, slower current and were now moving upstream. The still water reflected the moonlight in a shimmering silver path that stretched from the far shore to the very edge of the canoe. Nowhere on her small river at home was there a stretch of water so still and so wide that the moon could make such a path—a path on which Walk Before now came towards her from the far bank. She knew him for his bearing; the tilt of his head, the slow rhythm of his gait, the gentle way he reached for her. She felt him lightly stroke her face, thanking the gods for her in his prayer.

TWO

Chief Sun was high in the sky when Gray Willow was kicked awake. The paddlers were already reversing the craft when she jumped for the bank where Husband and Elder Brother waited with their burden. She couldn't know if they, like she, had slept through the entire journey upstream but the pace they set suggested they were refreshed enough to hurry towards their destination.

They trudged beside the Great River for the rest of the day, sometimes towards the waking place of Chief Sun, usually towards Cold Maker. The rushing water roared a threat to any who might place a foot too close to the steep edge of a path that was no path at all. Wind carried grit and dust to pepper their skin, clog their lungs, blind their eyes.

They climbed over boulders bigger than her lodge and ducked under bushes that she didn't know. Just before dark the men found a thicket of tall, leafy shrubs, crept inside, and gently lowered the woman to the ground. They curled beside her, trusting her to listen for approaching danger, and fell immediately to sleep.

Gray Willow checked the baby and helped him suckle at his mother's breast then fed the woman more berry leaves. She was still concerned that the afterbirth hadn't been expelled and she mentioned that to the Great God of All in her silent prayer. Then she, too, curled into a ball and slept.

The second day was worse than the first. The river below thundered so boldly it seemed to Gray Willow as if the sky and the river had traded places and it made her dizzy. Each boulder was larger and more difficult to scale than the last and the unrelenting wind was biting and bitter. And oh, how her body needed sustenance.

Towards the end of the second day they turned from the riverside, this time walking towards the sleeping place of Chief Sun. The path broadened through a small delta where a smaller river rushed madly into the great one. Then, once again, they took a barely discernable path and began climbing rapidly.

This little stream, still on her right, sang a different song than did the mighty one. This was shallow water, hurtling downhill, tumbling over rocks and between steep banks; but should she lose her footing or her grip, the result would be the same.

The food they offered had given her strength though she'd not eaten even a crumble, but that strength had waned long ago. Only her concern for the woman ahead of her kept her feet moving one in front of the other.

She focused on her prayers to keep her mind off her own tired body and reminded herself to not mumble them aloud. Yesterday the men had stopped and, gesturing tersely, scolded her for praying aloud though she hadn't believed they could hear her whisperings over the roar of that river. She directed her breathing towards the back of the new mother and saw her head bob in sleep. She used her eyes to bore through the blankets and watch the woman's heart beat.

The men stepped to either side of a log that lay in the middle of the path. Worn flat and smooth, silvery with age, it filled the pathway from just beneath the woman's sling to where Grey Willow trudged. She stepped to the top of the log and walked with ease behind her patient.

When the men stopped to rest, Gray Willow, at last coming to the realization that the log on which she had been walking was an unusually long one, looked behind her. No log stretched across and between the boulders over which the men had just scrambled. Neither was there now a wide, silvery log stretching ahead of them.

Again they turned to follow a smaller creek, leaving the major tributary behind. Trees and shrubs spoke to her in an unknown language. They grew in dense profusion along the sides of the little stream and made it impossible to stay on dry land.

The men took to the creek bed and Gray Willow, after a moment of hesitation, stepped into the icy water. The chill jolted her awake and numbed her feet to the smarting of the pebbles. She yearned for the creeks of home, lazy and murky, into which she could wade to pull tasty roots with her toes by playfully wriggling them into the cool soothing ooze.

The men waded upstream to a tiny sandy beach where two boulders marked the beginning of a trail. Passing between the markers in her scramble from the rocky creek bed, Gray Willow saw that one of the boulders bore the marks of a Holy Man. She couldn't take the time to study the image pecked into it. Perhaps, if they stopped to rest, the men would allow her to come back and pray at the stone.

Elder brother made a calling sound. It could have been a whistle, she thought, except that it came from his throat like a scream. It was not a sound she recognized but the call was answered immediately and soon Others were rushing down the path to meet them, to ease their burden, to welcome them home. Gray Willow herself was hoisted by two men and hurried along the trail, her feet dangling several inches above the ground.

The new mother was rushed with her son into a warm, dark, smoky tipi and Gray Willow was chucked in behind her as if she was simply baggage Wife had brought for the journey. Immediately on Gray Willow's heels came a grandmother, older than the mother of Gray Willow but not so old as to be ready to be sent into the forest on her final journey. The weakened wife, now resting on a bed of animal hides, cried out in pain and Gray Willow rushed to her side. With the help of the old woman, she eased the birth of a twin—a gusty noisome daughter.

Gray Willow rubbed both babies with rabbit fur dipped in the warm herbed water brought in by Grandmother. She pondered the twins. It was as if the firstborn recognized the gravity of their plight so came quickly and made no immediate demands on his mother. Did he, cradled there on his mother's abdomen, draw strength and courage from the proximity of the sibling with whom he had been entwined for so long? And did his closeness, so near that she could hear his heartbeat, keep the girl quiet in the womb until she could face a saner, safer, world? The daughter's first breath, a shout of complaint and censure, testified to her resentment of the extra confinement. And here was now a mother with two babies while Gray Willow herself still had none.

A young girl, not yet old enough for the ceremony, stooped through the flap of the tipi. She lugged a battered black iron pot half filled with hot, aromatic soup to a tripod that stood over a small depression in which burned a bed of ashy coals. She glanced at the new mother who was being attended by Grandmother then slipped stealthily to the mat where Gray Willow was bathing the babies. She gazed at the newborns in awe then looked at Gray Willow. Her eyes widened and she bolted from the shelter.

Gray Willow shivered and watched the dark sky through the opening at the top of the tipi. It had been raining. Not the gentle rain of her homeland but a thunderous downpour in which she dreamed she could hear the startled wail of her daughter, frightened by each resounding clap of Thunder.

She was sweating from the horrors of the nightmare and was reluctant to close her eyes again lest it recur. She wanted to take a walk to the trees and knew she wouldn't be able to wait till morning when the little girl would come again to take her there. She wrapped her feet in her tattered ribbons of fur, stepped from the tipi, and followed the path the girl had shown her a few hours before.

She strolled slowly back to the tipi, taking deep breaths of the newly cleansed air. Nights were getting much colder and she pondered her chance of surviving a winter of searching. And where would she begin her quest this time? These people had led her so far from her course she'd not be able to pick up the thread of her journey. She'd have to begin again but could do that only after she'd figured out how to re-cross that great river. Yet her daughter called. The dream had strengthened that certainty. She stood before her most recent home, raised her eyes to the Great God of All, spread her arms in supplication, and stood silent, ready to receive His guidance.

Above her to the right, the clouds parted to reveal a nearly full moon in that part of the sky where Chief Sun died at the end of each day. To her left, the moist air captured the moonlight and mirrored it back to her, creating a narrow silver arc that completely bridged the valley side to side.

Unable to stifle the joy brought by the omen of the moonbow, Gray Willow began to hum her Gratitude Song, quietly though, so as not to wake any of the Others. She hummed and stepped and then, without being aware of the transition, burst into the song and the dance of her mothers. She was brought up short by the sound of a familiar cry in a distant tipi.

Gray Willow sat on the damp earth and watched the man draw symbols in the dirt with a stick. The girl with the flattened forehead, the one these Others called Redwing, played within her reach. Nearby, wary and watchful, squatted the woman who called herself Mother-to-Redwing.

The man's stick told Gray Willow he had been fishing the great river with his people when they were attacked by a group of horse riders who stole their medicine woman. In the ensuing chase one of the raiders dropped a small bundle of hides. The husband of Mother-to-Redwing heard a cry come from the bundle and stopped to retrieve it. He accepted the deformed child inside as a gift from one of his gods—an answer to one of his prayers—and he brought the baby home to his childless wife.

His people had assumed that the child and the raiders who had dropped her were of the Deformed

People from across the river. They were upset by the little servant girl's report of Gray Willow's similar deformity. They had come to him, demanding that he send away this stranger.

He was agitated now. His stick moved so rapidly through the drying soil that his lines were no longer sharp and, likewise, his meaning not always clear.

"You are her mother. You have come here to take her away," his stick accused.

"Mother-to-Redwing has nursed this baby, as one should cherish a gift from the gods, for ten moons." The old man dropped his stick and held up both hands, palms forward, fingers splayed, so that Gray Willow could count each and every moon if she wanted to. After giving her plenty of time to do so, the man picked up his narrative.

The stick showed Gray Willow that the new mother she herself had saved was the medicine woman taken by the raiders; that the healer's husband and elder brother had journeyed long to find the woman and bring her home—her and her wretched twins, children of Those With Flat Heads. With that name he spat and jabbed his stick sharply through the picture he'd just drawn. "Because of those babies, our healer is weak and cannot help her people now," his stick said. "The raiders had just as well killed all of us down there by the river that day.

"Will these children have flat heads like you and this child?" his stick asked. "Will you carry away the child this woman has mothered and go back to your raiders?"

Gray Willow held the eyes of the man. She had assumed these people were the same Others who had raided her village and stolen her daughter. Likewise, these Others thought it was her people who had made war on their fishing camp, stolen their medicine woman and tried to make her their own by planting their seeds in her. If that wasn't enough, these Others were certain Gray Willow would take away a child that, despite her difference, they had loved as their own for nearly a year. Yet they had not treated Gray Willow the way many Others would have done to someone likely to be the cause of so much pain. They had let her live.

Remembering some of the things Walk Before had said about the many differences in the ways of Others, she thoughtfully, respectfully, moved her hand through the man's symbols and, with her old, crooked finger, began drawing her own symbols to tell of the raid on her own village and of her quest to find her child.

Like the old man she spoke while she drew. The cadence of her words, spoken to the rhythm of her finger strokes, mesmerized her listeners. "The two born to your Medicine Woman will not look like me or my child. I am not of the raiders," she finished.

"The Great God of All took away my child and gave her to the woman who calls herself Mother-to-Redwing. I must accept His decision. If you will allow it, I will bind myself to your people. I will help your medicine woman. Until she is strong I will be healer to your people. And I will be Nurse-to-Redwing into the forever."

THREE

She was named Sia for her coppery skin and her deep-red berry-like mouth. She was proud to be named for the bearberry—one of the plants that were so important to the health of her family. Perhaps it was the sacredness of this shrub that made her mother, Redwing, give her such an honored name.

Her dark hair fell evenly from the top of her head straight to below her shoulders. Her mother would pinch Sia's front locks tightly between two willow twigs that had lain in the stream for a full night and then, taking a firebrand from the cooking pit, she would singe the hair from in front of her daughter's eyes. Now it framed her round face and accentuated her pert little nose.

Early this morning Sia had carefully maneuvered along the stream's edge, careful to not fall into the cold water and disturb Salmon, while she followed in the footsteps of her mother and her young sister, Tsaltsaleken. Chief Sun had warmed her shoulders and the trilling of Meadowlark had made her smile. Redwing was telling them of their mothers and grandmothers while the three of them gathered clusters of the tiny blue elderberries, all coated so beautifully with that characteristic white powder.

Redwing told of the fever that, long ago, had halved the number of their lodges; of the women who died and of their sisters who were taken as wife by a brother-in-law or an uncle; of the men who died, leaving their wives, mothers, and daughters to take their own lives rather than risk the alternatives—starvation perhaps, or the humiliation of being sold for slaves to Others or as wives to the white men—Those People—who rode into these foothills looking for furs or gold.

Those People were adventurers, Redwing had said. While a few were good men, most were the rejects of their own society. It was while she was telling of bounty hunters who were paid by Those People to take Indian scalps that they heard the hoofbeats. By the clang of iron on rock they realized, too late, that the oncoming horse was shod—a custom of the very people they were discussing. It was as if they could be summoned by the speaking of their name.

Redwing had dropped the basket of berries, grabbed one child under each arm and ran the few short steps towards a cut in the bluff. She fell forward, using her momentum to pitch the girls further forward and down the bank. "Run!" she'd hissed, "Hide!" Then she rose, spinning, to face the danger.

Redwing was beautiful. Her hair, the color of the black bird for which she was named, fell straight and thick from the slightly elevated crown of her head. Her eyes, made elliptical by the unusual shape of that head had captured the imagination of more than a few suitors. Her beauty would keep her alive while she was bartered and sold—won and lost—from hand to grubby hand until she was no longer so. She would will her soul to die long before her natural beauty could fade. Redwing knew this as Truth.

The rope was already flying through the air when Redwing thrust her digging stick with a strength made supernatural by the willing. Straight and sturdy, it had been tempered in the embers of her own fire-pit and was stronger and sharper than any carried by all of the other women of her village. The lasso shushed past her ears and dropped over her shoulders. An imperceptible flick of the wrist tightened it at the perfect moment—one learned through years of practice by the killer—to render a captive immobile. It forced home the digging stick. Redwing's dark eyes gazed steadily into the cruel ones of the bounty hunter. Blood and bubbles oozed through her half-smile at the look of anger on the face of the rider. Her smile broadened into a grimace. Her spirit hovered ever so briefly as her body, devoid of life, folded to the ground. The spirit cupped her hands before her mouth, blew a gentle kiss towards her daughters, and wafted gently towards the sun. Earth resisted at first, then slowly accepted the blood of Redwing as it spread onto the carpet of tiny white elderberries.

FOUR

Her mother's desperate push sent Sia sliding down the rocky incline on her face. She grabbed tiny Tsaltsaleken by the hand and, blinded by blood, pain, and terror, sped with her through the tall brush. The small silvery leaves of the sage snagged her flying tresses. The barbed stems tore her bare arms and tugged at her doeskin dress. Sharp stones and spiny grasses ripped her shoeless feet leaving a bloody trail across the cruel surface of the landscape.

She tripped and again pitched forward to roll and tumble through the dust. The moment was one of such turbulence—legs and arms, brush and dust, hitting, bumping, flying—she thought she had been sent on a journey by Wind. Still clutching the hand of her sister, she was thrust against the slender trunk of Crab Apple.

The tree had gathered her sisters and made a chamber for the young girls—shaded, cool and quiet. Before Sia could wonder at Her presence here they heard the man outside, breathing hard and cursing. They heard his horse, milling and stomping, snorting a protest of the man's harsh handling. They huddled together, afraid to move, afraid to breathe, afraid to whisper a prayer for the safety of their mother, afraid even to weep for her absence lest the sound of a tear dropping to earth might reveal their presence.

When they woke, all was still. Not even Grasshopper was singing in the heat. Slowly, Sia rose and peeked cautiously between the slender weeping branches of the trees into the fading sunlight. The grass was higher than she remembered it being when they fell into the little den. She could not hear the creek that had giggled so cheerfully this morning. She remembered they had crossed it once on their way to the berry thicket but was it now before them or behind them?

Tsaltsaleken grabbed her arm and pointed. Far across the flat was Grandfather; old, stooped, and walking with a stick. He stopped to examine the ground then hobbled slowly on his way.

"Grandfather is looking for us," she whispered. "If we run and catch him he will tell us how to find our family."

The old man disappeared down a little wash. They had never seen this Grandfather at any of their camps but the girls hurried on in his wake. The trail they found would have been invisible had they not been so certain this was the spot where they had last seen him. A clump of dried grass was tamped and broken but nowhere in the deep dust of the hot scrubland could they find the mark of his walking stick or the print of a moccasin.

The frenzied activity caused the wound on Sia's face to bleed again and she stopped to gather a spider's web woven thickly beneath the leaves of the tsaltsaleken – the plant for which her sister had been named. She pressed it against her face to stop the bleeding.

Again Tsaltsaleken grabbed her arm and this time pointed to a spot in the dust. Something wet had dropped here. Sia knelt to finger the tiny spot. It was not her blood. Sweat, perhaps? Not theirs certainly, they were too young still. The girls circled the spot in ever-widening concentric circles. When they found a second drop they repeated the process until they had found a third. Though the tracking was still slow, they now had an idea of the direction the weeping Grandfather had taken.

Sia couldn't have said why she thought of him thus, or why she was certain he was a Grandfather rather than one of the witches sometimes sent by neighboring villagers to frighten their family away from prime hunting spots. Nor did she care to dwell on the reason the mysterious droplets did not immediately evaporate in the late afternoon heat.

Tear by tear the girls followed the trail of the old man. Several times Tsaltsaleken jumped up and pointed excitedly ahead but by the time Sia was able to wipe away the blood and focus on the horizon, there was no one ahead of them. At some point near the bottom of the draw she realized that they were now following a real path—or was this the work of Water, after a visit by Rain, seeking the company of his brothers and flowing to the stream? They crept along the gully, watching and listening for danger as they had been taught to do.

They reached the stream and Sia recognized the twin boulders where, long-ago, a wise man had pecked lines on the face of one of the rocks; a place where their own strange grandmother so often visited to say her prayers. Sia shoved Tsaltsaleken into the shadow of one of the boulders then slipped into the icy shoal to wash the blood from her face. Refreshed, she scanned the hillside above the creek then motioned Tsaltsaleken into the water. Staying beneath the overhang of the elderberry and chokecherry, the girls silently made their way upstream and along the path that led to their family village. She stood at a turning in the path and wrapped both arms protectively around her little sister.

Mourning fires had been lit and the drummers were singing their spirit-going-away songs. With a flash of insight Sia knew for whom they were singing. She knew from where the turbulent, life-saving, wind had come, she knew the name of Crab Apple and of Grandfather.

Mournful wailing came from the lodge of their mother's nurse. Sia's heart ached for her grandmother, the woman who called herself Nurse-to-Redwing. By custom, mothers and close grandmothers of the dead were barred from participating in burial preparations lest the spirit of the departed be made reluctant to leave Earth. However, Redwing's true mother had long ago given herself as slave to the woman who called herself Mother-of-Redwing, thus, unless the Holy man intervened, it would be Gray Willow's duty, and her agony, to prepare her own daughter's mutilated body for the Spirit-Going-Away ceremony.

Hand-in-hand the sisters made their way towards the drummers' circle. In the flick of an eyelid one of the drummers burst forth with a loud joyous song of thanksgiving. Startled, the other drummers halted their mournful dirge to gawk at him, only to join in his song when they, too, saw the girls on the path.

FIVE

Sia's heart had turned to stone. Her breath came in jagged spasms and she thought her chest would burst. Yet from somewhere inside herself she found the strength to sit stoically in the tipi of Grandfather Weh-ho Tan. She sensed rather than felt Tsaltsaleken trembling beside her and slipped her small arm around the smaller one's shoulder, holding her warmly just as her mother had done for Sia so many times. She would miss the earthly presence of her mother but knew that the spirit of The-One-Who-Is-Now-Gone would always be with her. She accepted without question that her mother's spirit was the wind that had blown the girls into the sheltering haven of Crab Apple. Even as she accepted, she ached for her mother's touch.

The-One-Who-Is-Now-Gone had often told of man's upwardly spiraling walk that begins below the earth, circles through this world of mortal beings, then, finally, wafts upwards to a life among the spirits. Death enhanced the essence of a person, she'd said. A loving person's soul grew more so, the wise grew wiser. And just as the spirit of a bad person became evil, one's enemies could develop great depths of ill will.

To shield them from this potential hostility, the girls had been whisked into the tipi of the chief; kept away from the remains of their mortal mother; cloistered here with only Grandfather and a distant grandmother to attend them until after the Feast-of-the-Dead. Grandfather had gently explained that a spirit's search for the path to its starwalk is confusing at first—so disorienting that the living would not speak her name for a full year lest her spirit think they were calling to her and thus distract her from her search.

"Sometimes a spirit must choose between fighting Hostiles and searching for way to starwalk. Sometimes a spirit will jump into body of deer or wapiti in order to more easily bound about in search of path and to avoid Evil Ones from below."

It would be unfair to the spirit of The-One-Who-Is-Now-Gone to ask it to protect these daughters from the spirits of the Hostiles at the same time she was making her own difficult transition. "We must take away need to fight—allow her spirit to search unimpeded for her path. We will protect you here until ceremonies are finished."

He worried that their mother's initial exertion on behalf of the girls might already have slowed the ascent of her spirit into the clouds. It would be important, therefore, for everyone to offer many prayers for her.

"Sho-Lan Ti, our holiest man, will direct Spirit-Going-Away ceremony. He will choose which women will have honor of fitting your mother for final rest. He will choose who will dig grave and who will cook for visitors. He will order cleaning of tipi of She-Who-Is-Now-Gone and will remove all belongings. He will apportion those things as he sees fit. None of these tasks need worry you.

Word of the death of their mother had spread quickly and many had come to help, he told them. First, the chosen women would cleanse her body with a mixture of herbs that would be uniquely her own. This would make her spirit forever recognizable when it visited members of her family who still lived.

While they worked, the women simultaneously chanted their own individual songs of death to the mutilated corpse. Each song would be in praise of the woman's beauty, her good deeds; her love for her husband, her daughters, her mother, and her people. Each song would thank She-Who-Is-Now-Gone for a kindness done, a gift given.

Sia knew the songs would help her mother find her starwalk, would alert the gods to the special value of the one now entering their sphere—and could keep a cleansing woman from thinking too deeply about her sad task.

Women not chosen to help with the cleansing would be preparing a feast that would signal the end of the three-day ritual—a final sacrament held so that all, stranger and loved one alike, could rejoice in their trust that The-One-Who-Is-Now-Gone had successfully found the path by which she could begin her final journey.

He explained that for three days the soul of their mother would be in danger from the spirits below the earth who would steal it if they could. In order to help frighten the Evil Ones, the drummers would drum and the women would sing. The large fires burning throughout the village would not be allowed to wane and The-One-Who-Is-Now-Gone would not for a single moment be left unattended.

Relatives, friends, and visitors, all going about their assigned roles in the ritual, added their own songs to those of the cleansing women so the drumming and the death songs throbbed through the village. The dismal cadence made Weh-ho Tan speak louder than he thought fitting and he paused often to give his throat a rest.

Just as grieving loved ones might tempt their mother's soul to linger, so too might belongings that had held a special place in her heart. Therefore, all of her earthly belongings would be removed from her home by the funeral director and his gravediggers.

The finest items were carried to her grave so they could provide comfort to her spirit on her starwalk; small items were given to the funeral director, the gravediggers, and cooks in payment for their efforts. With the exception of one cherished item for each of her daughters, all that remained would then be given to friends and neighbors. These two special items would be kept by the funeral director for a year before they would be passed to the girls in a gifting ceremony. This waiting period, like the name-speaking taboo, ensured that the memories evoked by the handling of so personal an item could not call back the spirit of their mother while it was still in a confused state.

It was indicative of the esteem the villagers held for The-One-Who-Is-Now-Gone, Grandfather had added, that nearly every man in the village came forward to help empty her tipi and to dig her grave.

Once their mother had been cleansed, dressed in her finest clothes, and fitted with new moccasins, the women would carry her to her own, now emptied, tipi. Only then would the people of the village be allowed to visit her. Again, each villager would say his own prayer for the newly released spirit. Like the songs before, the prayers would take the form of praise and thanks.

Sia twitched her nose and tried to take her mind from the pain of the gash she'd suffered that morning. Grandmother had put wet leaves over the wound and that had eased the worst of the burning but now her face, from the peak of her hairline to the tip of her nose, was in desperate need of attention. She focused her eyes on the lines of Grandfather's face and imagined herself a little spider, following the roads to this place or that.

Grandfather noticed the sharp scrutiny and called for the grandmother who sat without. He ordered food and warm tea for the girls and medicine for Sia's face. He sipped his own brew and watched over the edge of his tin cup while the girls ate. When the woman had gone, he resumed his lesson.

The spirit-going-away ritual, he explained, must be performed with exact correctness lest the spirit of the deceased be offended by an omission or a mistake in one of the steps. Only the women who had helped cleanse the body would carry it to her tipi to lie in peace until all who wished to had said their farewells. Then they, with the help of the gravediggers, would carry the burden to her final resting place. Here she would be placed in the ground, her head to the west, with her favorite belongings.

"Unlike our neighbors east of this place, our customs do not call for sacrifice of slaves, or lesser wives, or even favorite pack animals," he assured the girls. "We believe gods will provide those things as is their wisdom to do so."

Again, songs would be sung by the women, but quietly this time—low murmurs intended to ease the spirit's travel rather than the spirit-frightening noisome chants of the past two days. A lone drummer would stand with the gravediggers on one side of the grave. They would face the south, the direction from which the evil spirits might make one final attempt to steal the soul of The-One-Who-Is-Now-Gone. The women would stand opposite, eyes cast upon the body, watchful for spirit movement lest her soul had chosen to linger.

"Sho-Lan Ti will sprinkle blessed water over her and will make offerings to four winds and to sky and to earth. He is offering game to East so Chief Sun can feast as soon as he arises and offering grains to West so he has food before He sleeps. To North, he offers hides against the chill, and to South, feathers of Eagle to shade the site. To Sky he will offer smoke of sage bundle and to Earth, drops of water.

"Each offering to winds is a small bundle of these things in addition to herbs and medicines and gifts that spirit of She-Who-Is-Now-Gone will be pleased to present to other spirits she will meet along her way. He will tuck each bundle around her. He will say words of prayer to Mother Earth and to Father Sky and will ask Chief Sun to shine on her. Finally, he will sprinkle a handful of dust over She-Who-Is-Now-Gone. This is sign for attending women and gravediggers to complete burial.

"They will walk single-file around grave, men following women, all while singing of attributes of She-Who-Is-Now-Gone. After third time around, women will walk back to village. To look behind is forbidden. It is over.

"Sho-Lan Ti will again address She-Who-Is-Now-Gone. He will ask her to remain in spirit clouds. He will say he knows she could choose a difficult and arduous journey—return to beneath earth and begin life-spiral as another soul. He will ask that, should she do so, she choose a new life wisely and always remember with kindness, us who so loved this spirit now gone.

"Gravediggers will bury mortal remains of She-Who-Is-Now-Gone then they, like women, return to village, not looking back. Sho-Lan Ti will build small warming fire at head of resting place. It will be kept alight for one moon so her spirit can come and warm itself."

Sia was certain her sister slept now in the warmth and dimness of Grandfather's home. Her own lids drooped and her head had bobbed once or twice. She pulled the little one closer to her and again focused on the old man's face. Had the cadence of his narrative changed? His tone had certainly softened. It was as if he were no longer teaching the etiquette of the spirit-going-away ceremony but seeing his own burial ritual.

"Honored women go directly into cleansing hut to bathe with herbs and to drink purifying tea. This will remove death pollution that has fallen on them. Gravediggers now come to hut to bathe and drink tea. Finally, Sho-Lan Ti will return and himself be cleansed. Then Feast-of-the-Dead will begin."

Grandfather began to quietly sing a haunting melody. The old woman slipped into the tipi and murmured a barely audible question.

Grandfather shook his head slowly and almost smiled. "I could not have gone on much longer. Little One dropped off long ago. Strong one held to last word. You did not put enough medicine in tea—theirs or mine."

May your feet walk the earth in kindness,
May your spirit ride the winds with joy,
May your heart sing with thanksgiving,
And may you be one with the ALL.

May you ever have Love on your shoulder
May you always have Peace at your side
May you always have Them to protect you
And may you be one with the ALL.

SIX

'Briela wedged her back more snuggly against the gunwales of the little ship. She frowned towards the sails and sent forth a quick silent prayer that they stay full and fast. Dominic had told her not to worry. They would dock in San Francisco in less than a week and the baby wasn't due for another three. He would have two weeks, even more, God willing, to retain a mid-wife to attend her; to find a room to rent where she could have her lying-in and await her deliverance.

She had insisted he make those arrangements the moment they docked—even before he began his search for a ship that would eventually take them further north. When he chaffed at the prospect of a delay in his plans, she reminded him gently that he had, after all, promised all those things to her father.

Truth be told, she didn't expect their time in San Francisco to be any easier than that spent on this cramped clammy ship, bobbing for countless days out of Panama Harbor. They knew no one in San Francisco—no one in all of California. She had no heart for lying-in, either. She had always been exuberant, 'annoyingly active' her mother called her, but she was apprehensive about this birth so would accept confinement as a necessary element of the journey. She intended to be strong and supportive, nursing a robust son, when they reached the wild country of the upper Columbia River.

Dom had spoken many times of going west just as soon as his enlistment in the Army was served; voiced his intention to Christianize every savage that was native to the territory; every miner and every Yellow Devil who had found his way to the Oregon country from the East and the Far East.

She'd argued against all of it. She wanted him to stay in Charleston, build his own plantation perhaps. She had even come to accept the idea that he might go into a trade though the life of a tradesman's wife would be much less grand than the one she led at home as the debutante daughter of a plantation owner.

But even if a tradesman's wife, she would never let herself be so debased as to be unable to demonstrate, in all but the highest socially elite circles of the city, her skills as a hostess. A few doors would remain closed to her certainly, but snobbery wouldn't intimidate her. She would simply be creative. The idea of actually having to make an effort to achieve the status she sought quite intrigued her. She was certain she could become the hostess of events to which an invitation would be the most sought-after chit in a social season. She would simply charm Dom into staying in Charleston.

She was delighted, even a bit smug, when he set out for Ohio on the very day he was decommissioned from the Army. It pleased her that he was anxious to complete any unfinished family business there and return to Charleston for good. When he returned a few months later it was with boxes and crates and barrels of furnishings. She was somewhat dismayed when he insisted those containers remain tightly closed and referred to them as *provisions*. She took to her bed in shock the day after their wedding.

Daddy had taken Dom into the parlor and outlined his plan for the two of them. Dom would oversee the plantation just yonder from Daddy and Momma. When it was making money, Daddy and his friends would make Dom a full partner.

It was a most generous offer but Dom had declined. His trip to Ohio, he said, had convinced him that the diverging political policies of the industrialized New England states and the agricultural-dependent Carolina's would only—could only—grow more hostile. He didn't want to participate in the armed conflict he was sure would ensue.

She'd soon realized she had conceived a child on their wedding night; another weapon in her arsenal she'd thought, but another error in judgment. He didn't even consider changing his mind.

Now she watched the gray sails butt the gravid sky and wondered if she could have justified a refusal to travel. It was only a few months into the marriage...her first child...so many additional preparations...her mother, her mother's mother, and her mother before her, all notoriously weak child-bearers. Was it not irresponsible and selfish of him to drag her along on this grand plan of his?

When it was clear he could not change Dom's mind, Daddy had taken them into the library of his fine white house and spoken most severely. He allowed it wasn't proper to lay this kind of information before a woman, but he wanted Gabriela to be able to find her way back to Charleston if something of a disastrous nature, God forbid, should befall her husband. He'd refused to allow any discussion of taking his daughter in a wagon of any kind across a land of so many unknowns. He had booked passage for them on a fine ship that would take them to the Port of Colon.

Colon, he'd told them, was one of the western-most tax-free ports in the Caribbean Sea. In the South American country of Columbia—an apanage of the family of Christopher Columbus—it was on a narrow isthmus that connected Columbia with Costa Rica. Rum–runners, buccaneers, and purveyors of all imaginable goods had built a donkey road across that arm of land to connect Colon with the city of Panama, another free port—this one on the Pacific Ocean side of the isthmus.

In Panama Harbor, Dom could find a ship to take him and his new wife to San Francisco and, from there, another to the Columbia River country. Dom had no choice but to agree and he spent the next weeks arranging for the shipment of his provisions.

Late in the night, just before their departure, Daddy had again called Gabriela into his library. This time, his words of caution were for her alone. It made him blush to speak of matters of such a profane nature with a woman, especially his daughter, he'd said, but her mother insisted that he do so.

Pirates and freebooters—he went on to say—indeed, thieves and criminals of all sorts were drawn by the lack of regulation to any tax-free port. The easy access they provided to the open seas made either of those two ports, Colon and Panama City, as bad a city as any in the world; worse than most.

Riding the burro caravan across the low narrow stretch of mountains would be the worst part of the trip, he'd warned. Not solely because of the physical discomfort of riding the burros. That part of it would take only a few days at most and he was certain she could endure that. Goodness knew, he's spent enough money on riding lessons for her.

His concern was with the greedy and desperate men who profited from the trail and from all who used it. Against that, he had something to give her that would help ensure a safe journey from Panama Harbor to the Columbia River. He was sending treasure in the care of a business associate.

Again he reverted to his own prejudices. On the grounds that she was a woman, even though his own daughter, he refused to say what the treasure was. He brought out of his desk a casket that gleamed golden in the candlelight.

It was a narrow box of about four fingers deep, six or eight fingers wide, and eight or more fingers long. She would not have been able to cover it with her hand. Indeed, when he grasped it from the top with his own burly paw his fingers barely gripped the edges. The top was inlaid with blue and white stone set into a pattern that suggested a family crest though she didn't recognize it as something she'd seen before. The sides, too, carried the blue and white motif with additional black accents at the corners. She was not allowed to touch it, to lift it, or even get close enough to study it, so she simply accepted that it would one day be hers.

Besides carrying the treasure, the business associate he'd mentioned would keep a watchful eye on Dom and 'Briela. He'd been instructed to stay in the shadows in order to watch for others who might be targeting the young couple. Should there be trouble, the man would step in to help but, barring that, neither 'Briela nor her husband would see him until they had reached Panama Harbor and booked their passage to San Francisco. At that time, the man would hand the box to 'Briela and return to

Charleston with his report. And, as with the treasure, Daddy thought it not fitting to tell 'Briela who was to be her guardian angel.

But no one had bid them *Bon voyage* in Panama City. No one had handed 'Briela the beautiful box that had gleamed so brilliantly in the candlelight of Daddy's library. And no one had stepped in to help on either of the two occasions Dom had been set upon by a thug; a giant of a man who vanished from the hubbub when 'Briela came running.

She watched the captain's approach. The seas were rising, he said; a storm was brewing. She rose and accepted his proffered hand but declined his gesture at the ladder, opting instead to stroll alone, eight small paces across the deck and eight paces back, inhaling the salty air.

The below deck was so cramped, stuffy and smelly it exacerbated the nausea that had plagued her throughout her pregnancy and she dreaded the closeness of the quarters but loathed even more the prospect of having to listen again to the predictions of old Missus Schneider; a fellow passenger who seldom came topside. The woman was the eldest of seventeen children and had borne eight of her own, making her an expert in her own mind. 'Briela had made it clear on several occasions that she had no intentions of taking the woman's advice—any of it. She would deliver with a doctor in attendance (though, in her heart, she knew it was much more likely to be a midwife) and have her lying-in at a clean and proper hotel no matter what the woman suggested.

Probably because there wasn't much else to talk about, and possibly because the woman couldn't remain silent, Missus Schneider continued to prophesy.

"If you have morning sickness your baby will have a hairy body."

"I do not have morning sickness, Missus Schneider."

I have been sick from the moment I conceived. That is precisely thirty-three weeks. And precisely the number of weeks I have been married to Dom and making these gowns in preparation for the Blessed Event. And if being with child isn't sickening enough, I'm in a rolling boat with a yammering woman who gives me no peace.

"You're very thin. You're supposed to be eating for two. You'll have a hard delivery – I've seen them last for days."

I shall eat for ten and remain thin so long as I keep tossing my food to the fishes within minutes after I've eaten it.

"You carry him very low. Boys ride low. Girls stay way up high under your lungs and you just can't hardly breathe once it gets on to being your time. You can count on having a boy."

"Thank you, Missus Schneider."

I, too, am certain I shall have a son. Not because of your folk wisdom but because the firstborn child for many generations of my mother's family has been a boy. We will name him Dominic, for his father.

"You know, when I was your age..."

"The light here is poor for sewing, Missus Schneider. I believe I'll go topside."

Again the captain brought a caution about the imminence of a storm and again, 'Briela declined to seek shelter below deck. She took her seat at the rail and picked up her handwork, sewing as fine a seam as the rocking boat would allow.

A small crate below was filled with all the neatly folded garments she had sewn while sitting on this makeshift stool. She was reminded of the story of Joseph and his coat of many colors. Like that one, this pale flannel gown, the final one, was pieced from leftover scraps. It had taken her this long to get the hang of making a fine seam so this would also be the finest, she reckoned. She was a bit vexed when she realized that she'd soon have to come up with another project; something that would give her cause to continue to avoid Missus Schneider.

She peered closely at the fabric in order to send the needle through the perfect spot. A few more stitches were all she needed but the light had gone and a rolling motion had been added to the rocking of the little ship. She bit her lip and squinted in concentration.

The explosion of light and sound knocked her to the deck. Sailors' shouts added to the sudden noise of huge hailstones pelting the deck and all who had not sought shelter below. Dom was with her in an instant, throwing his heavy coat over her and pulling her to her feet. He rushed her to the ladder. Neither noticed the small puddle of amniotic fluid that was blending with the hail and washing into the sea.

Thirty minutes later Gabriela Eadrich LeGrau snugged her tiny daughter to her chest. Blue-eyed Letitia had a whisper of dark, downy hair on her head and she was beautiful. 'Briela gazed over the top of the baby's head and smiled into the loving eyes of her husband.

SEVEN

Moise huddled on the cracked wooden wagon seat, his mind awhirl with flashes of disjointed memories. Each jolt of the rickety contraption set off another fit of spasmodic shivering from the cold and the fear. His father, sitting as if stone beside him, was a teamster who hauled elixir to the many silver and gold mines that dotted the mountains on either side of their valley and beyond. His favorite destination was by far, the boisterous little settlement of Ruby.

He'd taken Moise there with him one time. He'd made Moise stay on the wagon but even from there Moise had heard and seen things previously unimaginable and still unexplainable. On their return, Mam was coldly furious. The mixture Da called *elixir* was really *nitro-something*. It was frighteningly dangerous...could blow up for any reason...or for no reason at all. Maybe because the elixir was so like him, Da was the best at carrying it from one place to another she'd said.

For the first time in his life Moise questioned his mother. If something were as volatile as that, why would Da not keep his wagon in better—safer—condition? Did he not care that a jolting wagon could trigger an explosion? Did the man not fear death? Had he seen so much of it in his life that his own death was of no consequence? Mam had simply wrapped him in a gentle hug and whispered that Da hadn't always been like this.

Moise grieved for his mother, now resting in her unmarked grave. He ached for his little sister, Dora; wanted to vomit when her image flashed through his consciousness. He hadn't realized how much her spirit had contributed to his own sanity. He missed her quiet industriousness. She never complained, didn't chatter incessantly like their one-time visitor, Amelie, had done. When Moise remarked to his mother about Amelie's chattering, Mam laughed and said Amelie's tongue was tied in the middle and loose at both ends.

He'd met Amelie just once, when her father was moving his family and his herd of goats upriver towards the high peaks at the head of the valley. Their colorful caravan had rolled towards the hill where Moise and Dora were picking currants and it brought more noise and excitement than Moise had ever seen outside the gatherings at Mam's village. Two wooden wagons led the way. They looked like big boxes painted in bright shades of yellows and oranges and trimmed in greens and reds. They were followed by a smaller wagon laden with things hidden by a large brightly painted canvas covering. Behind the wagons came the small herd of white goats that were being kept in check by several energetic black dogs and a few dusty young drovers.

Moise and Dora had watched in fascination at the working dogs, the strange white herd animals, and the big beautiful boxes. Timidly they'd followed the caravan until a girl of about Dora's size had jumped from the lead wagon and ran back to them. Within a few paces, she'd had them laughing and playing along beside the wagons as they crept down the hill towards the homestead and the river. The wagons were her family's homes she'd said and the drovers, her brothers and cousins. They were Basques, she'd said, raising goats for their milk and cheese, their meat and skins. Moise had never heard of goats, of cheese, or of Basques.

The caravan drew to a stop at the homestead amid a swirl of dust and clinking harness and the lead driver had stepped down. He'd asked Da's permission to camp for the night on the flat between the creek and the river. Their conversation was brief. When the man reclaimed his perch on the wagon he'd turned to his companion with a terse remark before clucking the horses in motion. Moise had only understood the words "black-hearted Frenchman." He was sorry to see them go; wished they had camped by the river.

He remembered the man's comment and it puzzled him. Was that his father's name? Mam's people called her Sia but he'd only ever known his father as *Da*. He wondered briefly what Mam's people called him.

He'd known with a foreboding certainty the day before yesterday that Da was planning something unforgivable although Mam had once said Da didn't have to plan ways to hurt people—it came naturally to him now. Da had spoken to him and Dora only in kicks and curses since Mam took sick. Her children had watched him bury her at daybreak out in the little south pasture where Da had dug a deep hole several days earlier.

Da had sneered when Moise asked about the hole; said it was for the crab apple tree he thought to move, "knowin' how yer Mam loves that tree." Now stark in its dormancy its vivid summer fruit had provided the only color in their drab existence. Moise thought it much too large to be moved without killing the roots. Was that bright color the tree's death sentence? Did he refuse hospitality to the Basques because their brightly colored wagons emphasized the darkness of his own low, log hut?

Before the autumn rain could smooth the dirt on Mam's bier Da had filled the south pasture with his underfed cattle, tossed a few things into the wagon, and whipped the horse into a trot. His children had scrambled aboard then huddled together in the back, shivering in the weak dusk.

The temperature dropped steadily as the day darkened into night. When it was too dark to continue the journey Da had stopped, shoved the children onto the ground then curled up in his bedroll in the narrow wagon bed. He neither unhitched the horse nor built a fire. He ate nothing. The children had crawled under the wagon and, with their backs against a wagon wheel, they'd again huddled beneath their single wool blanket and gnawed on a few dry roots Dora had secreted into her apron pocket.

Moise had sat awake, alert and afraid; afraid of Da, afraid for Dora. Mostly, though he was afraid of the rattlesnakes that slithered through the cool of the night using the heat-seeking pits above their nostrils to locate their prey. Mam said he was too big to be prey. That didn't stop his heart from lurching every time he saw or heard one—or thought he did.

They'd wondered where they were. Da had driven north and followed a rocky winding track along the river rather than heading over the hill to the east, the route they took when going to Mam's people.

The next morning they'd been curious and watchful when Da turned from what had become a rutted roadway. He followed two barely discernable wheel tracks through the sparse scrubby pines and the stunted sagebrush that marked the beginning of the foothills, the end of the scrubland. Moise had noticed many of the plants his mother loved—yarrow for its relief of fevers, stoneseed for internal bleeding—and the elderberry that she'd hated, but he couldn't rouse any interest in them. He knew Dora saw them, too. Neither felt safe enough to speak of them; of her.

Cresting a small rise, they'd seen below them the semi-permanent camp of the bounty hunters. Before Mam took sick a group of the hard, filthy men had come to their homestead looking for a place to camp. Looking for information on her people, too, Mam had said. She'd hustled her children into the root cellar and there, while sorting through spring vegetables, talked of bounty hunters and of her own mother's death.

Da drove right into the hunters' camp, swung down from the wagon seat and strode assertively into a dirty tent. The circular tent with upright sides seemed high but was dwarfed by Da. He'd come back to the wagon with a grimy tote-sack half full of what might have been food and tossed the bag into the back of the wagon. He grabbed ten-year-old Dora by her upper arm and, with one motion yanked her off the wagon seat and dropped her, sprawling, at the feet of the leering cook who'd followed from inside the tent. Before she could recover her feet he had mounted the wagon and was driving away. Moise had turned and seen his little sister held in the grip of the dirty-aproned man.

Her look of terror had torn his heart from his chest and surely matched his own.

"Da?" he'd croaked in disbelief. The blow came faster and harder than he could ever have imagined.

When he came to his senses he was lying in the back of the jolting wagon. The stars above were crisp and clear and he shivered violently from the cold. Still, he knew with paralytic certainty that he was in Hell.

🜨

Moise wrapped the thin blanket tighter around his shoulders, gritted his teeth against the bumping of the wagon, and thought of Mam and the stories she'd told—thoughts and dreams and stories as jumbled and confused as his spirit.

Mam, he knew, was proud that her skin was coppery colored like that of her mother's people, not brown like the people who came from where the Chief Sun rises. Her hands were small and dainty with strong pointed fingers. She said that was because her mother's people had retained the old ways of gathering berries and roots for food. Many of the Others had turned to hunting the buffalo but working with the tough hides of so strong a beast turned a young woman's hands into those of Grandmother, she'd said.

He knew her mother, Redwing, had been stolen as a babe from her mother who was called Gray Willow; knew Gray Willow had followed the marauders, alone and on foot until, many months later, she had found the camp of the woman who now claimed her daughter as her own; knew Gray Willow had offered herself as slave, risking degradation and even sacrifice, to this woman just so she could be near her daughter.

Mam kept her long shiny black hair plaited and wound around her head in a coil. He had only once seen her long braids hanging down, stretching over her ears and down her back, falling beyond the beaded leather belt she often wore. On that day, Da had returned earlier than anticipated from a trip hauling elixir to the mines at Ruby. In a fit of anger for which there was no known reason, he had spurred his horse into the garden, grabbed the braids of the hoeing woman and dragged her behind his horse into the barn.

Moise ran to get Dora to hide with her across the creek in the root cellar just like Mam had made him promise to do. As he sped with her through the bunchgrass he looked back and saw Mam's sister, Tsaltsaleken, and her father, Skakuluk, enter the barn.

He ran to the little den and propped the wad of hides across the somewhat-circular opening. The two children hid behind the dwindled piles of roots until Mam came to get them at the dusk of that summer evening. Neither Tsaltsaleken nor Skakuluk were anywhere to be seen. Neither was Da. And unlike other times when Da had dragged Mam to the barn, she showed no signs of injury. But Moise never again saw his mother with her braids down.

Mam had a scar that ran from beneath her bangs to the end of her nose. It was a constant source of ridicule from Da. Only recently, the day the Indian hunters had come into the farmyard, had Mam told them how she came to be scarred so. To save her daughters, her mother had shoved them over and down a sandy bluff. The girls had been saved by Crab Apple, but Sia would always bear the scar that told of her mother's sacrifice. Now her only prayer was to keep cruelty and devastation from being visited on her children.

She had looked at marriage to the strong assertive young homesteader as a promise of stability and protection but the man left home for longer and longer periods of time. The first trip started just days after Moise was born. It had lasted nearly a year.

When the man returned, bragging of booty and plunder, he had changed—at first, angry and volatile but as the days wore on he became secretive and solitary. Soon long dark periods of resentful brooding would culminate in violent rages against every living thing. It was as if, she'd said, some part of that plunder had taken possession of him and had taken away the man's ability to love and to be loved. Then a war started somewhere and he went away to fight.

It was during his brooding days that Mam began digging the root cellar. Somewhere to hide the children, she'd said, somewhere they would be safe. At first, the cave was little more than a shelter under a small ledge. Shielded from casual observance by thick clumps of elderberry and chokecherry that grew along the riverbank, it deepened tempest-by-tempest and hurt-by-hurt until it was so deep it was unsafe to dig further into the bank.

One morning, after Da had ridden away, she'd found an aromatic board lying beneath the crab apple tree and quickly spirited it to the root cellar. After that, two or three of the wide, rough-hewn slabs would appear each time Da left for a trip to the mines.

Now she enlisted Moise and Dora to help enlarge the cave. Each day they took a different route to the hole in the riverbank so no path would reveal its whereabouts. Dora was barely old enough to walk but Mam had given her a sheep-horn spoon and let her dig in the coarse pebbly soil high above the water's course. When they had brought in enough planks to line the sides, back, and top of the little cave, the supply stopped—just as mysteriously as it had begun.

Mam had scarified a few old pieces of deer hide with the surrounding gravel to mask their gray-brown color, stuffed them into the opening, and anchored them with a few large rocks. Seldom had their cache been invaded. The badger-eviction had been a particularly interesting adventure and, despite his misery, Moise smiled at the memory.

Throughout the digging of the tunnel and cellar Mam taught them how to carefully wade the creek then weave their way through the brush to reach the circular opening that led to the chamber beyond. No leaves could be pulled from branches to show where they had passed. No twigs could be snapped to alert a stalker to their presence. He wondered if he would ever revisit their haven there above the laughing waters of the river Mam called *Met-how;* if ever he would retrieve the treasure he had buried in the floor.

He didn't know why Mam died. He was sure it had something to do with her belly growing so big and her not being able to get out of bed. But why hadn't she sent for Tsaltsaleken to bring herbs? He had always been certain of the bond between the two sisters and knew that they talked to each other with their minds. If Mam was afraid, her sister would soon be with her. If Tsaltsaleken was sad, Mam would bundle up the children and trek across the ridge to find her. He knew Tsaltsaleken could have saved her if only Mam had wished for her.

Da had tried to doctor Mam. Moise had seen him put medicine in her tea the last few nights. When she went to sleep that last night he had put some drops onto a cloth and laid it gently over her face. That was to keep the light out of her eyes...wasn't it? The breeze had carried the sweetish heady smell of the medicine to the chink between the logs where Moise watched, curious and still.

Way back when he could first remember, Mam had said tsaltsaleken was her family's name for the plant the neighbors called sunflowers but Da said was balsamroot. Moise liked using the Indian word though it annoyed his father—or because it did. He loved his aunt. Her bright showy nature contrasted sharply with Mam's quiet intensity. Mam's family name was "Sia" and her personality had taken on the characteristics of the deeply hued bearberry whose name she carried. And, like their namesakes, the sunny Tsaltsaleken and the passionate Sia were of equal importance to the vitality of the family.

The stars swam above him and he saw his Mam in the swirling specks of light. He squeezed his eyes shut trying to burn the image in his brain. Lest Da hear above the creaking of harness and the clatter of hooves, he only mouthed his prayer.

"Oh, Mam! Please hurry. Dora needs your help."

EIGHT

Son-of-Striker had been several days without food and nearly as many without water. Heat from the autumn sun radiated from the boulder on which he rested to watch the canyon below. His body glistened with sweat even though it had snowed that morning and it would be freezing here before moonrise. Watching the spring-fed creek from the rocks above he forced himself to think about the water; to not want it.

The quest had been a difficult one. He would have started it moons ago but had been stricken with the White-Man's illness and lain unconscious on his bed of wapiti blankets for several days. Herbs from his mother's medicine pouch and her constant prayers had saved his life but his recovery had been grueling.

And now that he was here, alone and eager, no visions came to him; no beings to emulate for the rest of his life save Squirrel and Jay—each more brazen than brave. Had the White-Man's illness stolen the fierce Totem he was certain the gods had saved for him and him alone? He knew the plants that would send his mind into another realm and so give him the vision he wanted. He'd seen them growing profusely on the hillside, tempting him with their promise of an easier way. He'd resisted so far, wanting his vision to come from the gods rather than from the ground. He would continue to search.

He saw a fleeting shadow on the path below. He focused on the narrow bare patch of ground but nothing tangible appeared. It must be Raven or Coyote playing their Trickster games. Still, he watched.

A girl, not yet old enough for the ceremony staggered into view. She hurried to the creek and, bending from the waist, reached between her legs to grab the hem at the back of her White-Man's dress. She pulled it between her legs and tucked it into the front of her apron at her waist then knelt, scooping water with cupped hands, to drink as if consumed by great thirst. She sat on the bank; her feet dangled at the water's surface. After a short rest she regained her feet, wobbled and clutched at a spindly shrub for support.

She stepped from the stream and stopped to gaze upwards towards the ledge on which he lay hidden. She crossed the sandy path, picked something from a bush, and put it into her mouth. Again. And again.

Puzzled, he edged further to the face of the cliff. What could she be eating? He knew it could be neither the plump purple sarvisberry nor the tart tiny red currant—they had withered with the late summer sun—but he didn't doubt that she was eating something. His stomach roared with envy.

The girl stopped eating and stared motionless at the path downstream then turned and ran upstream to the bend where the creek curved from the northeast to take a more southerly direction. Here she stopped then slowly turned, peering in all directions as if looking for something once seen but no longer visible. Again she ran to the next curve in the path then stopped as if bewildered. The next spurt of flailing legs and flying hair took her beyond his vision.

He dared not follow to see what was amiss. His quest, no matter how successful, would be annulled should he speak before returning to the family for the cleansing ceremony and the gathering of the elders. Not until he was directed to tell of receiving the gift of a Totem would he be allowed a voice. But this time it would be as a man of the family.

A sound reached him from far down stream. A stone carelessly knocked into the water? Son-of-Striker watched the lower path and through the sparsely leaved brush saw a White Man tromping up the trail. Now he saw a second. They stopped; peered closely at the ground. They were following the girl. He knew this with a certainty he could not explain. Nor would he have been able to describe or justify to the elders the deep fear he felt for the child. For the first time, alarm drove his quest from his mind and he stood to race to the creek.

A hand touched his shoulder—gently but impelling. Startled, he turned to face his arrester but nothing visible faced him there on the rocky ledge so high above the wild stream. No human hand reached out to prevent a plunge down and across the scree of granite. Rain sent by the Sky Chief perhaps? A gust of frigid air blew his straight black locks away from his face, taking his breath and drying his sweat. Ah, Wind. It was probably Wind who'd stayed his descent.

He heard the horse before he saw Her and instinctively knew Her for the goddess that She was. She exploded from the point where he had last seen the girl. Thrower-of-Fire marked the path of Her pale gleaming hooves with parallel streaks of silver. Thunder roared the first warning as the goddess sped down the narrow path, sure of Her destination. Rain had covered Her coppery coat with tiny drops that glistened like dust from a thousand stars. Her tail, darker than Beaver's coat, stood proudly, the long threads of silk billowing behind Her like the dire flag of Hell—compelling in its beauty, terrifying in its glory. Her neck was arched and Her mane, like the silken hairs of Her tail, threw back the light as if Sun, Himself, had put Fire there. Along the path She flew, straight to the evil that followed the girl.

Startled, the two men dove from Her path, one to each side. They cursed Her as She spun on Her hind hooves and came at them again. From his vantage point the boy could see the blaze that ran down Her oddly dished face. From under Her forelock to the tip of Her nose the narrow white streak emphasized the length of Her excruciatingly beautiful head. He watched in fascination as She drove again and again at the men, pushing them further and further back the way they had come. He watched long after Her screams had stopped and their curses had faded to silence.

Still he watched for Her return. He watched and waited until he realized the jagged rocks of the ledge had penetrated the dark skin of his chest. Only then did he raise himself and make his way carefully to the path. He stepped silently into the icy edge of the stream, hiding behind the last few leathery leaves of the bearberry lest the evil that had walked the path that day return to avenge itself on the horse and the girl.

He reached the place where the girl had rested. One shiny plump sarvisberry glistened at the edge of the water. Impossible at this time of year, but there it was. He looked along the edge of the scree for heavy foliage that would herald the presence of such a bush. He saw only the stark barren branches of the elder, the currant, and the willow. No sarvisberry grew here...nor here...nor here. Who was this child whom the gods themselves chose to feed?

Next the boy turned his attention to the ground. From his vantage point on the bluff the goddess had appeared smaller than any of the few horses belonging to his family—no bigger than a young filly in fact. He tried to implant the image in his memory so he could relate every detail to the elders. He would measure her hoof mark against the palm of his hand so they would be able to judge her size. He stepped cautiously to the bank and peered closely at the packed soil along the path. There were no prints. Not here...nor here...nor here further down towards the fray.

Here though, marks of heavy boots scrabbling hither and there gouged the mud and ripped up the stream grasses. Amongst them he found a narrow piece of hide almost as long as his bare foot. Upon examination, he found it was actually two pieces of narrow leather bound one to the other. At one end something small and dense had been sewn to fit snuggly between the pieces. The two leather thongs at the unweighted end he tied around his wrist and found that, when held and snapped in just such a way, the heavy end might become a formidable weapon at close range.

Prowling further he found a filthy fabric bag large enough to fit over a man's head. Inside was a small dirty rag with a peculiar odor. He pulled it from its hiding place and raised it toward his nose. Even before he could inhale deeply, his eyes began to water and his senses to swirl. Again, as with the strange weapon, he was aware of the presence of profound evil and he shivered.

Then, careful to leave no prints of his own on the path, he stepped silently into the creek. He surveyed the scene of the fracas and he knew. A Goddess could bring Thunder with Her hooves, could summon Lightening—the Thrower of Fire—with Her power, could use Rain to give Her coat brilliance, could call with the screams of Panther. And only a Goddess could drive away evil without leaving hoof prints in the mud.

Horse had chosen Son-of-Striker. Not the mundane beast that served his family in so many ways, but this small proud force that streaked to the rescue of a child without touching the path—this glistening beauty the color of Fox with Her rippling coils of muscle, Her upright tail and arched neck, Her sharp flashing hooves, Her strangely dished face with its long narrow blaze, and Her chilling scream. This was his gift from the gods—his Totem.

He closed his eyes, opened his arms, and raised his face Heavenward in a silent prayer of reverence. Normally he would sing a song of gratitude and step the dance of joy but today he was fearful. He sensed there was something yet undone, a debt of honor by which he was inescapably bound to the horse.

Cautiously he moved upstream, still using the understory to hide his movements, his brown willowy body gliding around and through sparse bare branches and making no sound. He slipped past the resting place; a phantom—alert, undaunted by the frigid water cascading around his legs.

At the bend, the stream had washed away large chunks of the bank and he crouched, sheltering beneath this low overhang as he worked his way against the flow. The undercurrent made forward movement difficult. He felt the streambed with his foot, checking for loose stones that had the potential for rolling—for sending him splashing noisily into the icy stream to alert a watcher as he, himself, had been alerted just a short time ago. Step by silent step he moved towards the point where the path diverged from the creek's swath—the place where he had last seen the girl.

He crouched for many minutes watching the path and the forest through which the water ran. He moved nothing save his eyes. His ears were alert to the slightest change in the call of Raven, the chatter of Squirrel. Satisfied, he stepped to the bank and, still avoiding the muddy path, followed the girl's prints.

She had run, stopped and turned, then run again. And vanished. Again he gazed in wonderment. Who was this child the gods themselves would feed? And protect? And hide? Where had she gone?

Ahead of him was a tree that he had not noticed in all of his fourteen summers of using this path. It was taller than the surrounding scrub so should have been visible from far away. How could he have missed it in all these years? Was it, perhaps, a second vision?

The tree was broad too, with dense sweeping branches that touched the ground around it. The needles were short and overlapping so they provided a barrier to the rain now softly crying to the earth. The tree gave off a strange crisp scent.

Mindful of the odiferous cloth he still carried in the dirty bag he sniffed lightly this time, his nostrils flaring softly. He stepped forward, broke off just the tip of a twig and studied it more closely, sniffed more deeply. He took several steps back and studied every aspect of the tree so he could describe it to the elders in the very way he would describe every inch of his Totem.

He approached the tree again, parting the boughs so he could see the trunk of this stranger before him. He stepped into a warm, dry chamber higher than his head and so wide he could have sat against the trunk and stretched his legs straight out before him without touching the sweeping boughs—could have sat just as the girl before him was sitting now.

He gave no notice of his astonishment save a slight narrowing of his eyes. Unlike his Totem, this creature was mortal and he realized she was examining the lithe brown figure before her with a curiosity that matched his own.

"Mama said to wait here for you," she stated.

He stared for a moment longer, hoping she would say something he could understand, then he extended his arm and swung his forearm in a motion that indicated she was to follow. He stepped from the chamber beneath the aromatic branches. He heard the whisper of the boughs and knew she was there behind him. He walked several paces before turning to take one last look at the strange tree.

The rain had stopped, the wind had died, and the spot where the tree had stood was shrouded in a dense, iridescent fog.

NINE

The wagon sat cold and silent. Puzzled, Moise forced himself to waken fully and pull himself onto the wagon seat. He studied his surroundings. They were stopped in front of one of the saloons in Ruby. He recognized the place from the time Da had brought him along to help haul elixir from the madcap town to one of the silver mines. The building, closed and barred against the pre-dawn chill, was dark save for the dim glow of a lantern hanging beside a door in the side alley.

Da hadn't told him to wait here though Moise knew what would happen if Da came back to find him gone. But what if he did jump down and run back to find Dora? What direction would he take? He'd been in and out of consciousness. In his wakeful moments he'd been searching the stars for Mam rather than watching the road for landmarks. How...?

His head and shoulders were suddenly enveloped by a heavy hide that stank of rotted meat. His arms were forced to his sides and he felt a rope being pulled taut around him. He kicked out and swung his head like a wild ram. He connected with something solid—another's head perhaps?

He jerked the rawhide away only to have it thrown over him again. In that brief second he thought he saw Da standing under the overhang at the side door of the saloon. He called out but the man stepped back into the deeper shadows. Moise's throat was gripped vise-like and he struggled to remain conscious. A smelly rag was pushed against his face. It had a sweetish smell that reminded Moise of the medicine that Da had given Mam to help her sleep. A light exploded in his mind. To stop her fighting, too?

His recollections of the next few days were vague and muddy. Was it a few days? One? Two? Should the time have been measured in hours instead of days? He couldn't even guess. He was sitting astride a horse, trussed like a shock of corn with the rawhide covering him head to hip. Now, though, shards of daylight peeked through the gaps between the ragged bottoms of the stinking shroud and the skinny horse. That meant his eyes were no longer covered as they had been at first. His hands were still bound. Snow swirled around the animal's hooves and the wind howled a gale. Never before in his twelve years had he felt this cold or heard the wind wail with such sorrow.

Heavy hands hauled him from the back of the now stationary animal, rousing him from his stupor. Lying motionless and silent in the snow he tried to bring his mind alert.

"I say we quit jammin' that stuff in 'is face so's 'e wakes up then we make him fetch firewood. Do 'im good to move aroun'. We ain't gonna git more'an a buck 'r so each if 'e cain't move aroun' some."

"We told his ol' man we'd deliver him ta the Pierced-Noses. Sooner we do 'at, the better. Ain't no meaner bully this side o' the Pearly Gates an' I don't want 'im 'oundin' my tail he e'er thought we'd lost his kid somewhurs. 'Sides, ye don' know. Kid might'a picked up his daddy's ways. Mayhap he's meaner'n the both of us. We leave 'im tied."

"Do ye s'pose he wasn't joshin' us? Ye s'pose he really did sell his little'un to those barbarinians?"

"Quit usin' big words if ye don' know wut they mean."

"I know there ain't no word big enough ner bad enough fer that Devil. Makes e'en yer pockets shrivel up squeamish-like knowin' whur thet money come from an' why."

Moise woke at dawn to find his ropes had been removed and he could, for the first time since his capture, move his arms. He was manhandled into a sitting position then the dirty, untreated hide was yanked from his head.

"You talk, boy?" snarled the taller of his captors. The man's left eye was swollen nearly shut and the skin around it had darkened into a large bruise.

The boy stared back wide-eyed. His lips moved but no sound came. He tried to rise but his arms and legs remained frozen in the same twisted positions in which they had been tied for so long.

One of the men jerked him to his feet. "Git on over there behind those trees and do what ye gotta do. Don't be tryin' ta run off 'r we'll leave ye here to freeze ta death!" he shouted to Moise's retreating back.

Amid the grove of naked trees, Moise did think of running. He knew the two men were almost as afraid of him as they were of his father. He could run but, like his captors, he was more afraid of what was behind him than what lay ahead and he had no way of knowing which was which. He had a remarkable sense of direction and a memory for places he had been that was unmatched by anyone he knew—few though that number might be—but on this journey he had been drugged and blindfolded. He would need more time to get his bearings than these two would give him.

On his way back to the meager fire he picked up an armload of dead branches. He dumped them before his startled captors. "Firewood," he said flatly.

"Boone," said the shorter man, extending a rancid piece of meat affixed to sharp stick.

Moise eyed the man and shook his head. Even though he wouldn't let his eyes wander to the meat, his stomach reminded him and all within hearing distance that he hadn't eaten in days.

The man guffawed and shoved the stick towards Moise. "Here. G'wan. Take it. Eat. Keep yer strength up. This 'ere's Gavin," he finished, pointing to the taller man.

Moise reached timidly across the distance between the two and accepted the stick. He bit down then swallowed the rotten meat before the taste could reach his brain then shook his head in declination of the offer of a second piece. He knew he would soon be sickened by the one piece, not only because of its condition but because of his own starved state as well.

The men finished their breakfast then scraped snow on the fire and again bound his arms to his sides with the ill-kept rope. Mam would have admonished them to keep their rope clean. Dirty, poorly conditioned tools would not work for you for very long. They would break in a moment of stress, she would tell them.

They boosted him up to the saddle but this time left his wrists free. They again tossed the rawhide over his head but didn't wrap it as they had before. Were they so confident of his impotence they thought he wouldn't try to escape?

Now that the air could circulate inside the shroud he came to realize how much warmth the horse had been generating. Against his will he began to relax, nodding again into a drugged sleep.

The shroud of cowhide hadn't been replaced after the midday stop and he'd been able to observe his surroundings. The jagged snowbound mountains he was used to had given way to low rolling hills. The forest with its green understory of shrubs from which his family gleaned so many foods and medicines was behind them now as well. The wind-whipped flatland through which they'd ridden was made a dull brown by dormant grasses he couldn't identify. He'd wished more than once for the return of the shroud to ward off the bone-chilling wind.

They'd ridden at a quick pace until they came to a ridge overlooking a wide river. It was dusk but they stopped here, waiting for something. They'd tried to get him to eat more of the rotten meat but he'd refused, reinforcing his refusal by vomiting into the shrubs. With just enough light left to see the way to the river, they'd remounted and started down the hill.

Now they led him slowly across a large floor of heavy wooden planks that had been built to extend into the water. He thought it seemed more like a giant table with two far legs that were huge round tree trunks sunk into the riverbed. The sign said it was the Fort Okanogan Landing.

Water slapped softly against the wood and a stench hung in the air. A massive shape loomed dark and still in the water—a larger structure than he had ever seen—and was tied to the table with ropes that were bigger around than his arms.

They rode between stacks of wooden boxes and crates that watched, silent and accusing. The tread of the horses sounded hollow and haunting. It was the hour between the onset of darkness and the full-on blackness of night; that brief span of time when even the familiar can startle—the unfamiliar can terrify. Moise shivered with a chill of foreboding.

"You swim, boy?"

Moise jerked his head in a brief negative.

"See that light yonder?"

Again Moise was silent, responding with only a slight nod of his head. He peered into the blackness at a pinpoint of light far across the widest body of water he had ever seen.

"We're gittin' on 'is yere boat and goin' ta thet light. Ye make e'en a pretense o' trouble and we'll pitch ye o'er the side so fast ye won't e'en make a shada."

Moise nodded his acceptance and the men led his horse up a steep, wooden ramp into the belly of the boat.

TEN

Dora was growing vexed with the dark young man. She was certain he could not know the danger that lay behind them but she had no knowledge of how to convey her urgency. She had tried to explain in both the language of her mother's people and that of her father but there seemed no point in talking to this one. He acted like he didn't understand. She wanted to run up behind him and give him a shove to make him walk faster, even if it meant she herself would be forced to run, but she had never touched a boy's skin before. And this boy, perhaps two or three years older than her brother, was *all* skin. Only her fear of the two men and her confidence in her mother's wisdom kept her striding a pace behind.

Her father had thrown her to the ground and the man with the dirty apron had grabbed her up as if she were a nugget of gold tossed at his feet. She was too stunned to cry out. She looked at Moise and willed him to help her. She heard his bleat of disbelief and saw her father slam him with his fist into the bed of the wagon. It was the last she'd seen of her beloved brother.

The ugly man took her into the tent and shoved her to the ground against one of the uprights. He picked up a one-legged stand that had been leaning against a tree stump, jammed it into the ground and straddled it, sitting himself opposite the stump from Dora.

Once balanced on the wobbly one-legged stool, he picked up a bloody cleaver and began whacking big chunks of fly-blown meat into smaller chunks of equally revolting goop. He whistled tunelessly through gaps in his black, decaying teeth and eyed her every time the cleaver slammed onto the stump he was using as a butchering block. Blood oozed down the sides of the dead wood and black flies swarmed over all, their iridescent wings accentuating the movement of the dark undulating blanket.

The man stopped chopping to spear smaller bits of too-old meat onto dry willow sticks and leaned those against a frame built over a too-smoky, too-hot fire.

If she'd been at home she would be helping Mam smoke the day's kill. Not because she was expected to but because she loved working with her mother, listening to the woman hum traditional songs or retell family legends and explain her traditions. If Mam were here she would tell the filthy man that he should use chokecherry or cottonwood, even willow, for his fire. His piney wood was too smoky and would throw off sparks.

Dora was too frightened to speak, too terrified to move. She couldn't even think with the cook leering at her—willing her to squirm, to give him an excuse to attack. Closing her eyes against his grin of anticipation and the heavy smoke in the tent only brought images from the stories Mam had told when they were hiding in the root cellar. She focused on the fire and wished her father there. He would be one day. She clung to that certainty.

Like one of Da's tantrums, the flames shot into the air with a violent roar. And, like she did when Da exploded at home, Dora jumped and ran for the river. She darted away from the startled cook who seemed unable to decide whether to grab the escaping prize or extinguish the fire that was already consuming a wall of the dirty tent. She sped past a frightened mule that was tugging at his tether and well on his way to breaking it. She leapt over a narrow ditch meant to divert a trickle of water to the livestock and, with an open path shining before her, ran upstream with wind in her feet.

Twice she saw Mam ahead on the path, smiling encouragement and reaching out to her. Her mother pulled her forward to the next bend in the path, the next curve of the creek, always just a few steps away. When Dora thought she could run no further there was a bank where she could sit to catch her breath, water to sip and berries to eat. She hurried on then, but not far this time. She found Mam standing beside a beautiful tree. The woman reached out and pulled aside a sweeping bough to reveal a small chamber inside.

"Wait here. It is safe. Help will come."

Dora darted towards the opening and, as she passed through, felt a loving hand caress her shoulder. She looked back to see only the boughs of the mysterious tree swaying into place.

The boy led her along several paths, each more obscure than the last. The land was drier here than at home though she wouldn't ever have imagined there was life-sustaining land anywhere that was more dry and barren than was Da's farm.

She was making every effort to step where he stepped just as Mam had taught her to do. Once he stopped, turned and watched her catch up to him, then seemed to almost smile before turning to continue his journey. She could, perhaps, have imagined that smile but from that time on he seemed to be walking without touching the ground, as if he were talking to someone in his mind like Mam and her sister, Tsaltsalaken, often did.

Just on dusk the young man stopped. She realized she had started thinking of him as such but couldn't have pinpointed the moment when she stopped thinking of him as a boy. They stood at the edge of a long, steep ridge. Below, clustered along both sides of a pitiful stream, were eight or ten tipis. Smoke wafted upwards from a single cooking fire. The far-off beat of a prayer drum reached them even here.

He spread his arms, threw back his head and stood motionless. Dora recognized the act of prayer and bowed her head, stilled her thoughts, opened her heart. A peace descended on her like none she'd known before.

A pebble landed at her feet to rouse her from her contemplation. Her guide stood watching but once he seemed sure that she would follow he turned and strode down the hillside to the village. Dora, her skirt still tucked into her apron, slid and slipped along behind.

The two marched with confidence into the village; the new man, now with his own Totem, being trailed closely by the ramrod straight, courageous girl-child who matched him step for step. Looking neither right nor left, he went directly towards the largest tipi in the village and stooped himself inside. She would have followed him straight into the men's lodge where burned the Sacred Fire had not one of the women grabbed her to encircle her in a loving hug.

ELEVEN

Jill paced in the shade of the apple trees, her phone pressed to her ear. "She drives me NUTS, that's all. Not only is she opinionated and arbitrary, but she's rude as well."

"Send her back. Tell Professor Martin she isn't working out."

"I can't," sighed Jill. "Most of the time I'd like to, but she's a good archaeologist. I can't let the archaeology suffer just because a member of the team lacks social skills or doesn't like my *tall person persona*. It wouldn't be so strained if there were more of us or if we weren't sharing quarters."

"Won't Patterson rent you another cabin?"

"Ha," Jill snorted. "Bad enough he refused to give us permission to dig here. Then he sells us this dinky corner of his property for more money than what the whole orchard is worth and does that only because he's convinced it's going to wash away into the river someday else he'd have trees planted here. Then he rents us his three picker-shacks for rates that would qualify him as a slum-lord in any city in the world. I wouldn't ask to rent another one if he did have one available."

"Jill, you agreed to his terms, exorbitant as his prices were."

"Only because I KNOW there is something important here—something worth digging for or Ben wouldn't have led me here."

"Patterson doesn't care why you wanted it. He only knew that you did and that you would pay whatever he asked. Are you regretting that decision?"

"No, of course not. But are you sure there is nothing in that sales contract that will void it if we should find something of monetary rather than historic value?"

"It was a sound contract and he has accepted—and cashed—your check. So dig without worry. Hey, I have this great idea. Dig a tunnel to the Bahamas so we can go there this winter.

"Meanwhile, do you want me to bring a few tents?"

"*No* to the Bahamas, and *no* to the tents. We'll do all right with the three cabins; men in one, women in one, lab in the kitchen unit—along with the shower, toilet, and no-reception-television. We need time away from each other but he needs the cabins in less than a month for his picking crew so we have to be out of here by then. We have no time to spare for a holiday."

"You can't be finished by then, can you?"

"Have to be. We've excavated the area closest to the riverbank—the part most in danger of eroding—but the area the deer's leg broke through is still another two meters back. Judging from the way the silt and gravel has settled, I'd say there was a long narrow tunnel leading from the bank into a den so whoever used the den was pretty small."

"Who?"

"Okay, *whom*ever, if that's what you mean. Not *what* certainly, because of those sawn timbers. It's exciting so I don't want to give it up. If we don't finish excavating before Patterson needs his cabins, we'll cover what we can with a tarp then backfill everything. That'll make it easier to start up again next spring—and hide it from the pot-hunters."

"Will Martin send students next spring? By the way, where are the students now?"

"The underclassmen have gone. They'd signed on for only four weeks and we used all of that out at the homestead because that's where the school agreed to pay us to dig. The three grad-students are the only ones still here but they'll be heading back in about a month whether we've finished or not."

"I knew all that. I meant, where are your three helpers right now?"

"Rising and shining. They're all early risers. I barely have time to meditate in the mornings before they're ready to go.

"Anyway, I didn't phone just to complain. You're probably thinking I'm the poster-child for the Rainy-Day Woman. I wanted to find out if the lab had sent any of the results...and to hear your voice."

"Good addendum." Lane Bragg smiled into the phone. "There is a packet here from the lab as well as a message from your mother. I'll drive both down this afternoon. Then you'll have a face to put with the voice."

"Always a good thing," she smiled. "What did Mom want?"

"You to come in out of the heat, as usual, and I don't disagree. But her message says she found something buried on the north side of the barn—opposite where your students excavated. Wants you to leave what you're doing way down there and go way out where she is to dig it up—in a professional manner, of course."

"What is it?"

"She wouldn't tell me. I can only tell you that she was more excited than I've ever seen her."

"Oh, brother. Should I be phoning Andy? Send him out to tell her to cease-and-desist?"

"I doubt it. He's been out there more often than you have since you gave him that business card. He's probably the one who insisted she leave whatever it is alone until you've seen it."

"Bless his heart. I was going to say it didn't sound like Mom to wait for a go-ahead from me or anyone else."

"I have another great idea. You can't finish the dig at the Patterson place in the three weeks you'll have the cabins. On the other hand, you might be able to excavate whatever your mom's found in that period of time or even less. So think about this...cover the Patterson site, take extra time to hide it well. Then pack up your gear and your specimens and reports and all that, take the weekend off, then start digging at Wolf Creek on Monday."

"That could work. It's tempting. I'll see what these three think."

"You're not arguing? No second opinion? Wow! I might really have had a great idea for once in a row!

"I'll phone Andy. And...just because I love you so much, I'll drive out to the Station and pick up some of Frank's lasagna for you and your shovel bums. The rest of us will eat while you read reports."

"Sure and you will. Seriously, while you're talking Frank out of a pan of lasagna, ask if he can house the crew at The Station for the weekend, will you?"

"Ask and ye shall receive, my dear. I was put on this earth to do your bidding."

Jill laughed, added a few comments, then disconnected and stepped from the quiet cover of the apple orchard.

This morning, as she did every morning while working at a site, she'd slipped from her sleeping bag at dawn—later this week than last—and put the coffee on to brew. Then she'd taken her cell phone and strolled to the orchard where she meditated before doing her stretching routine. She'd started this habit during her first marriage when she thought God was the only person she could ask for wisdom and guidance. Gradually her prayers evolved into a period of time during which she no longer asked for God's help but simply opened her mind to whatever He had for her that morning. Sometimes insight came quickly; some days she would sit there, cross-legged and quiet, and simply appreciate the peacefulness of the moment. The phone call to Lane came third on her morning list and he'd teased her about that many times.

"Are you telling me I come after your God and your meditating?" he would often ask.

"Yes. I am and you do."

"I'm okay with that."

Now the sun was threatening to breach the tops of the eastern hills and the three members of her crew were standing at the door of the kitchen cabin drinking coffee and discussing the work ahead.

She marveled that the four of them were working together again. She had sent Professor Martin a request for two or three experienced people who could help excavate and help supervise an additional three or four underclassmen who were willing to dig and take instruction. She'd hoped for Bill and Tracker. They were a given, like peanut butter and jelly. They'd worked together since their first field school experience and were an asset to any team. But her heart sank when she saw the third passenger step out of the van. Gem Belmont had come late to the crew and had, from the first encounter, rankled all of them.

Jill tried to ignore the verbal sniping between Gem and the men because, despite their differing opinions, the work was going well. Even so, she knew the project could not be finished before winter. Lane was right—this would be a good time to button it up—cover everything, backfill, then spend the next three weeks out on Wolf Creek. Surely it wouldn't take them more than three weeks to excavate whatever her mother had found.

"**You** mean that haunted place?"

"Belle's Creek Station used to have a surprising resident Bill, but he was harmless and sad—just lost was all. Anyway, we sent him to his rest a long time ago and you're getting sidetracked. What do you think about the idea of covering this site, staying at the Station for the weekend, and then going back out to Wolf Creek for the last few weeks of the schedule? Or would you rather just hide this site and go home early even though the rest of the month should give us great digging weather?"

Tracker, like his friend, was more interested in the gossip about spirits than in making plans. "That cop that was out here said your mom's place on Wolf Creek is haunted, too. He said a woman who'd lived there died in a snowstorm and if she doesn't like you, she makes it snow, no matter what time of year it is."

Jill sighed and turned to Gem. "Are you afraid of spirits, too?"

"We ain't scared o' no ghosts," the men quipped in unison.

Gem smiled and looked over at the dig site. "I...like this place. There is something here I can feel. It was a safe place. I agree that we won't do it justice by trying to hurry the process, but I'm afraid if I leave now I'll never find out what is here. Will you promise to invite me back when you work on it again?"

Startled, Jill studied the other woman. The men were behind her, emphatically shaking their heads and it was all Jill could do to stay focused on Gem's face.

"Despite what these morons say about me," Gem finished, without turning to look at the men.

Jill chuckled. "All of you are good people—excellent archaeologists so I'm glad you're helping with this project. I know you're as curious as I am about that den. I know you recognize that archaeology is more than just excavation, education, and preservation—that it's also about interpretation. Those feelings Gem has about this place go a long way towards helping with the interpretation part. All I can promise is that I will give each of you plenty of notice before I start working here again. And I would be pleased and proud to finish this project with any or all of you on board.

"And by the way, guys...if Wolf Creek *is* haunted, the spirits will be the people who *don't* cast shadows when they shake their heads and wave their arms."

"**Tell** Frank this ain't the Yeager sisters' lasagna," said Jill with a grin.

"You've said that before," interrupted Tracker. "What's the joke?"

"What makes an inside joke special is that it's private," shrugged Lane.

"And they're usually so lame they *have* to be kept private," added Jill. "But Lane is referring to the first time we met. He'd brought a pan of lasagna from a café run by the Yeager sisters. He said it was the best in the world."

"It was love at first bite."

"So," continued Jill, ignoring his interruption, "when Lane's brother-in-law started cooking at The Station, he started making his version of lasagna. It's very good, but we remind Lane that, in his opinion, Frank's can only, and ever, be second best."

"Since we're, apparently, going to be spending a couple of nights there, tell us about The Station," suggested Gem. "I thought you said Frank ran it. Now you say he's the cook."

"Both. Lane will tell all. I'm going to my room. I'll leave the four of you to clean up while I wade through these reports."

"Way way back before the dawn of man...oh, wait. You're not dinosaur people. I don't have to go that far back."

"Thanks for bringing the reports. And the food. Don't leave without saying good-bye," Jill interrupted as she headed for the door.

"Wouldn't dream of it. Go. Work while we polish up our technique for delivering oral history. Since we don't have to go all the way back to the dawn of man I'll have time to tell tales about you while you're gone."

"Don't bore them with details. They've probably heard it all, anyway. There's not much to do here after dark but brag about our exploits." Jill winked at Lane then closed the door softly behind her.

"Really, she doesn't talk about herself. She talks about you a lot, though. And your sister, Jennifer," said Bill.

Lane turned to run water into the sink lest the others see him blush. "Not having to talk about me will shorten the narrative considerably."

"I'm still waiting to hear about The Station."

"Belle's Creek Station started out as nothing more than an overnight camping spot for teamsters who hauled supplies to the miners up in the Slate Creek Coulee. Then one guy, Merle Magruder, decided to provide a few amenities and call it the Black Bear freight depot. Not that he did much. Just threw hides over logs at first; built a corral and brought in a few extra mules. Then he married Jill's great-grandmother who pressed him to build a better house.

"After he died, Jill's great-grandmother sold it to the Normans. That was about the time my family was homesteading next door. The Normans ran it as a hotel called the Red Blanket Lodge. Then the late Miss Norman ran it as Belle's Creek Station—named after Jill's great-grandmother. When Miss Norman died, she left it to Jill, who didn't want a thing to do with it, but came up from Oregon to look at it. That's when she was stranded for the Thanksgiving weekend by a freak snowstorm with Frank, my ranch foreman; Jennifer, my sister; and a passel of other folks.

"Crystal Miller was one of the guests that weekend. She's helping Jill's mom tear down, or fix up, the old homestead out on Wolf Creek. You've met her.

"My sister married Frank and they have a son. Not very old. Jill and I were married about a year ago. She lives with me on the Bragg Homestead and turned the running of The Station over to Frank and Jennifer."

"A storyteller you ain't," grumbled Gem. "You'd better learn to do a lot better before you and Miss Jill have children. Kids'll have nightmares, you tell bedtime stories like that."

"Like what?" asked Lane as if deeply wounded.

"Like a court document. Give us details. Tell it like you lived it!"

"You're the only one who wants to hear it."

"Not so," argued Bill. "We want to hear your version. Jill always sounds like she's telling only part of it...like she's keeping part of the story a secret."

Lane poured himself a cup of freshly brewed coffee. "Mark Twain said that an audience hungry to hear more is the mark of a good storyteller. That's Jill all over. Leaves just enough out so as she doesn't quite answer your questions."

He retook his chair at the table and set the cup down with a crack. "It'll cost you, then. Bill, how about a shot of that 'shine you keep under your bed."

"'Shine?! That's good Kentucky bour...."

"Thought it might be," smiled Lane. "Set 'em up. I have a saga for you!"

TWELVE

Moise wished for the sweet-smelling medicine his captors had used to subdue him in Ruby. Maybe if he were drugged he wouldn't notice the bitter cold or the bitter hatred for his father that had been growing inside him since they'd crossed the river. He wished for the stinking shroud that had protected him from the wind but his captors had split it down the middle and each took half and bundled himself inside the rancid pelt to try to stay warm. For Moise there was nothing save his tattered shirt of worn ticking.

He couldn't understand many of the men's words. They talked like Da did after he'd had too much whiskey. His mother had been a stickler for speaking the White Man's words just the way they were written in the book and the only book Da would let them have in the house was a Bible. Mam said he would toss it on the fire if he ever learned she was using it to teach the children to read. He was afraid of people who could read, she'd told them.

She'd gone so far as to cut the book from its cover at the front and back spine. When they had their lessons, she carefully lifted the book from beneath the cover so as not to disturb the dust that had built up on top. Perhaps Da didn't really glance at it each night to see if it had been opened. But it sure seemed as if he did.

The children had few opportunities to practice speaking the words they were learning to print and read. The farm was visited by none save society's outcasts; people as violent and tormented as Da; people from whom Mam hid the children. As a consequence, Moise's vocabulary was astounding for a boy his age but his speech, a mixture of Bible English, the French of his father, and the languages of his mother's peoples, was incomprehensible to all but those who loved him most.

They were nearing the end of the day and riding east. The wind had died but his captors remained wrapped to their eyelids in their rawhide cloaks and were paying little attention to their prisoner. For the first time on the journey his horse had been allowed to lag behind and the animal seemed content to follow at a plod.

They rode under the overhanging branch of a barren oak tree and, without a thought to the consequences, Moise reached up, grabbed the limb, and hoisted himself onto the branch. The riderless horse made no protest but continued at his steady pace behind the others. The tree wore no leaves to rustle and give him away, nor did it block his view of his captors. He watched them slowly make their way into the darkness.

When he thought it was safe to move, he wriggled his way upwards through the stark branches until he found a crotch small enough to hold him securely. Here he could watch, sleep some, and listen to the curious winds that whispered in the night. What did the voices say?

He opened his eyes but otherwise remained motionless; sensed rather than heard nearby movement. The moon was low, the night still young. He heard the dried grass rustle, one blade whispering to another. He tilted his head in tiny increments. Below him a stag stood on alert. Had he picked up Moise's scent or was there something else to alert the skittish critter?

Moise again moved his head slowly, using his eyes and peripheral vision to scan the countryside. There were no horses sighing or stamping against the chill—he could discount Boone and Gavin. He watched for something that might be stalking the deer but could see nothing in the darkness.

He worked his way down the tree, ever alert to sounds and movement on the barren land but now even the plant-life was silent and still. He descended through the branches with agonizing slowness then rested on a limb directly above the stag. He took a deep muted breath and deftly dropped onto the back of the startled animal.

With a snort, the deer jumped straight into the air. His back arced sharply as he twisted his head to touch his flank while, in that same split-second, folded in the middle so his front hooves must surely have touched the back ones. In an eye-blink, his wind-milling feet hit the ground and gained a foothold. He darted through prickly sage and careened across the dusty, rocky grassland with Moise flopping grotesquely on his back, hanging onto the antlers for his very life, and wondering what on Earth he had just done.

Whether from weakness or from sudden insight, Moise released his grip on the deer. He flew through the air and came finally to rest after bumping and sliding across the ground like the balled weeds sent across the landscape by Wind. Bloodied and sore, he lay motionless, trying to reckon the extent of his injuries.

He took deep slow breaths and cursed himself. Groggy and disoriented, he wondered how far he might have been carried and if stupidity, like the works of angels, was real only if witnessed by another's eyes. He would ask his mother. She would know. Warmth like an embrace engulfed him and he sunk into blackness without having moved from his furrow.

He woke and rolled onto his back, clamping his teeth to keep from yowling. The sparse shrubs grew taller than his head—had he been able to stand. The sky was the white-blue of a cloudless winter day. The sun, just above the horizon, gave no warmth.

He moved his left forearm, bending at the elbow to use only the barest amount of energy, and patted the parts of his body he could reach. The bloody gouges on his chest had been caked with dust and dried to a soft scab. Maybe the cold had kept him from bleeding to death here amid the sage and greasewood.

He listened for sounds that would tell him where he was and thought he heard a small creek whispering not so far away. He grabbed a handhold of the gray twigs of a nearby bush and, by twisting from the waist, pulled himself into a sitting position to take further stock of his wounds.

He could feel cold pebbles on the backs of his legs so reckoned the legs of his breeches had been as ravaged as the front of his shirt. He would further assess the damage when he found the creek. When he had rested he would come back to this spot and backtrack the panicked flight of the stag. From the oak tree he would retrace the route his captors had taken from the Great River. He had to get back to Mam's people. He had to find Dora.

But first, he had to stand. As bad as his legs and hips felt, his stomach felt worse—he couldn't possibly crawl and he knew he had to find water. He again grabbed a fistful of the prickly branches to pull himself upright. Instead, he fell to his back, pulling the clump of brush over himself as he lost consciousness.

Awake again, Moise surveyed his surroundings through a writhing haze. He was sitting in pool of springwater that bubbled from a large mound of tumbled boulders. He didn't remember finding the rocky pond and crawling into the tepid smelly depths. It didn't matter. He was sure it would all come back to him—the chill of scraped and naked legs, the dust sticking to his open wounds, the steep uneven terrain binding his feet to the ground. He was certain he would remember more in time.

He painstakingly urged the shredded remains of his shirt from his back and pulled his arms from the sleeves. Newly woven fabric or recently tanned hides might have withstood the tumbling and sliding of a boy across the scabland but Moise's clothing had been handed down and patched so many times they served no other purpose than to preserve one's dignity, Mam always said. The back and sleeves, frayed and torn, had not escaped the shredding the front had taken. His trousers had suffered in much the same way. Now they were useless in every way.

He forced himself to move from the warmth of the pool and shivered. The heat of the day had passed and it would soon be dark. He'd not be able to track his crawl to the water nor his wild ride on the stag. He draped his dripping rags over a bush then began to slowly circle the pool watching carefully for signs of his previous passing. He was so intent on examining the ground he was startled to come upon the bush where his clothes draped, still dripping. He rearranged the shirt to take better advantage of the waning light then moved several yards further from the edge of the pool and began another circle of the water.

He circled the pool in ever widening sweeps and still found no evidence of his having passed that way, but he did find a trickle of water springing from a small gravel bar. Unlike the pool, this water was fresh and cool and he knelt by the puddle and drank greedily from cupped hands. He returned to the pool, collected his damp garments and carried them to a large boulder where he again draped them for drying.

He carefully and painfully eased back into the pool and wedged his back into a small niche with the hope that the warmth of the water would protect him from the chill of the winter night. He fell asleep pondering the absence of any sign of his coming to the pool. And praying, as usual, for Dora's safety.

The birds called and jeered and Moise wondered how they could see to fly. The shrubs that grew on the slope were black mounds that huddled, still and silent, to watch him waken. The sky wasn't yet light though the darkest of the night had passed. He knew he should be stirring, rousing himself from the warmth of the pool, looking for the trail back to the tree. He adjusted his position and went back to sleep.

He opened his eyes and squinted at the silent mounds still huddled before him. The four men, just as unmoving as he, peered back. He first thought he must have found a village water source and these men had come to fetch the day's supply, but that could not explain their presence. He had seen no evidence of activity around the edges of the pool—not of his own; not of these men; not of even an animal. And if these men wanted water to be fetched they would not come themselves, they would send their women.

The men stood and waited expectantly. One raised a tanned-hide robe and held it forward, inviting Moise to step inside its warmth. Moise, puzzled, stood, squared his shoulders as best he could, and stepped from the bubbling pool.

THIRTEEN

The scabland was made up of thick clumps of tall sage, clumps that were impenetrable to any but the hares and voles that scurried across the gravelly sand and maybe to the coyotes that chased them. A few sparse groves of aspen dotted the high plains, warty indicators of a water source to those who knew the signs.

Moise stretched to step in the footprints of the leader who picked his way silently between the brush and boulders. But the days without food was taking a toll on his young body and several times his head seemed to spin. He'd have swooned were it not for the steadying hand of the guard at his back. Puzzled by the gentleness of that touch, he tried to keep his mind alert by analyzing his circumstances.

He supposed he was more curious than fearful despite his being a captive again. He wondered about the circling route they were taking through the scrub. He reckoned they'd been walking for close onto an hour now but, judging from the few landmarks he could remember, he was certain he could have found his way back to his clothes in a quarter of that.

He listened for the barely audible breathing of the men behind him. There had been three back there when they left the pool but, without looking back, he knew that two of them had, one by one, quietly slipped away and now only the one remained. Where had the others gone?

As if in answer to his pondering Moise smelled wood smoke and without warning he and his captors stood before the partially open end of a long, low, brush-covered structure the likes of which he had never seen. It looked like two of Da's lean-tos pushed together.

Two spindly poles had been affixed horizontally to either side of two aspens growing about two horse-lengths apart. Those crosspieces formed the peak of the roof. Parallel on either side, about as long a distance as two men could stretch foot-to-foot, were other crosspieces affixed about boy-height to nearby trees. Branches and hides placed between the high and low horizontal poles formed the sloped roof; hides hanging from the lower poles provided a break from the wind.

A tattered wisp of smoke escaped from the gap between the two higher crosspieces and was immediately dispatched to Sky by Wind. Small wonder they had been able to circle the small home in the shallow wash for an hour without seeing or smelling it.

The interior of the pole-and-hide house wasn't much warmer than the surrounding scrub but it did provide shelter from Wind who, with nothing to stand in His way, blew assertively across the flat land.

Moise was motioned to a small mat laid out on the ground against one of the support trees. A girl, not much smaller than he, handed him a strip of meat that had been roasting over the low flame of the communal fire. His captor made a low, guttural sound. The girl quickly pulled back the food and withdrew to a far corner.

From the end of the house opposite to the one Moise and his captor had entered came a woman carrying a ceramic bowl. This, along with a metal spoon, she placed at Moise's feet.

He raised a questioning glance to the man. At his nod, Moise lifted the bowl and guzzled the cold, congealed soup inside.

The woman smiled; appreciation of his appetite, perhaps? By the time she knelt to take away the spoon and the emptied bowl, Moise was feeling the warmth of the room. He saw others enter. These people were strangely fuzzy and deformed. Each one seemed to stand beside himself as if he were actually two or even three of the same being. Moise wanted to reach up to brush the film from before his eyes but he couldn't make his arms move. He leaned against the tree trunk and all went dark.

For several days Moise slept, woke, ate more cold soup, and slept again. The first time he woke, he found he'd been given a pillow and been covered with an additional animal hide. The second time, or perhaps the third, he had been clothed in soft buckskins. Even his shoeless feet had been shrouded in warm rabbit fur booties.

On this morning, he was brought awake by his blanket being quietly lifted away. He opened his eyes and watched the girl hold it in front of the small fire, turning and shaking it in the warmth of the embers. When it was warmed she turned and brought it to place over him once again. She saw him warily watching her and she laughed with a sound that reminded him of the tiny bells Amelie's goats wore.

His captor, short and dark, came in through what Moise thought of as the back door. He carried a small haunch of venison and with the help of the woman hung it above the fire to dry in the smoke. He turned to the watching Moise and motioned him up and outside.

The intensity of the cold startled the young man and he gasped then coughed. His captor spun and clamped a hand over Moise's mouth. His other hand he placed over his own mouth. Moise understood that the safety of the camp rested on their living undetected in this little swale and that silence was integral to their invisibility. He nodded to the eyes of his captor.

There were three women working outside the strange-looking longhouse. Two of them were cutting strips of meat from a gutted stag hanging from a tree. The other was hanging the meat on a rack built over a bed of coals. The wind and the heat would dry the smaller ribbons. The icy chill would freeze the rest.

The women chattered while they worked but in

tones so low it sounded like a small swarm of bees. He made an offer to help but the surprised women shooed him back inside where his captor now sat.

The man sat before the fire drinking something hot from a metal cup. He indicated another cup to Moise then passed a stick of venison across the fire. Moise solemnly chewed and swallowed the first meat he'd had since the rotted meat fed him by his earlier captors. He washed it down with the hot drink—a surprisingly sweet concoction of herbs.

Their breakfast finished, the man leaned forward and spoke. Moise stared. The man tried again. This time Moise shook his head in confusion. The third try was in a mixture of English and something Moise had never heard but he nodded and held up his thumb and index finger indicating he had understood a tiny bit of what the man had said.

"Nahtahk." The man patted his chest then drew a circle in the dirt. Though Moise missed some of the specifics he recognized the symbols for family groups and could guess at the relationships. When he no longer looked befuddled, Nahtahk, in broken English, sign, and more drawings, began his narrative.

His family, explained Nahtahk, had long ago been charged with the responsibility of protecting the Sacred Pool; of keeping its location a closely guarded secret. One wishing to bathe in her waters must first find the village of Nahtahk. If found worthy, he would be led by Nahtahk's family men to the pool by such a route and in such a way as to ensure he would not be able to find his way to the pool again. All that secrecy meant that Nahtahk's family must, themselves, remain aloof, small, and solitary. They moved often, hiding their longhouses in cottonwood groves or aspen swales. They worked and lived in quiet.

He explained that horses were noisy, active creatures so Nahtahk's family neither used nor kept them, but they certainly recognized their value to those who lived in other villages. Imagine the surprise then, of the three boys who were watching from beneath their deerhide hunting blind when Moise slipped into the barren oak and let a perfectly good mount walk away.

When darkness fell and Moise had not descended from his perch, the youngest son of Nahtahk's sister ran home to alert Nahtahk to the presence of an intruder. When the moon sank behind the western mountains, just before the coming of dawn, the four men of the family set out in search of this strange boy—one who would give up a horse and would sleep in a tree.

Throughout the night, the two sons of Nahtahk's son had waited beneath their blind. They shivered and whispered about the boy in the tree until sleep, at last, silenced their speculations. They were instantly alert when they heard the soft tread of the browsing stag. Just as cautious and still as the boy in the tree, the brothers peered from beneath the leather. When Moise dropped to the back of the stag, the older boy sped after him. The other stayed to tell his uncles what the boys had seen, though even the poorest of trackers could easily have traced the path of the bounding stag.

By mid-day, Nahtahk's elder grandson had found the furrow where Moise had been thrown from the stag. It was then that he heard the other two intruders riding hard in his direction. The boy hid again, and this time watched the two riders circle one clump of brush after another in an effort to find the one who was lost. They too could see the tracks of tumbling and sliding in the dirt but they could not find the boy-who-would-give-up-a-horse.

The grandson gave the men plenty of time to give up and be far away before sneaking from his cover to, himself, look for the stag rider. But as he stood to do so a woman appeared, lifted the strange boy in her arms, and carried him directly to the warm pool. She placed him gently in the water then stood, looked at Nahtahk's son, placed her finger over her lips in a request for secrecy, and stepped behind the boulders.

Nahtahk, with the men of his family, arrived at the Sacred Pool to find his grandson watching the sleeping Moise. Then they did what Moise had done. They'd backtracked again and again looking for sign of the woman. They had easily found where Moise had lain hidden by the brush he had pulled atop himself, but they had found no sign of the woman.

Moise shook his head in denial. "No woman. I crawled to the pool."

The man whistled softly and within seconds three boys stood before him. When he entered the longhouse the tallest of the three had nodded slightly to Moise as if in recognition, but now they stood straight and still before him with bowed heads. Nahtahk spoke; the tall boy responded quietly and with gestures Moise recognized but refused to accept.

Nahtahk turned to Moise and, repeating the gestures said, "Indian woman. Long black braids; long, beautiful face; round belly, full of child; marked here to here." The man drew a finger from his hairline, down his forehead, and to the tip of his nose. "Woman carried you. You not crawl. Pool well hidden—secret. No one knows it. Woman took you there."

FOURTEEN

All of his mother's peoples, from small family bands to large multi-family clans, traded with their neighbors for local goods, but it was at the trade fairs, many days walk down the Great River, where intertribal cooperation and communication were developed, fostered, and maintained. Here, for several weeks twice each year, men, women, and children alike would sing and dance, race and play, gossip and gamble, haggle and barter. Stories and ideas, especially religious and social concepts, were shared and debated in sacred gatherings and in general conversations; marriages were performed, births and passings were marked.

The young man who was called Moise by his father now called himself Ben and he wandered between the tipis and marveled at the festivity. He watched and listened in fascination, hoping to discuss the goings-on with the Black Robes with whom he'd spent the last few years.

Many of the goods brought to the gatherings were not original to those who brought them. People from far beyond the Great River brought items traded from peoples ever further away. So it was that people from near to where Cold-Maker lived were able to carry in their sacred bundles the vision-inducing buttons some traders called peyote which grew where Cold-Maker seldom visited. People from the mouth of the Great River were able to bring canoes—large enough to hold twenty paddlers on a side—that they had bartered from makers many days walk along the salty water's edge. Dancers at the fires could wear large frightening masks made from the hides of animals that had not been seen in this territory while alive.

Ben himself had traded all of his trade goods for a pouch made from the bright red iridescent scalp of the large bird that pecked its nest into the wood of dead trees. It had come from Nahtahk's cousin who lived not far from the Black Robes. The man was a shrewd trader and Ben knew he had probably paid too much for it, but, in all of his years, he had never seen something he'd wanted so badly.

The people who lived close to the Great River had easy access to salmon—the fish with the pale-red meat—and many large baskets of them were caught, dried, and traded every year. It was one of the two most important trade items at the gatherings. Those people, who called themselves by the names Umatilla and Yakima, drove hard bargains and amassed much wealth, forging strong trade alliances throughout the region.

Their proximity to the gathering place meant that they were also the most populous of the tribes at the trading fairs—their wives and daughters weren't pressed to walk from afar carrying their trade goods as were women from other regions. Assembling as one large family meant they had greater opportunities for mixing and meeting throughout the event, for arranging marriages to men and women from other tribes; marriages that would indisputably tie groups together into an even larger—richer and more powerful—family.

In these ways, they had controlled and manipulated their wealth and power to make themselves the socially and politically elite at the trade fair. Nahtahk had encouraged Ben to bring something to trade—toys, crucifixes, Rosaries, spoons—anything that would make the Umatilla's notice him. Nahtahk was certain Ben was worthy of a Umatilla bride.

The only trade items more important than the salmon were the slaves. The Indians preferred to own slaves from faraway places, believing there was less chance they would try to return to their homes. While traders would sometimes travel through an area selling their newest captives, the annual gathering was where those in the market for slaves had the largest selection.

Those Indians who called themselves by the names Modoc and Klamath brought many slaves captured in war raids. They called their captives Pit Rivers and Shastas and spat when they said those names.

The Chinookans from the mouth of the Great River brought people they had captured in raids too, but they also traded away some of their own people—orphans, contraries, law-breakers, or social misfits.   Ben was surprised to see the Chinookans had also brought White Men this year—men who had worked on large boats that had foundered and sank in a body of water that was so enormous as to be incomprehensible to him. He would only accept the stories of capture and salvage as true because he'd read about oceans in the books in the Black Robes' library.

Ben meandered along a path far from the frenzied hum of activity. He was deep in thought about the concept of slavery and was rehearsing his questions for the Black Robes and Nahtahk when he came upon a slave struggling with his owner. A scraggly pup was barking at the fracas and trying to bite the legs of the Umatilla.

The slave picked up a stone and slammed the Indian up 'side the head then turned to run but Ben stood in the narrow path. As with all slaves, the man's head had been shorn and he wore no clothes. His stance indicated he would not allow Ben to stop his escape.

"If this man is dead, you must die also." Ben said softly, squatting beside the downed man.

"English?" the slave grasped at the possibility that someone might understand what he had to say. "He wanting eat my dog!" He held out his arms and the pup leaped into his grasp.

Ben nodded and continued. "They will kill you now. They will throw *you* to *their* dogs."

The slave was retreating. "Keep dog. Kodiak. I am Russian sailor. They kill me. Not kill Kodiak. He save me when ship sink. I save him now."

The man thrust the dog at Ben's chest then turned and darted for the trees. Ben wanted to call after him; to warn him that he would need his dog for many things; to tell him to go upriver, not down, and north not south. Two spears found their mark before Ben could call out.

Still squatting beside the injured Umatilla, he held the squirming pup and tried to console a creature that should have been nothing more than a meal. He found himself reliving the days under the stinking shroud, feeling the sudden and violent loss of all he held in his heart. He ached afresh for the loss of Dorie and Mam.

He pulled the pup closer to his chest and nuzzled the back of its head. He didn't know if it was his empathy that made the pup stop struggling or a realization that his friend was beyond help, but, with a quiet whimper, the dog settled onto the dirt in front of Ben's knees.

The downed Indian stirred and when Ben tried to help him to his feet he slapped at Ben's hand and reached for the dog. The pup snapped and would have done the man an injury had not Ben grabbed him back. It was clear the man wanted the dog and Ben worried he would call to his friends, the two lancers who were yipping and crowing over the body of the dead Russian. He would be no match for the three of them.

He reached to his belt and loosed the beautiful scalp of the bright red bird and shook it vigorously towards the Indian. The man hesitated, looked at the snarling dog, grabbed the trophy and ran to join his friends. Ben picked up the pup and, rising to his feet, turned back towards the encampments before the Umatilla could change his mind. He didn't wait to see what the men did next.

He sat before the tipi, his new friend curled against him. The young dog's shivering had slowed to infrequent spasms that seemed to ease with Ben's quiet assurances. Still, Ben was reluctant to move until the dog had quieted even more.

He tinkered with several of the small bent *par fleche* rods Nahtahk had brought to the gathering. When he was a boy, Ben had seen his mother's people submerge fresh deerskin in a solution they'd made by pouring water through a basket of ashes. The hide was soaked, scraped, stretched and beaten to a transparent thinness. When dry, it was tough enough to use for the soles of moccasins; to make carrying baskets for the women, quivers for the hunters. While Nahtahk's small family had used the same method of soaking and stretching and beating and drying to make the same things, now they used the leftover bits and pieces to make the little knots Ben called puzzles.

He had learned to make them of iron when he lived with the Black Robes. The first summer he returned to Nahtahk's village he'd brought several to Nahtahk as gifts and was pleased by the old man's fascination with the twisted iron trinket. Ben knew the family had neither the capacity nor the desire to build a forge so was delighted the following summer when Nahtahk surprised him with the several he had fashioned from hide.

Nahtahk's family had always brought much to the autumn trading circle; chunks of smoked venison to trade for the pans or dishes used by his wives; the black, shiny cobbles he would trade to point-makers for more hunting tools; and the coyote tobacco to which he himself had become addicted. This year, almost as an afterthought, he had bundled several sets of the challenging little toys into a deerskin bale. He might be able to trade a few for trifles to take home to his daughter and granddaughters.

Now Ben linked two rods, then two from a different set. As he worked, he imagined many more shapes into which the rods could be bent and twisted. He shivered in the hot autumn sun.

He looked up at the group of traders who stood before him. All were watching him tinker with the small pieces of dried hide but the one who caused the spirit to run a finger down his spine was not among them. He continued to scan the crowd for the witch. In front of a tipi many steps away, two elders stood watching him. One dismissed him with a passing glance, focusing instead on the movement of his fingers. The other held his gaze with narrowed eyes and again Ben shivered.

Four winters before, Moise had left Nahtahk's family after the first freeze of autumn. When he reached the Black Robe's church and school on the banks of the Great River, those men first insisted that he rest there, then that he work to buy passage across the river. After that it was to learn a trade and to hone his speaking skills in order to communicate better with those who might know of Dorie's life. It was there he learned to make shoes for horses and parts for wagons—and to bend little scraps of iron into puzzling shapes.

He'd attended school and changed his names, pulling two almost at random from the Bible. He chose Benjamin, a given name that didn't remind him of Da, and a second one because the Black Robes said he must have a family name. He had never known Da's family name so adopted the first one that came to mind—Adam.

Every summer he went back to help Nahtahk's small family guard the Sacred Pool but after this autumn trade fair he would leave both the Black Robes and Nahtahk and go back to the valley where he had last seen his sister.

Now he rose and stood tall then turned and stepped deliberately into Nahtahk's tipi. He closed the flap and turned to sit cross-legged, facing the door, ready to face the witch. No one followed though he was certain the man stood without, his gaze piercing the hide of the structure.

Instead, it was Nahtahk who swept into the tipi demanding more toys. Ben indicated with a nod the remaining few that rested just inside the flap. Nahtahk, gregarious in his newfound fame, chuckled that they should have brought more bent rods than they did the chunks of shiny rock and the smoked venison. He strode from the tipi but failed to drop the flap completely into place. Ben watched the silver sliver of daylight and saw the moccasins of the witch, standing motionless where Ben had so recently sat.

The last morning of the gathering was always the most exciting and the most chaotic. Traders hurried to find buyers for their unsold items and buyers continued to haggle for even lower prices. The women, children, and slaves hurried to break camp and say their good-byes. Barking dogs and blowing dust dulled the senses to all else.

Ben worked to roll all of Nahtahk's purchases into the one deerskin that had previously held the little puzzles. It wasn't working. Nahtahk had traded for many more items than he had brought.

He grasped the bundle, one hand on each side of the bottom, and lifted it off the ground. He stood, turned, and found himself face to face with the witch.

The elder looked levelly at the young man who started then stared back. The man spoke. Ben remained silent. He had added Spanish and Latin from the Black Robes to his growing list of languages, but he was afraid of the witch and, though the words were strangely familiar, Ben didn't understand what the man had said.

The man raised his hand, palm forward and three times he opened his hand with splayed fingers. The fourth time he held up but one finger. Suspicious, Ben nodded hesitantly. He was indeed, that many summers. The witch murmured and turned away, leaving Ben to watch his retreating back.

FIFTEEN

Ben huddled under the juniper branches that formed the roof of the semi-subterranean chamber. They had watched the clouds build and roil from beyond the evening sky and had hurried to reach this rocky shelter before Thunder's Rain descended in her passion. Silently they'd dog-trotted across the prairie floor, chased by an angry Wind. Thunder was already shouting for earth-bound creatures to take cover against his violence when they finally reached this series of hollows that pitted the surrounding scree. Now they watched the furious torrent choke the thirsty hardpack and leave a sheet of water, waiting to be absorbed, covering the barren meadow.

They had all scrambled to gather branches to cover the top of the larger pit and now bundled themselves in their hide robes and hunkered down against the chill. Ben had used his robe to wrap Nahtahk's many purchases and now had nothing to cover himself or the fierce, scrawny pup that refused to leave his side.

He had learned long ago that by concentrating on something other than his immediate surroundings he could lessen whatever pain he might be feeling. Now he watched through the chinks in the stone walls at suicidal tumbleweeds bashing themselves against a distant rock wall or impaling themselves on the other prickly bundles that had been tossed ahead.

"Rabbits."

Ben started then turned to stare at the young Indian. He was the youngest of the group, close to Ben's own age. He'd built a low, smoky fire over which they would warm the red meat of their newly purchased fish and now, squinting against the smoke, grinned at Ben from across the drip that fell steadily from a gap in the juniper covering.

When Ben failed to respond the man continued. With broken English and much hand waving, his companion explained that the low curved stone fence was a trap into which runners, children usually, drove wild rabbits. The animals, unable or unwilling to jump the fence—he couldn't be sure he understood correctly—were trapped inside the curve and slaughtered by women who had lain in wait on the other side. This pit and the many surrounding it were part of a large temporary hunting camp that was used by the women year after year.

The young man stopped and waited now for Ben to respond. Questions were like the tumbleweeds bouncing past and Ben didn't know which to ask first. "English?"

"My wife, Kanit'sa, she teach to me. I am Striking Horse but Kanit'sa tells me in English, *Mus-n-touchit.*"

"Ya-ya-ya-ya-ya-ya-ya-ya!" The high-pitched yell came from the first of the older men who had stood to stare through a chink in the stones. Now all four of them were watching in great agitation and "Ya-ya-ing" in one form or another. Ben and Striking Horse turned to see a strangely marked horse being ridden across the prairie at what Ben could only assume was top speed. He wasn't sure whether the men were cheering the rider or deriding him. The rider pressed so low against the horse's neck that Ben, peering through the sheet of driving rain, couldn't see the lines that separated the two. Each hoof strike splattered horse and rider with dusty water.

As suddenly as it had started, the bedlam inside the pit stopped and the men now watched breathless and hopeful as if the rider had passed a certain point that seemed to make them think he might make it to the shelter. Within seconds the "Ya-ya-ing" recommenced but this time quietly, fervently, as if in prayer.

Thrower-of-Fire struck at the instant Thunder clapped. The small juniper under which the horse had just sped disintegrated into a smoldering ruin. The rider leaped from the back of the horse and, dragging it behind him, ran for the shelter of the pit in which the small group had collected. He was met at the entrance by all four of the elders brooking no argument, and waving him back to the trees. The rider hurried with the horse to another of the pits and stood with him, hand on hackamore, as the rain pounded them unmercifully.

"Iron Moccasin win horse in game with Palouse. Say she Good Fortune. Striker say may be—if spears from gods miss."

With a flash of insight Ben knew it wasn't the man they'd rejected but the horse—a thousand pounds of liquid would draw the spear of Thrower-of-Fire directly into their midst.

Ben continued to stare through the chinks at the sheets of driving rain, at the rider, at the unusual horse. It was the color of mud with a white rump dotted with mud splatters the rain could not wash away.

He sensed that the eldest man in the group was again watching him. As at the gathering, the older man's way of narrowing his eyes and looking at Ben as if he were reading an aura made Ben shiver. Striking Horse brought a newly-acquired buffalo robe from the bundle Ben had been carrying and draped it over Ben's shoulders. They stood together in silence and watched the storm pass with no ill effects.

He knew that now his work would begin. It was up to him, as the new member of the group—the dog—to bring firewood, water, and more juniper branches and this he set out to do in earnest, glad for the chance to be alone with his turmoil.

The erupting of the "Ya-ya-ya-ing" during the storm had masked the real reason for the shock that surely had registered on his face at that moment. He hadn't heard 'Musn't-Touch-It', Mam's nickname for Dora, since Mam died and Dorie was sold. That was more than five years ago. Where could this young man have heard that name?

He collected branches and brought them to the shelter then returned to the verge to gather more. He moved slowly, pondering the turn his life had just taken. For two days the men had been trudging north. They'd left behind the family of Nahtahk moving slowly behind their aging patriarch.

Ben felt sad but somehow betrayed. His old friend and mentor had dropped the idea of Ben marrying into the Umatillas—as if he'd stood a chance after the incident with the dog—and urged him, indeed ordered him, to travel instead with this new band. But he wouldn't, or couldn't, tell him why.

"When Sun rises, we will leave for high mountains. Maybe snow. Then down, down, down to Great River. Then walk into Morning Sun some days. Walk by river some days. Cross. Follow Met-how to home." Striking Horse had come, unnoticed, to help with the wood.

Striking Horse' description of their homeward journey seemed to Ben to be the one he would have taken alone had Nahtahk not interfered. It was the way to the valley where he had last seen Dorie.

Throughout the journey Striking Horse was friendly and gregarious, seemingly glad for a chance to practice speaking English. Ben, afraid to ask about Kanit'sa, asked instead about life in the village.

Striking Horse admitted being surprised when his father, Striker, insisted that Ben come with them. Yes, Nahtahk had spread the rumor that Ben was protected by the gods, but they already had one in their village they believed to be Special in that way. And he was certain his father didn't want Ben as a slave. They were different than the Chinook and the Modoc peoples they'd met at the trading circles. Those people relied on their slaves for much of the work done in the village. Here, in these wide, vast plains, the people valued their own independence so greatly they wouldn't dream of taking another's from him.

"Unless he was a very bad man. No, not even then. We would kill him if we couldn't change him. But not eat him like the Coastal peoples do. If he were very brave we would eat his heart so we could have his courage." Striking Horse continued to ramble and Ben, though he much preferred walking in silence, continued to listen lest the man make reference again to his wife.

Ben had wandered up and down the Great River while he was at the school of the Black Robes and now the horizon across the river became increasingly familiar. It was the one he'd seen every morning from the schoolhouse. Between the hills he'd named *Rounded Butte* and *Baldy Top* was the canyon through which the *Met-how* tumbled. It was up that river his home place had stood—Mam's cave had been dug far into the bank of that stream. It was up that river he must go one day to face the man he called Da. It was this little river, flowing into The Great River at just the right place, that created the eddies and undertows that widened The Great River and so made an upstream crossing on foot possible. By his reckoning they should be at the crossing well before nightfall. If he wanted to break from these men, there would be the place to do so.

Deep in thought, Ben failed to hear Iron Moccasin ride up to the group on his strangely marked mare. Only after the rider stopped dead in front of him did Ben come out of his reverie.

"English!" Iron Moccasin shouted while pointing up river. He motioned and shouted and danced his nervous horse around Ben.

The instant Ben came to realize he was expected to leap onto the back of the horse behind its rider he shook his head and backed away. But Iron Moccasin had reached down, grabbed Ben's arm, and turned to ride away. So Ben lunged for the mare, grabbed for the rider, and both men thudded to the ground. Iron Moccasin flew to his feet in rage, bouncing and stomping and railing.

Ben, reverting to tactics learned long ago, sent his mind to another place. He thought Iron Moccasin looked like a wasp fallen onto a hot skillet. A grunt from Striker brought the man silent for a moment before he grabbed a handful of mane, flung himself onto his horse, and rode madly upriver.

Puzzled and uncertain, Ben looked to the others for answers but they, with heads down and eyes to the ground, had resumed their trek as if nothing had interrupted their journey towards home.

Iron Moccasin soon returned, this time followed by another rider. The one, Ben assumed, who spoke only English. He seemed nervous—wary and watchful—but relaxed somewhat when Ben, in English, asked him his business.

He was one of three men hired to drive a herd of cattle from the Indian Agency in Yakima to the one in the Okanogan country. They'd not been able to find an easy place to ford the river with the herd so were looking for riders to help them cross. The Catholics had suggested they wait for the Indians who would be returning soon from the trading grounds.

Ben hadn't been on a horse since the day he'd hoisted himself into the barren oak tree five years ago, nor had he been around cattle since leaving Da's homestead just a few days before that.

"What're you paying?"

"Payin'?" the cowboy blurted.

Ben remained silent, watching the man in the way he imagined Striker, standing behind him, would be doing.

"Um...uh....Two head!"

"Each." A brave word, he knew, for a group of seven men that had but one horse and a dog between them.

"EACH?" the cowboy croaked. "Why that'd be ... ."

Ben waited patiently for the man to tally the count and when he realized it couldn't happen he said, "Fourteen."

"FOURTEEN?! We only got...thirty!"

"How do you know?"

"Agent said so!"

"Maybe you do, maybe you don't. You'll have none if you can't ford."

"We ain't payin' fourteen head. That'd only leave us...."

Ben again waited for the man to do the numbering then gave up. "Good luck to you," he said sincerely then he stepped around the man's horse and resumed his journey. He knew without turning that the others were following his lead.

The cowboy turned his mount and rode at a gallop up the dusty path just as Iron Moccasin had done earlier. But this time, Iron Moccasin rode sedately behind his kinsmen.

SIXTEEN

The tired men trudged up to the complex of the Black Robes. Ben knew they would be fed and sheltered for the night, as would all weary travelers. As would the three drovers who met them at the gate, barring the entrance with their bulk and their ire.

Before Ben could demand entrance, one of the priests came into the courtyard and shouted a greeting. The cowboys, rooted and belligerent like thorny greasewood, turned slightly to eye the priest.

"This is the man I was telling you about. The one who speaks English and knows the Indians and the river. He can find you the men to get you across."

"This yere's the kid tried to rob us," accused the cowboy.

"Ben?" asked the priest with raised brows.

"We want fourteen head as wages."

"Ben! They have only fifty. Even God asks for only ten per cent."

"Then let him ask his god to get his cattle across."

"He did, Ben, and God sent you."

"You have preached to me, Black Robe, that I can be sure my sins will come back to me—if not today then tomorrow or tomorrow or tomorrow. Maybe this man's god is already exacting his due for the man's intent to cheat us. He tells me he has thirty head, you say he has fifty. After we take the fourteen head God tells us to have, the drover will still reach Okanogan with more than he reckons he started with. Let him, instead, thank his god for the increase.

"Fourteen head. We choose which ones. We choose *after* we're across."

"That's a hard bargain. You have no Christian mercy for these poor drovers?"

"These *poor drovers* first tried to cheat the *stupid Indians*. And your Christian God has yet to show me mercy. Or kindness. Ever. When He does, Black Robe, I will return to the Indian Agency in Okanogan fourteen head of cattle in exchange for what we take tomorrow."

By the time the parties had reached an agreement and the priest put it on paper—fourteen head of cattle to be selected by Ben after the river crossing—the sun was low on the horizon. The cattle wouldn't cross with the sun in their eyes, that much Ben did remember, so it was early in the following morning that Iron Moccasin, on his strangely colored mount, led the small group to the camp of the drovers.

Ben reckoned they were getting a late start, but one of the riders was just breaking camp, a second was frantically trying to keep the small herd bunched together; the third rode up to Ben. "They'll have enough help now, they don't need me. I'm heading back to Wenatchee Landing. I'm a schoolteacher not a cowboy. Only signed on as a lark. Those two morons have been fighting and bickering since we started. Can't even keep the cattle going along a trail wide enough to drive a wagon through. One of them forgot the grub-box so this morning we're supposed to use dried cow-platters for plates. 'Just don't eat the bottom flapjack,' he says. Well, you can have 'em. Them and their cattle, too. Take *every* head away from them...serve 'em right." Without waiting for a response, he flicked his reins and rode around the knot of men standing on the path.

Iron Moccasin had sat his mare, watching the inept drovers. When he'd found what he was looking for he eased the horse into the small herd, dropped a rope over the horns of the lead cow, and coaxed her without rushing towards the trail. The milling took on a new motion as the remaining animals followed their leader. Ben and the men of Striker's family followed, whooping now and then to encourage stragglers and impress, or frighten, the drovers. The over-zealous drovers, once they caught up with the herd, spurred their horses wildly but ineffectively up and down the trail on either side of the cattle.

The sun was still low in the morning sky when the vertical riverbank dropped to a sandy beach. Here the river meandered through a wide, flat plain. Small, low-lying islands stretched from the near beach to a similar one on the western shore. They could see the Indian Agency, a short ride upstream on the opposite side. Without hesitation, Iron Moccasin, the sun now at his back, led the cow into the water and towards the nearest of the islands. He wove his way between and across the islands with the drovers riding beside the herd. The Indians waded behind.

After the negotiations of the day before, the long night's wait, and the tension of dealing with the unfamiliar, splashing across the river at a walk was anticlimactic and the drovers were angry. "We ain't giving you nothin'! You didn't do nothin' we couldn't a done."

Ben eyed them narrowly then shrugged one shoulder to Iron Moccasin. The rider turned slowly and began coaxing the lead cow back into the river. The drovers plunged their mounts into the river to turn the herd but this time Iron Moccasin had led the cattle into deep water. Frightened cattle, blinded now by the morning sun and unable to smell the familiar scent of their leader, plunged and thrashed in the deep cold river. Horses, reined and whipped, spun to do their riders' bidding, only to lose their footing in the depths. In the ensuing mayhem the drovers and their confused mounts washed downstream towards the rapids. By the time they had reached shore and ridden back to the scene of the chaos, the Indians had led the intact herd of cattle into the corrals at the Indian Agency.

It was midday before Ben was allowed to cut his fourteen head of cattle from the corral and leave the Agency. He had watched Striker for a nod of approval or an imperceptible shake of his head each time he chose an animal. These animals were here to be slaughtered. Ben saw no reason to leave the best ones to be eaten—better to take them to found a herd—a pitiful one maybe but one they could call their own. With good stewardship they themselves could supply the Agency with enough cattle for a good many people. But, *the best* in this case could in no way be synonymous with *good* and Ben knew a few of these would not make it through a hard winter.

A younger son of Striker, waiting for them at the Indian Agency, had shot for home on Iron Moccasin's Good Fortune as soon as the men arrived. He was to direct the villagers to haul logs and brush to the mouth of a nearby box canyon where they would corral the cows and the bull-calf they'd culled from the herd of derelicts.

The trek home would be long and arduous. Iron Moccasin had insisted on keeping the lead cow, belligerent though she was about leaving some of her herd behind. The other cows followed her, though not always well. The men trudged behind, hurrying the strays along. Having the cattle meant they would spend another night away from home but by keeping a steady pace and with no more gifts from the White Man's god, they could make it home tomorrow.

The sun sat round and red on the western horizon and Ben paused in his work to stare. The cattle had raised a cloud of fine dust that turned the sun into a crimson ball. Awesome as it was, it wasn't what held his attention. He'd seen that sun set behind those mountains. When he'd visited Mam's people? When he'd gone to Ruby to deliver the elixir with Da? He knew he had seen that skyline.

He realized that, once again, Striker was standing at a distance, staring at him. This time he held the old man's gaze.

Darkness was falling when Iron Moccasin led the herd to within sight of the village. The last miles had been especially treacherous for both man and beast. The cattle, sick and weak and with naturally poor night vision, stumbled continuously. Frightened by their blindness they wanted to drop where they stood or bolt at a blind run. Only the proximity of the lead cow and the gentle voices of the men urging them forward prevented an outright stampede.

They heard the chaos of childish laughter and much ya-ya-yaing coming from the ring of tipis. It was a puzzling sound and they picked up their pace, curious of the cause, then stopped and gaped, unable to move. A young boy was riding Iron Moccasin's lucky horse through the camp pulling a small bundle behind. As they watched in awe, the bundle stopped being dragged and began to chase Good Fortune.

The lucky horse ran between tipis and cooking fires, knocking poles and pots in every direction. The bobcat ran behind, skillfully dodging the wreckage and gaining ground on the horse. The boy clung tenaciously to Good Fortune's mane and, still gripping the rope with the lassoed bobcat at the other end was screaming, "Somebody shoot it! Somebody shoot it!"

The cattle took fright and bolted into the middle of the fray; the boy lost his grip on the rope; the lucky horse, with the hissing, snarling bobcat fast on his fetlocks and the boy glued tenaciously to her back, headed for the path in which the tired drovers stood, stock-still in wonderment. The men made no effort to stop the horse or the bobcat, but calmly stepped aside to let them pass.

At the sight of the men, however, the bobcat veered sharply and bounded towards the river, the rope still dragging from its neck. A single shot rang through the chaos and the unfortunate bobcat rolled lifelessly into the dirt.

The shot shook the boys from their high spirits and they immediately began to help encircle the milling cows. When the cows finally stood, huffing and bawling but not going anywhere, Striker roared a word, one that Ben didn't need to understand, and struck the ground with his walking stick.

The boys jumped to attention, their dusty faces tracked by the tears of their laughter. The two groups faced each other over the backs of the cows—the boys with saucer-like eyes and rigid spines, the men with cold immobile faces. Ben knew the sting of Striker's eyes—knew they could make even an innocent man shiver—and was in ambivalent empathy with the boys.

Striker grimly pointed his walking stick at the tallest of the youths—the one Ben had seen at the Indian Agency. The young boy stepped forward, hung his head in contrition or respect, Ben supposed it was both, and began his explanation.

While he was speaking, Iron Moccasin rode the sweating, huffing lucky horse into camp. Mounted behind and clutching him around the middle, rode the young perpetrator of the mayhem. He handed the boy down beside the taller boy then said a few terse words to Striker. Striker turned again to the boys. With a coldness that sent chills down Ben's spine he spoke to the group. With an emphatic "Ya!" and a wave of his stick he sent the boys scurrying to drive the cows from the camp. Then, with regal carriage, the men of the trading party strode into one of the damaged tipis.

Ben rummaged through the debris and found a water bucket that had sustained only minor damage. He found the path that led to the creek and stumbled through the darkness to the water. He brought back as much water as the dented pail would hold and took it to the tipi into which the men had stooped. He stood waiting outside the door. Strange muffled barks and snorts came from within. Striking Horse moved the flap aside and invited Ben inside.

The men were sitting around a small, smoky fire and all were in various stages of hilarity, holding their bellies, slapping their thighs, and rolling on the ground. Striking Horse placed the dented bucket on a large, flat stone then, grinning, motioned Ben outside.

"Women go to make corral for cows. Son of Iron Moccasin see Bobcat hiding near water path—very dangerous for small ones, he say. To save

139

babies, he jump on horse and catch Bobcat with rope. Bobcat not want to come here. Pull and pull. Then Bobcat say, *Why pull? I will chase!* Very funny Bobcat!

"Son of Iron Moccasin almost ready for vision quest. Get big head. Push other boys. Not kind. Now Bobcat make very funny Son of Iron Moccasin!

"My father tell my brother if he will be chief someday—after me—he must be wiser one and stop foolishness of other boys. He say to boys, bobcat with rope will die slow so he must shoot bobcat. He say the boys catch bobcat in fun but bobcat not die in fun. Son of Iron Moccasin must find dead cat and make nice headdress for his father before he allowed quest for totem.

"Men see very funny but boys must not know. Now boys take cows to women. Women and boys will guard. We sleep." He grinned and motioned Ben towards one of the smaller, almost intact, tipis.

Ben looked at the poles leaning precariously in every direction and shook his head with a hint of a smile. He dropped the buffalo rob to the ground beside the tipi and rolled into it. He patted Kodiak, who had dropped to the ground at his side, and gazed at the stars to begin his prayer for Dora. He was immediately asleep, tired beyond anything previously imaginable.

He woke once during the night, confused by a dream. He dreamed of Dora again. He dreamed she was speaking to him and patting his dog, but in the skewed reality that dreams take, the dream-Dora was an Indian.

SEVENTEEN

Lettie hugged her knees closer to her chest. She'd have pulled the quilt over her shoulders to ward off the chill but was wary of waking Blue-Belle. She gazed at the smaller form beside her; felt rather than saw the girl's presence in this mid-night blackness.

Belle stirred and murmured. The younger one was so demure folks would have found her easy to overlook had she not been so exquisitely beautiful. Like her mother, and her mother's mother, she was fair of skin and blessed with baby-fine pale hair and light blue eyes that made one think of the delicate little flowers produced when the wild borage proclaimed the onset of spring in this high desert—the little blue bells to which she owed her nickname. She had a whimsical smile that made one wonder if the child knew something the observer didn't and a voice so sweet and soft one felt one should listen twice just to catch what she said. "If it pleases God, don't let her become the scolding, bitter woman our mother has become," whispered Lettie rolling her eyes to the roof of the cold barren cabin.

Her earliest memory was of a time when she was about the age of three years, perhaps as many as four. She had found a hen's egg beneath the prickly, woody stems of a sage bush. Even now she could feel her delight. Mama would be so pleased. She grabbed the egg and ran as fast as her shoeless feet could go over the gravelly scrubland. The chickens had scratched through the arid crust in several places, making small dust filled pockets of dry powder in which to fluff and flutter, expurgating themselves of ticks and other parasitic vermin. She could still see the indentations; feel the warm powder squirt between her toes as she ran, slapping into the little wallows and dodging the surface detritus that made up the floor of the prairie. Pealing, "Mama! Mama!" she sped towards the prairie wagon Papa had borrowed.

But Mama, meeting her in the shade of their temporary home, had not been pleased. She'd scolded Lettie, shouted at her to come fetch Mama next time rather than bring the precious egg.

Several years later Lettie had talked with Papa of her memories. He explained that rattlesnakes, attracted to both the shade of the bush and the egg lying at its base, were a serious danger here at their new home and besides that, Mama feared Lettie would trip in one of the hen wallows and break a leg. They knew of no one who was trained in bone setting here in Washington Territory and no mother wished a poorly knitted bone on a four-year-old child. Twelve years had passed since then. A log bungalow had replaced the wagon, Belle had come into the world, but Lettie could still feel the sting of that early reprimand—never mind snakebite or broken bones.

Lettie more closely resembled the man she adored so much—active and irrepressible but as plain as milk-cheese. And while Belle's smile might suggest amusement Lettie's grin left no doubt. Papa often declared that if God hadn't given Lettie ears to stop it, her grin would have wrapped all the way around her head.

Like her father, Lettie possessed a sharp intelligence and quick wit. Last year she had become frustrated with the burrs in her long wavy hair so, bending at the waist, had gathered the dark mop atop her head and used the shears Papa saved for cutting the wagon canvas to whack off even the finest strand that dared extend beyond her encircling fist. Now she smiled and ran her fingers through the shock of curls. She loved it like this. It was worth all of Mama's shrieking and the half-hearted switching Papa gave her. Mama didn't know that Lettie did the same thing every few weeks in order to keep it shorter than was thought fitting, though she had once remarked that it seemed to be taking an awfully long time to grow back.

Papa knew. One evening while she sat reading by the light of a tallow candle he had stood beside her chair.

"Reading again, Lettie? What is it this time? You could do with a little more devotional reading and less of those penny-dreadfuls. I cannot suppose you find them uplifting. I do not know where you find them at all." While he spoke he dropped a few short dark hairs in her lap.

"The ones by these English women, Bronte and Austen, were given to me by Missus Coopersmith at the harvest festival last fall because her daughters find no pleasure in reading. The pamphlets belong to my friend Dora who finds them at the Mission in Okanogan. She lends them to me when she is finished with them. When I have returned them to her, she returns them to the Mission House. Mister Ben Franklin is credited with instituting the first lending library in the United States. Did you know that,

Papa?" Quietly, slowly, she had picked up the hairs, reached them toward the candle, and dropped them in the flame.

"Your papa is right, Lettie," contributed her mother from the bed where she rested. "All that reading cannot be beneficial. It will be the ruination of your eyesight and it will give you lofty ideas."

"But Mama, where could I get new stories to tell my sister at bedtime? I cannot *imagine* them." She was correct in her assumption that her mother would acquiesce to anything that would make life easier for her favorite of the two girls. There were no further comments from the darkened corner of the room.

She tucked the woolen patchwork quilt more tightly around her sister while she, herself, continued to shiver periodically. She fingered the quilt, another gift from Missus Coopersmith who had called it her Twenty-Year quilt—sewing on it for brief moments as often as she could spare the time and the will. Those were the two things most difficult to come by in this remote region, she'd explained, but she had an endless and abundant supply of worn out clothing.

"Frocks wears out so fast in this Hell, 'tseems the yard-goods comes that way a'ready." The largest pieces of usable cloth would go to mend still wearable garments. Only the tiniest of remnants, in whatever shape, were patched together to make a crazy quilt.

Her life was in that quilt, she'd told Lettie. "Not sure if that word *crazy* means the patte'n or the maker but that quilt knows more of me than any person does...been a better friend, sure. Was with me times I was happy, times I was so tired I thought I couldn't put in another stitch, times I bawled like a baby. The night my Momma died I put on that little patch there.

When I heard you's were homesteading so nearby to me, I was so excited I could hardly keep the seams straight right here. This here one.... Well, less said the better about that."

The woman never revealed what that particular patch had meant to her. A week after she'd made them a gift of the quilt and the books she was bitten several times by a rattlesnake and died. Mama refused to sleep under the quilt but Lettie thought it un-Christian-like to waste a gift that had meant so much to the giver. She was a bit squeamish about the mystery patch though, and often wondered about it. She was glad it was near a corner that she could tuck under the tick and not have to see regularly.

Belle whimpered. "Lettie, go back to sleep," her father scolded softly from her parents' bed below the loft. It always amazed her that he could hear and identify the rustling of the bedstraw in their mat on the loft floor. How did he know it was she, sitting in the dark, pondering, and not some rodent scurrying across the planks?

She sighed softly and slid down beneath the covers. She snuggled against her sister's back then, tickled by a wisp of blond hair, sneezed once before whispering, "'Night, Papa."

He did not respond but she knew he heard and she slept the better for knowing.

EIGHTEEN

Ben had lived up here in the high graze for most of the summer, guarding the small scraggly herd that belonged to Striker's extended family. He'd never thought himself a cowboy though he'd learned to sit a horse from Blackheart the Frenchman and recognized that he must have picked up a least a smattering of animal husbandry from that same man—his father. He himself had persuaded Striker to trade two good horses for a young breed-cow to supplement the in-bred herd of scrawny ones he'd bartered from the Indian Agency. He was the one who had led the three healthiest cows across the ridge to a rancher named Charlton who willingly sold Ben the services of his best bull in exchange for some much-needed repair work on his farm wagons.

Until now he'd never thought the night a lonely time. He'd always felt safest then; been more comfortable dealing with critters that stole through the blackness on four legs going about the honest business of stalking their prey than with the charlatans who strode boldly about in the daylight on two feet and with two faces.

He wasn't surprised that this new feeling of emptiness was sharpest in the deep of night when the silence was heavy, when the stars rained down a

148

stunning brilliance and the moon's light blurred the edges of the harsh landscape. By day he kept himself busy—riding round the cattle, keeping a close eye on the three yearling heifers that would be the saving of the herd, snaring a rabbit or a bird for eating—but the onset of night brought again this unfamiliar yearning.

Striking Horse had twice ridden up to this high place of solitude to bring food and news and Ben would surely have welcomed another of those visits. But he knew he wanted more. He ached for the sound of a voice, a smile of greeting, the tinkle of laughter on a regular basis.

Did he also want to leave the family of Striker? Now that he knew Dora was safe and happy in her life with Striking Horse could he return to the Black Robes and a life of study—or to Fort Okanagan and the settled life of a blacksmith?

Kanit'sa had accompanied her husband on his second visit. Though she assured Ben her visit was to check on his well being, she'd seemed restless and distracted. He thought it was because she wanted to search for huckleberries but when she left the men to their visiting she set off in the other direction. The men followed, watchful and worried.

He couldn't say who first heard the humming. It wasn't like the humming of the women of the village but very like his sister's humming when she thought no one could hear. The men instinctively stepped into the cover of the sparse shrubbery but Kanit'sa strode ahead, unafraid. Ben pointed to a branch on a nearby willow and Striking Horse nodded and pointed to another. Neither wanted Kanit'sa, if she had seen them dart for cover, to think they were fearful of the strange noise.

They caught up with her as she stopped atop a small rise that looked down on a field of grass and flowers. Dancing and humming through the little glade were two girls—one a young woman about his sister's age, the other was several years younger. Ben watched in fascination. They spun slowly with arms outstretched, dipping and swaying in rhythm to their humming. The cadence increased and the humming turned to song and laughter as they skipped and ran through the flowers. The elder of the two had short curly brown hair that caught the sun and nearly blinded him with its brilliance.

"Close your mouth, big brother, your heart is showing," teased Kanit'sa with a smile. She turned and walked confidently towards the two girls.

Ben clamped his teeth together, spun on his heel and strode back the way he had come.

The cattle had wandered further into a box canyon than he had planned to let them. He didn't know this place but the steep walls would keep the herd from straying too far and so allow him time to follow a nearby creek to see what lay upstream. At dusk he would push them to a treeless wallow where they could bed for the night—away from marauders stalking from above. Tomorrow would be soon enough to push them back to their home range.

He rode upstream without hurrying. The creek meandered as if reluctant to leave its source; as if it too had no place to go and plenty of time to get there. Just on dark he fed Kodiak a part of the dinner rabbit, hobbled his horse beneath an old cottonwood tree and tossed his rope over a low branch. He shinnied up to rest on the perch and, as part of his evening ritual, cursed his unreasonable fear of rattlesnakes. He tied himself to the limb and went to sleep thinking of the dancing girl.

When he opened his eyes the night had nearly passed. The full moon paled the sparkle of the stars and he could make out the shapes of sage and stone against the ashen soil of the high desert. The thinnest thread of gray iced the eastern horizon. The new day was here. He listened for danger lurking in the predawn night and, hearing nothing out of the ordinary, untied the knots that had secured him to the tree during his sleep.

He left the dog with the little mare where she was hobbled and went in search of water. He strode to the top of a low berm and instantly dropped to his belly. In a small vale through which the little stream flowed stood a squatter's shack. A prosperous squatter by the look of things; a low cowshed with a lean-to attached where chickens could roost, a smokehouse, even a fenced plot outside the front door. Front door? Most places around here had but one. But if he could judge by the paths that disappeared under an overhang at the back of the shack, there was a back door as well.

What interested Ben most, however, was the small dam upstream of the home. The berm on which he lay edged a shallow pond above that dam. Without considering the consequences he slithered down the bank and into the water. He rolled into the deep basin and let the cold water work its wonders on his body and take with it the dust and insects that had been building up in his clothing and on his skin for weeks.

It was full on daylight, though well before sunrise, when he rolled over the top of the dam into the creek then pulled himself from the whirling water and, in a crouch, scurried up the bank and out of sight of the cabin.

NINETEEN

Lettie crawled slowly across the cold wooden floor of the loft. She stealthily lifted a lower corner of the old canvas flap that covered a small square opening in the western wall and peered into the coming dawn. In winter Papa nailed animal hides across the opening on the outside. He stuffed dried grasses into the nook before affixing another hide on the inside. The system served to keep out most of the cold wind that blew steadily and strongly along the nearby creek but made the loft too cave-like for Lettie's liking.

When spring finally arrived she was long past feeling like a beast gone to den for the long winter—a bear, she often thought. Bears exuded an aura of curiosity and independence—running away from Papa just out of range of his shouts and stones then wandering back, a bit at a time, as if testing the range at which he would let them sit on their haunches and watch the activity around the little log home. Papa called them impudent. Funny...he had called her that yesterday. But she'd also seen the bears when they prowled around the cougars' kills. At those times they were alarmingly powerful and courageous and it was that indomitable attitude that she most wished for herself.

When the hides were removed in the spring Mama simply covered the opening with a piece of worn canvas from that old prairie wagon to keep out the mosquitoes and bats at night, the swifts and swallows during the daytime, and it was this curtain that Lettie moved aside. She was certain she had heard something out there in the darkness. Not the screech of an owl or a nighthawk. Not the scream of a cougar or the yip of a coyote nor the struggle or agonized last cry of their prey. It was something so quiet Daddy could not have heard it in his windowless corner below else he would already have been at the door with the shotgun on his arm.

She squinted towards the rock weir they had built across the creek to hold back the runoff from the spring higher up and so provide the family with an ample supply of water throughout the sweltering summers. She held her breath while she tried to analyze the sound she was certain had wakened her but that she had not heard since rising. Maybe it had been in her dream. Maybe she should just go back to bed until she heard Papa building a fire in the cookstove. But she watched—breathless, unmoving—and wasn't even a little surprised when she saw the creature she'd known was there. The man pulled himself over the berm that sided the pond and slipped into the cool water.

She concentrated on a small pocket over by the boulders she knew to be especially cold and clear and bubbly then watched the man settle himself into a reclining position there between the big stones with nothing more than his head above the water. Did he sleep? How could she warn him that Papa would soon be up—snarly as a porcupine until he'd had his coffee drink? Papa wouldn't take lightly the finding of a body in his reservoir. He'd be even more angry if he found a real live man in it. With the chastity of two daughters to protect he didn't look with favor on men who wandered too close to his family. Lettie smiled at her lack of wonderment and thought again of the bears.

The man moved his head slowly from side to side. His eyes seemed to rest on the tiny square opening where Lettie knelt. She knew he couldn't see her and was certain beyond doubt that she could only be imagining that his eyes met hers from this great distance. Still....

She waggled the edge of the curtain ever so briefly then watched, fascinated, as he pushed himself over the top of the weir into the free-flowing creek. He stood and in the gray of the coming day Lettie could see that his garb resembled the clothing worn by the nearby Indians, though enough different to make her curious. He stepped into the cover of the willows but now there was enough light to reveal the horse beyond the thicket standing patiently, waiting for the rider to finish his bath. She had been right. She had heard the quiet snort of a cautious animal entering into unfamiliar territory.

"Need I go put it out of its misery?"

Though spoken quietly, the question caused Lettie to start and drop the curtain. Only with the greatest effort was she able to bite back a shriek, a sound certain to awaken her mother and Belle. She turned towards the interior of the cabin with a hand on her breast, glad for scant light to reveal any hint of a blush. Panting, she responded to her father's quiet question. "I think not. It moved away from the spring."

"Bear?"

Lettie blushed at the image the question conjured. "Not quite," was what she wanted to say. Instead she settled for a simple, "No, I'm sure not.

"My, how you startled me. I didn't hear you rise. Good morning, Papa."

"Not surprised, the way you were staring out that window. If not a bear, what was it?"

"You tell me I can identify critters from far away with a high degree of accuracy so I must be careful in my answer in order to preserve my reputation. I believe it to be a young buck—perhaps in search of a mate."

"Daughter!" He was stern, scandalized by her reference to a forbidden thought. "Not a fawn? A buck then?"

"Big for a fawn, Daddy. And I believe a yearling female would not have wandered far from her parent unless a hunter had taken the doe."

"Huh," the man snorted then turned and strode through the kitchen door.

Lettie knew he was heading for the privy that stood beyond the garden and that he would be there awhile. She stole another glance out the window then carefully descended the rickety ladder into the kitchen and began the morning ritual.

Each night before going to bed Mama slipped a few eggs into the coffee pot filled with cold water. This pot she placed on the back of the stove where the damped-down fire would cook the eggs during the night. Two of these would be her breakfast. It was her largest meal of the day and Lettie worried for her health.

A small roast of smoked venison or bear, infrequently of beef, was put into the oven to also take advantage of the nighttime fire and Lettie reminded herself always that they could thank Papa's foresight in having this kitchen stove shipped out from Charleston before that horrible war started. Most other women in the territory still cooked at the fireplace—a backbreaking job if ever Lettie could imagine one.

She opened the damper, shook the grate to sift the cold ashes into the ash-bin, then stoked the remaining embers with kindling and stove wood. She dipped the eggs from the water and slid the pot to the already warming stovetop. It had broken into a rolling boil by the time Papa returned to the kitchen. He took the pot to the back stoop where he splashed enough of the boiling water into a metal basin of cold water to comfortably wash his hands and face. Only after he returned the pot to the stovetop did Lettie repeat her, "Good morning, Papa," and slip out the back door for her turn in the privy.

Papa, she knew, would begin collecting the flour, bacon drippings, and soured dough so Lettie could make the biscuits in which he took great pride. By then the coffee water would be boiling again and he would toss in the coffee grinds—his one true luxury in this life of paucity. While the coffee brewed he peeled Mama's eggs, often helping himself to one or two, depending on how many she had boiled.

Lettie, on her return to the house, washed in the water Daddy had left in the basin on the bench beside the door. She poured the cooled water on the patch of ground Mama laughingly called her onion patch and watched it sink into the thirsty soil. On the opposite side of the door was the cooling cupboard, situated to take maximum advantage of the shade of the overhang. From this cupboard Lettie took the jar of heavy cream she and Papa would dump lavishly into their hot strong coffee. She dipped cream into the poured coffee then each one took a heavy mug and stepped out to the lean-to. There they sat, sipped their coffee, watched the sky lighten, and speculated on what the day would bring.

It was a ritual that had become almost ceremonial in its performance and its gratification. Emptied coffee mugs signaled the end of the rite; time for Papa to go to the barn to milk Behayma, the cow; for Lettie to make biscuits, warm any meat and gravy left after last night's meal, then sing a morning song to waken Mama and Blue-Belle.

She was beginning to realize how the simple event of a breakfast meal could set the tone for the entire day. If Belle was particularly chatty or Mama too disapproving, Papa would leave the table without finishing his meal; head outside to clear more land, repair a fence, or build another lean-to. Lettie knew he developed his sermons out there in the silence of their hillside but wondered if his mealtime huffs weren't an attempt to exert more control over the three of them. Mama, too, would waft from the table like steam escaping a warm pan. She often spent the day out of doors, working in the solitude of her garden. The cooking and household chores were left to Lettie and Belle to manage—or not, as they saw fit.

Lettie began her chores by hauling the ashes from last night's fire out to the wooden ash crate. The coarse, oblong box was made of thick boards salvaged from the prairie wagon Papa had first borrowed, then purchased, from one or another of the nearby homesteaders who had used it to travel here from Ohio. The long sides of the box were shaped like an open-bottomed vee. The ashes were kept clean and dry until the day Mama chose to pour water over them to make lye for her soap.

But Mama hadn't made either lye or soap in a long while. Mama hadn't done much of anything but don her big sunbonnet and wander through the garden for most of the summer. Papa said she was ill, but not from something a body could see.

Mama had grown up in a grand white house in a city called Charleston. Here in the Washington Territory she'd had to live in a borrowed prairie wagon while Papa finished building a cabin. The first one he built was a room sunk about three feet below the surface of the ground. Logs were stacked from the surface of the sandy soil to about four feet higher still, giving the room a height of nearly 7 feet—high enough so Papa could stand upright comfortably, but nothing to compare to the ten and twelve foot ceilings in the mansion where Mama was raised. And if living in a semi-subterranean dirt-floored one-room shack wasn't enough of an insult, snow melt and spring rains gushed into the chamber from beneath the logs and flooded them out. So Mama had to spend a second summer living in the borrowed prairie wagon.

This cabin was palatial compared to that first shack. Papa decided the problem was not that he had built a semi-subterranean house but that he had built it on flat, sandy ground. He searched the area and finally claimed land on a hillside with a spring near by.

Neighbors in this new territory were few but formidable. They came with their families and camped on the grounds while the men built Mama a cabin that had a real wood-plank floor, a front door, and a window in the loft. But Mama still pined for her Charleston home even though Papa said it probably belonged to the Yankees by now. Mama cried when he said that so he never said it again.

Mama'd had servants, too and lots of neighbors and parties and more food than they could eat. Lettie understood the concept of servants; the families in her books had them. But she couldn't, in her wildest fantasies, imagine what it must be like to have other people do your work for you. Boring? She'd once

159

reckoned it must have been so. Mama said that's why they had parties, then she took to her bed and didn't get up for two days running.

Out here in the Washington Territory they weren't even close enough to other people to have a town they could put a name to. Their closest neighbor (if one didn't count the Indians and Mama surely didn't count the Indians) was nearly a day's walk away so any visit was a three-day event. As it would be both unseemly and unwise for three women to trek through the countryside alone, Papa would have to accompany them. That left no one to milk the cow or close up the hens. Papa had planned to show Lettie, in time, how to drive the horse so she could take Mama calling and leave him home to do the chores but before he could do so their beloved Dolly was attacked by a mountain lion and Papa had to shoot her. Then he hung her in the smokehouse just as he would have done a stag. Lettie reckoned that was when Mama went to eating only eggs.

Mama didn't feel up to social calls now anyway even though Papa said it'd do her good since her only other chance to visit with women was at the harvest festival each fall. That, too, set Mama off on another crying spell.

Despite his awareness that Mama could do with a coze, Papa went alone on Sundays to the weekly gatherings. He walked away just after the evening milking on Saturday and came home in time for the morning milking on Monday. That left Lettie to milk the cow on Sundays because Mama wouldn't do it—just couldn't bring herself to touch that cow. So why, wondered Lettie, didn't he take Mama with him on Sundays? Was it because he thought she should be taking care of Lettie and Belle?

"Huh!' she snorted.

Lettie sat on a stump in the lean-to sorting through the box of dried beans. She watched Mama wander aimlessly through the vegetable patch and marveled at the idea of a family having more than enough food. How much was that? Though they themselves seemed to be better off than the neighbors they so seldom visited, she couldn't imagine having more than enough. Did it mean one didn't have to put the noontime dinner on the stove as soon as breakfast was finished? Didn't have to put aside meat and gravy for tomorrow's breakfast and still salvage enough scraps from dinner for a bowl of soup before bed? Mama said folks in Charleston ate their *main* meal in the evening, just like those people in the books. How could they see to cook at night? It would take more candles than they could make to provide enough light to do her main cooking at night. Well, soup at night would just have to do for this family.

She'd heard about Mama's upbringing many times in the past but had never given it much thought. It was all so very far from her own reality it could have come from one of her fictionals. Maybe because Mama was growing sadder by the day her stories were preying on Lettie's mind. Or perhaps she was beginning to realize what Mama, as a young woman, might have felt about the dashing, handsome army officer from Ohio.

Lettie washed the beans and put them in a pot of water to soak and soften. They would go into the oven tonight and be combined with the leftover roast for breakfast tomorrow. She went through the motions of cleaning the kitchen corner of the cabin but couldn't have said what she did or how she did it.

He was a stranger, of course, but something had seemed familiar about that man. There were so few men around she wouldn't have forgotten meeting one. When had she even seen a man other than Papa? She hadn't spoken to anyone who didn't live right here in this house since the harvest festival at the Coopersmiths'. That was when Missus Coopersmith gave Mama the quilt and just before she got herself snake bit. And that was something else Lettie had begun to wonder about. How did Missus Coopersmith get snake bit so late in the year? Didn't the rattlesnakes go to ground when the nights turned cold? She'd ask her Indian friend, Dora—Kanit'sa the Indians called her but Mama had a feeling against the Indians so Lettie used her friend's White Man name.

"That's it!" she said aloud and the sudden noise in the silent cabin startled even her. The two men watching from the hillside when Dora came to visit a few weeks back! One of them! Dora said he was her brother! What was he doing bathing in Papa's pond?

Lettie moved through the rest of the day in bewilderment. Her thoughts tumbled from her mother's childhood to Dora's life in the tiny village. Did Dora have it so bad? Was Mama's family better? More comfortable for a child? But was it fair to raise a girl to womanhood without helping her develop an inner strength—a sense of purpose? If Mama had developed more character would she have seen how selfish she'd been in marrying simply to establish her own household? Was it selfishness that made Mama think she could marry a man with values so different from her own and change him to fit into her idea of a perfect life?

TWENTY

It was the first bath he'd had since coming to the high pasture and he'd have luxuriated in the pool for hours if he hadn't caught the tiniest flick of movement from a window high up under the eaves. He was marveling at a home so palatial as to have a window when he realized that he was trespassing—a sin for which he could be shot on sight or hanged later.

He reminded himself several times throughout the day that he was supposed to be moving the herd out of the canyon but found himself thinking about that bath. When he found a spindly, out of place, soap plant, the decision was no longer his.

"That there's a sign from God," he grinned. He dismounted and pulled off a few of the scraggly, parched leaves. He was careful to leave a few for the brothers and sisters of Chief Sun just as Mam had taught him to do. He slid the treasure into his medicine pouch and for most of the day thought of the wash he would have when darkness fell.

The shadows had long disappeared in the canyon when he hobbled his horse a short distance from the herd, bundled his saddle and gear against a large boulder, took his rope and blanket and struck out across the meadow—no need to follow the meanderings of the creek this time. He could keep straight towards the far off round knob of a hill Da had called Teach's Top and arrive at the squatter's palace before it was full-on dark.

He nibbled on the cold meat from his noon meal and tossed bits and pieces to the dog. He picked a few late berries while he walked, mindful to give darkness a chance to overtake him. The setting sun painted the canyon tops with the burnished gold of late summer, fixing the picture in a gilded frame—the cowboy and his dog striding through the long shadows of the valley.

He crept to the little hillock where he could watch the pond but stopped dead before reaching the brink. With a racing heart he listened to that same humming sound he'd heard when he was with Kanit'sa and Striking Horse—the sound he'd been unable to drive from his mind.

He forced his forearms to bear the weight of his upper body while he peered over the bank. The young woman, now in a white shift, was twirling slowly through the small fenced square in front of the shack. Her arms, like before, straight out from her sides, her curly brown cap framing her face, lifted to the moon. She moved slowly, meditatively as if sorting her thoughts.

Ben watched in awe as she spun; two, three, four times around the enclosure. Midway through the fourth turn a man came to the door and ordered the woman back inside. She bowed solemnly to him, her left foot curled behind her right, her left arm extended fully into the air, her right arm folded neatly across her waist. Then with a few quick light steps she ran past him into the house, kissing him lightly on the cheek as she passed.

Ben scooted back to a point where he was sure he could stand without being seen then loped back towards his herd, energized and confused. His plans for the days ahead were now so muddled he couldn't remember what needed doing first or what came next.

Oh, she danced through the flow'rs
And my heart skipped a beat.
My tongue got tangled in my own big feet.
She had big dark eyes like those of a deer
And a great big grin that stretched from ear to ear.

He sang to the dog then cursed himself for a muddle-head all the way back then tossed and flopped throughout the night. When the moon moved high enough to shine in his eyes he realized he'd been thrown so far off balance he'd made his bed on the ground next to his gear. But no self-respecting snake would have dared approach so agitated a victim.

Daylight brought no relief. He continued to thrash and dither about. He saddled and mounted the mare only to dismount and stride across the land as if he were going somewhere and knew where that somewhere was. His job, once bordering on tedium, now seemed trivial as well. He went through the motions of keeping the cattle together but knew he was simply waiting for night to fall. And when night came, what then?

As soon as Mama put on her sunbonnet and left the house, Lettie sent Belle to fetch stove wood. The girl was good and obedient but Lettie knew her sister was easily distracted. After an armload of the dried pine was dumped into the woodbox, Belle would swing through the garden to visit with Mama, then back to the woodpile to bring another armload or, on a good day, two. If Papa were working close by Belle would run to him for a bit of a chat before bringing a few more sticks of wood.

Lettie hurried to slice what was left of the breakfast venison roast and wrapped it in a dampened cloth—all but one thicker-than-usual slice—and took it to the outside cooler. She scanned the garden and, as expected, saw her sister sitting in the dirt beside Mama. She hurried back inside, scurried up the ladder to the loft, pulled her Sunday scarf from a peg on the wall, and scooted back down.

She filched an old buckskin shirt of Papa's from the mending basket and paused at the eating table long enough to wrap two biscuits and the slice of meat first in a piece of old flour sack then in the square of the brightly patterned silk—the gift Papa had bought for her long ago when their ship from Charleston docked in San Francisco. She bundled it all in the old shirt and tucked it back into the sewing basket where she could retrieve it just prior to taking her bedtime walk to the privy.

She needn't have hurried so. Belle had been drafted to help Mama twist the spiraling beanstalks around and up the squeaky shafts of the fast-growing corn. The leaves of the bean plants would shade the corn roots, keeping them from dehydrating too rapidly, and the tough cornstalks would hold the bean pods off the ground. The trick, learned by Lettie from the Indians across the valley and passed on to Mama as something she'd read in a book, increased the yield of both vegetables with less effort than the methods the neighbors used. The task would take Belle and Mama all of the morning.

"**You're** certain it was a buck in the creek yesterday morning?" Papa had just stuffed a spoonful of the venison-bean stew into his mouth and Lettie had to analyze the noises he was making before she could respond.

"No, Papa, not certain at all. Something woke me—a sound I didn't recognize. It was too dark to clearly see what it was that moved across the weir and into the willows."

Lettie had been raised with a strong sense of *sin*. She reasoned, however, that sins of commission were different, and much more weighty than sins of omission though she had never had the temerity to discuss it philosophically with her father. So, whether because of her sense of pride—and her fear of Hell—or because of his legendary ability to sniff out an untruth, she would not lie to Papa. But she had no qualms about leaving out a vivid description of what she'd seen yesterday in their water reservoir.

"Horse tracks in the mud. Dolly's been dead these two years so they're not hers. Sure you don't know anything about those?"

"Maybe that was the sound that woke me. I'm certain it was not a horse that was in our creek. Oh Papa! I did love Dolly so and miss her incredibly. Do you think God sent us a horse of our own after all this time?"

Briela spoke quietly from the dark corner of the cabin. "I had riding lessons when I was a child. When on our way here we had to ride little burros across the isthmus to get from the Caribbean Sea to the Pacific Ocean. The handlers offered to help me onto a burro but I said I would just as lief walk and those grinning Natives made me do so for nearly a mile. It is why you are not a boy, Letitia. Something..."

168

Papa interrupted to rail at Lettie for asking God for stuff-and-things and Lettie, fearful of what he might do if he learned of the little bundle of biscuits in the sewing basket, bowed her head and listened without interruption.

He hid upstream, curious, until the sliver of moon had reached its full brilliance. The girl did not come. He crept silently to the hummock and realized that the dog was scooting along on his belly right beside him. He patted the dog's head and grinned at the picture the two of them must have made and then he halted.

He stared at a small parcel that rested where he had lain the night before. Not taking his focus from the direction of the cabin he slithered backwards to the thicket and, patting the ground, found a long branch that had been broken from a nearby grove of shrubs and left to dry beside the path.

Soundlessly he brought the stick to the hillock and poked at the bundle. It was pliable but noiseless. After a few more jabs with the stick he pulled the packet towards him. Rolled inside a worn buckskin shirt were a slab of dried meat and two drying biscuits.

He had eaten only berries today. Still, he was wary. He tasted one of the biscuits, then the other, then the slab of meat. He was considering which was tastiest—which to save for last—when the humming started. He raised his dark head only high enough to peer over the sparse grass clumps and watched the woman dance with her moon shadow. She seemed more animated tonight. If last night's dance was one of meditation, tonight's was one of delight.

Before she could make more than a full twirl around the little enclosure the man appeared at the door and called the woman inside. As before, the girl tripped towards the house but this time the man stopped her with a severe scold. She bowed her head and nodded acquiescence then smoothly slid inside. Tonight's curtsy had been every bit as elaborate as the one of the previous evening but it almost seemed as if the hand, raised high into the pale night, was waving ever so slightly in the direction of the hillock.

The man scanned the creek, the squat shed where a cow had softly lowed, the hills beyond. Then he stepped back into the cabin and closed the door.

TWENTY-ONE

"*Papa*, please! Take her with you. She is only fragile from being wrapped inside this dim cave. Her spirit dies in the darkness. She has remained inside most of this long summer because of the heat. Now she must get out and be renewed else she will have no strength to make it through this dreary winter fast approaching!"

"Letitia! There are no facilities at any of the ranches for a delicate woman, not even for so brief a stop as a double night's lodging. This Sabbath I will be boarding with the new homesteaders, the Bragg family and it will be near onto dark when I arrive there. I can neither expose her to their poverty nor them to her fragility. You must do your duty by her here." With that final scold he passed the pail of milk into her reluctant hand and strode across the yard towards the path that led to the valley.

"I doubt God was a farmer, Blue-Belle. There never is a full day to rest on a farm." Lettie had just come into the not-yet-warmed kitchen from milking the cow and was relieved to see Belle peeling Mama's breakfast eggs in the dim kitchen corner.

Lettie tensed at her sister's immediate and incessant chatter. Neither she nor Papa spoke much in the mornings and Lettie had come to appreciate the silent companionship. Never mind, Belle was up and helping. She was grateful for that.

"Well?"

Startled, Lettie turned from her own task of straining the milk. "What?"

"You've not heard a word I said! Where do your thoughts go, and how do they go so far and so quickly?" Belle was hurt but still she spoke with that little knowing smile.

"I'm sorry, Sister. I was thinking about the milk I was straining. Behayma is starting to dry up. I know so little about such things. It could be due to the cooling weather but perhaps she needs to be bred again.

"What is it you were telling me?"

"I said, we should take a picnic to the meadow. We've not seen your friend Dora all this long summer. Maybe she will be there to dig autumn roots. You can ask her about the cow. And her brother," she added with a twinkle.

"Blue-Belle, there was frost on the garden again this morning. We've been fortunate so far but we cannot push God's grace. We must pull the beans and hang them to dry then pull up the corn and stack it. That surely will take us a week! And either your big hen was fox food or has found a place in the woods to nest and set some eggs—strangely late I think. I had hoped to find her before the eggs get too old for eating. Winters get so deep even a few of the fully-grown hens won't survive so you know what chance a late hatchling will have. The squashes can wait till last but soon they will have to be carried to the boulder pit and covered with branches."

Lettie had been moving through the kitchen corner like a brisk wind while she scolded—moving the pot from one side of the stove to the other, picking up a plate and putting it right back down in the same spot—and her agitation was such that it brought Mama to the kitchen corner.

"My, it is cozy and warm here," she murmured. She sat gingerly on one of Papa's handmade stools and gazed around this section of the cabin as if seeing it for the first time. "Is there tea? Are those my eggs?"

"Mama, would you like to take a walk after our Sunday worship? We could picnic in the meadow."

"Oh, my little Blue-Belle," her mother cooed. "You know, I think I would like nothing better had I my shoes."

"I'll help you, Mama. Sit here in your rocking chair and I'll bring the tea Lettie has brewed. You can sip it while we have our Devotional then we'll go for our picnic."

"Picnic?"

"In the meadow, Mama, like we just said."

"Meadow? I can't go to a meadow, child. I can go only to the privy or the garden," she said airily. She rose and wandered back towards her dark corner. "I have no shoes, you see. No walking shoes, no dancing shoes. No shoes at all."

"Mama?"

"Papa burned my shoes months ago, Blue-Belle."

Lettie saw Belle lurch as if struck a violent physical blow. The younger sister tottered and would have fallen to the floor had Lettie not rushed to her with the stool their mother had just vacated. She ran to the stove and tossed a handful of Papa's precious coffee into the still-simmering water. He'd be angry with her. Again. She shook her head against the questions raised by that thought and rushed to grab the Hymnal. She thrust it into her sister's hands and commanded, "Sing, Blue-Belle! Sing to Mama."

She ran back to the stove and was already straining a cup of coffee for Belle so could not stop the girl when, in a high-pitched quavering voice she began, *"In the swe-e-et, By-and-By...."*

Oh, Great, thought Lettie. *An entire book of hymns and she picks The Funeral Hymn of the Frontier!* But before she could out-sing her with a more joyous hymn, Mama had joined in and the two sang all the way through all the verses, each and every one connected by the chorus.

With the hymn ringing in her ears, Lettie, for the first time in her life, began to wonder about her father's motives.

If Baker's Peak was the throne of God, the foothills to the east were His raiment. Leaves of reddening maples and tanning oaks stirred above the flickering yellow of aspens—sparkling threads in sumptuous brocade. Dark green meandering vales and steep shadowy canyons marked the folds of His garments, and small meadows, like this one, were the jewels that proclaimed it exquisite.

To watch their meadow in autumn was to overload the senses. The few flowers not yet gone to seed bowed their heavy heads in awe of the intensity with which the pale drying grasses reflected the sun. Grasshoppers clicked incessantly to provide a rhythmic beat to the meadowlarks and redwings that swooped and sang with abandon. Butterflies bustled from stem to seedpod and back again like bubbles rising above a waterfall. Now and then a breeze would whisper through the trees above their heads, sending a few more leaves into their laps.

The girls sat shoulder to shoulder against the trunk of the ancient oak, not thinking, not speaking; simply being there. Despite Belle's admitted prayer, neither Dora nor Ben put in an appearance and when the shadows lengthened to touch the center of the meadow, they rose in silence and found the path that would take them home.

From a resting spot halfway down the hillside the girls looked below to their home, knowing they must go there but reluctant to leave the tranquility of the meadow. As they watched, two men strode from the back-door overhang towards the cowshed. They mounted horses that had been standing in the lee of the shed and rode towards the trail that led to the valley.

"Maybe that was Ben!" Belle blurted. So certain was she that God had answered her prayers she grabbed Lettie's hand and dragged her at a run down the path.

Lettie protested and, after the initial shock, broke away from her sister's grasp. "No! Blue-Belle wait! Something is wrong!

"Listen to me!" she scolded. "First, neither man walked like Dora's Ben. Don't ask me to tell you how that is because I can't. I just know. And second, why did they hide their horses behind the cowshed?

"Something frightful is happening, Blue-Belle. Yes, let us hurry. But only to make certain Mama is okay."

"**Oh**, Letitia. You've had callers. You've only just missed them. They waited on the back stoop for hours. I'm afraid Papa will be exasperated with us."

Lettie's mind whirled. One second she was thinking it might have Ben after all then immediately reminded herself Mama wouldn't have let an Indian sit on her back stoop—not for a minute, especially not for hours.

"Why would he be vexed with either of us, Mama?"

"The men had waited ever so long when I overheard one tell the other that it was plain they wouldn't be finding what they wanted here. I said if they had but told me they were wanting a meal I could have saved them hours of time in that I could have said my cook had gone for a walk."

Lettie laughed until her sides hurt then hugged her wide-eyed mother and laughed some more. At last she asked the befuddled woman, "That explains why he might be vexed with you, but why, my precious Mama, would my loving Papa be vexed with me?"

"My dear! He sent them. One was that trying Mister Coopersmith. I find it difficult to converse with him because I am much distracted by his quizzical name."

She sighed heavily at the girls' puzzled frowns. "Oh, never mind. It's my own private amusement. I was very skilled once at determining a young suitor's heritage by knowing the meaning of his name. It could be helpful in avoiding inappropriate callers. In this case, you see, a cooper is a man who makes barrels from wood and a smith is a man who makes things from metal. It's as if Mister Coopersmith were named twice, *Mister Barrelmaker Ironmonger.*"

She stared into the distance as if seeing a place and time of which the girls knew naught then twitched as if pinched awake. "All that aside," she said slowly, "his companion was the new neighbor, a Mister Stark."

"Stark? Do we know him?"

"I don't believe you've met. But I do wish your father were here. I've had the most puzzling experience."

"Tell us what it was, Mama. Perhaps we can help."

"Oh, I'm sure not," she said airily. "It's just that, when I overheard that Mister Stark talking to Mister Coopersmith out under the stoop, when I couldn't see his face but could only hear his voice, I had a vision! I imagined I saw my treasure! Isn't that strange? I hadn't thought of that in just *years*. Before I could ask Mister Stark why that would be so, he asked about a herd of cattle the Indians were said to be running nearby. Papa told them you would show them where the Indians are."

"Mama ...?"

"I explained that it would be most inappropriate to send a woman out riding alone with two men. I said I thought I had overheard you tell your sister you'd heard there were cattle now as near as Wolf Creek Canyon so perhaps we could buy beef again."

"Mama! Wolf Creek Canyon is near Mister Charlton's land and is a fair day's ride east of here! Those cattle were an hour's ride w...."

"Yes, dear, but it was the first name that came to mind."

"Oh-h-h, Mama."

Lettie could only stand and stare—rendered speechless by the knowledge that her mother had lied. And had knowingly done so to help the Indians.

TWENTY-TWO

The summer had been a particularly long and dry one. Water oozed from the spring with agonizing slowness and trickled lethargically to the pond. The reservoir, always shallow this time of year, was now barely deep enough to fill the bucket above a quarter when she dipped water for the kitchen. She knew it wouldn't deepen till after the first of the autumn rains. Filtering sludge for water in the summer, breaking ice for water in the winter—all in all a dreadful place. She was thankful they had but one cow and a few rangy chickens to try to keep alive.

She was already straining the morning's milk when Papa stalked through the door. Lettie and Belle greeted him warmly but, with no word of response, he went directly to bed and to sleep. It was as if a stranger had thrust his way into their midst. Wide-eyed, the girls took tea and two peeled eggs to Mama, rocking mindlessly in her chair, then grabbed the two remaining eggs and stepped outside.

Should the girls now wait for Papa's direction before proceeding with their work? Would he be angry at their moving ahead without his approval? Would he be just as angry if they had done nothing to prepare for the upcoming winter? Puzzled, they focused their

179

efforts on the garden, working throughout the day pulling beanstalks and carrying the heavy vines to the lean-to to hang them by their roots on the rafters. Here the pods would dry and provide both food for the winter and seed for the spring planting. The dried vines would be fed to the cow. Neither of them spoke of Papa's bad mood. It was something so strange they wouldn't have known what questions to ask or of whom one would ask such questions.

Lettie slid the pot of corn chowder to the back of the stove. "We have an abundance of corn and potatoes. We're awash with Behayma's rich milk. Onions are plentiful. Toss in bacon or chicken for a bit of a change. Small wonder, Sis, that corn chowder is the commonest supper here."

Belle had taken the pan of biscuits from the oven and was splitting and buttering one for each of them—two for Papa. Like they had done that morning, they looked at each other in wide-eyed amazement when Papa took his bowl of soup and his biscuits and left the house. The women ate their supper in a troubled silence.

Papa returned to the house and flung his bowl into a pan of wash-water warming on the stove. "Lettie, I sent someone here yesterday for your help and you weren't here to give it!"

"No, Papa. Blue-Belle and I had..."

"I care only that you were not here on a Sunday. Your life is much too easy. I have been lax with your discipline. It is time you had responsibilities!"

"Yes, Papa," muttered the confused child.

"Widower Coopersmith has asked for permission to call on you and I have granted it."

Lettie rose and cried, "Papa! No!"

"Mister Coopersmith is proving on a new homestead of 160 acres abutting his old one. In this new Washington Territory he is entitled to double that amount if he takes a wife. He has a cabin nearly as large as this one and will be building another to prove his claim."

"Papa! We were inside that cabin at last year's harvest festival. I deny it is a cabin. It is a windowless, floorless, one-room hovel with two beds—both built three feet off the dirt floor to keep fleas and rats off the beds and mud off the furnishings. He has three dull daughters still at home, all of whom sleep in one of those beds and all are older than I! I would be drudge to the four of them!"

"He has need of a wife! A man has needs.... I have given him my blessing. He shall call and you shall receive him."

"Papa, I cannot. The man has no teeth!"

"You shall not refuse an offer based on a man's appearance!"

"But you married Mama because she was beautiful!"

Lettie met her father's speechless stare and was more than a little grateful she was out of striking range of his large fist. She knew her father, despite his love for her, would not tolerate defiance but, even though she was as shocked by her outburst as he, she could not bring herself to take back her assertion. Instead, she pressed on, taking advantage of his stunned silence.

"It is truth. You say she is sick and I have come to know why. You knew she had no taste for Christianizing the Indians, for traveling, for leaving her own mama and her life of frivolity. You knew she lacked the stamina, even the desire, to be a frontier woman. Yet you vied for her hand and you won her by leading her to believe you could be persuaded to stay in Charleston if she married you. Instead, you gathered up your gorgeous prize and within months set sail for the west, tearing her from her luxuries and depositing her into this desolate keep. Her life may have had no purpose in your eyes, Papa, but it was the only one she knew and she deserved better than what you have given her.

"Why did you trick her? I'm hopeful you were so dazzled by her beauty your reasoning was muddled, because I don't want to believe you are a deliberately cruel man. But, if you will marry for beauty, I shall refuse a proposal for the lack of it. Now strike me if you will. I have said quite enough."

Dominic glared at this stranger before him then turned and stomped out of the cabin, slamming the door as he went.

Lettie watched him leave and took a long, jagged breath. Her mother's arms encircled her from behind and the woman laid her head against Lettie's back and wept. Lettie turned and hugged her mother with a depth of feeling she'd not realized she felt before now.

Papa failed to return home that evening and the following evening as well. Like they usually did in his absence, the girls carried on with the chores and the care of their mother. At mid-morning on Wednesday, Mister Coopersmith drove his team of horses to the lean-to. Perched beside him on the springboard seat was Papa, stony and silent. Following the wagon were two riders. Lettie recognized one as Mister Charlton who had helped build mama's house.

Mama slipped up behind Lettie and whispered, "That one on the brown horse is the one who was here on Sunday, wanting to know where the Indians were."

Papa went inside the cabin and made sure the fire in the cooking stove had not yet been lit to take the chill off the evening. He emptied the ashes—an action that stunned Lettie because he had never before done so—and then dropped the ash-bucket unceremoniously onto the kitchen floor. He loosened the wire that held the stovepipe in place then nodded to the other men.

The woman had been so intent on watching Papa they hadn't seen the men take two long poles of freshly cut pine from the wagon. At Papa's signal, they slid the poles beneath the stove and, with one on each corner, they lifted the heavy iron contraption and carted it to the wagon. While three of them tied the cooking stove to the wagon, Mister Charlton came to address Lettie.

"You seem a bit surprised. I had no idea he didn't tell you what is going on. We're borrowing the cooking stove for the harvest festival, you see. We'll build a covered area so the women can cook out of doors.

"This month will have five Sundays. The congregation—all five of us men—voted to hold the annual fall festival on Sunday next—it being the fifth Sunday—at my ranch. Your father felt it was unholy to celebrate anything on a Sunday so encouraged us to hold the festival on Saturday. That way, any out-of-towners can camp on the ranch grounds and be in attendance for Sunday's services. We have just ten days to make preparations and get the word to folks.

"Here's a notice Coopersmith and my wife inked up. The women just about have the festival meal all planned out. The men have already built a platform for leading the song services, Pastor LeGrau will give Bible readings and sermonettes between the sings. All you women can congregate around the stove to get in plenty of visiting while you cook the evening meal. Older children will supervise games and races for the younger ones. It's all here on this sheet.

"I hope you ladies will be able to attend again this year." He tipped his hat to the three women who stood beneath the lean-to with gaping mouths and even wider eyes.

✸

Lettie's hands shook as she spread the swatch of faded fabric on the eating table. She could not bring herself to read it. She could only think that whatever heat had seeped into the room during the day was fast escaping through the hole in the chimney. They had no fireplace like other homesteaders did so she would have to build a campfire outside to boil water and to heat a stone to put at Mama's feet during the night.

But what if Papa never came back or never brought the cooking stove? Could she and Belle care for Mama during the winter? She knew with certainty they could not. Food wouldn't be the problem. Not early on. She could whack small chunks of meat off the haunch of venison hanging in the smokehouse and drape them over the campfire to roast. And she knew Papa hadn't taken his hunting rifle. He had often told her it was a fine rifle, but he'd never taught her how to use it—just like he had failed to teach her to drive the horse and wagon.

Lettie was still rushing around to make the house livable for the night when it came time for milking Behayma again. And while she milked she wondered about moving Mama and Belle into the hayloft; or maybe Behayma to the lean-to. She wasn't

184

certain she would be able to fend for herself if she were alone through the upcoming winter. How could she possibly take care of a sick woman, a young girl, a cow and a flock of chickens?

The hypnotic rhythm of the milk splishing quietly into the bucket lulled her deeper into her reverie. With intense sadness she examined the man she loved above all others. *Why didn't Papa take Mama with him on Sundays? They had only his word that the families with whom he stayed would not welcome the once-beautiful debutante. He seemed so strong and sure. Was he, instead, so weak and fearful that he wouldn't, couldn't, let other men even meet his wife and daughters? And did he, indeed, travel to town to preach the Gospel as he professed?*

Questions with no answers rippled through her growing awareness, each creating others until her mind and emotions were in a tangled web.

Determined to severely question her mother, Lettie returned to the dark cabin just in time to overhear Mama sadly sigh to Belle, "Daddy said I would die if I rode in a prairie schooner. He put us on a ship instead. But he died of the summer fever before we ever made our first port of call, and his business associate must have stolen my treasure, I suppose. Do you think he was the same man who tried twice to kill your father? Had I been allowed to choose, I would just as lief been left with Daddy to die of summer fever in Charleston."

Her intent to scold forgotten, Lettie wanted nothing more now than to distract her mother from dwelling on things that could not be changed. "Blue-Belle, please read to us the notice of the harvest festival Mister Charlton has left."

"I cannot! It is illegible and nonsensical. It is maddening."

"Please do remember, girls, that not everyone has had the privilege of even the pretense of an education. You are fortunate in your upbringing."

"I see no harm in being uneducated," replied the younger daughter. "It is pathetic to be stupid. It is inexcusable to be stupid as well as to be so vain one refuses to ask for help with so small a task as writing an invitation."

"So bad as that?" asked Lettie, startled by the outburst.

"Worse. I envision him laboring, tongue gripped between toothless gums, over every letter. Yet his grammar and spelling are so poor one wonders what he is trying to communicate. In leaving out a comma or a full-stop—I don't know which he might have intended—he writes that our father is the strangest! It is not only the grammar and spelling! He indicates that we *ladies* are supposed to go to great lengths simply to have one of the MEN bid on the opportunity to share a luncheon with us. AND," she added scathingly, "the proceeds of said auction will be awarded to the MAN who has the prize winning vegetable!"

Lettie stared open-mouthed at her sister then saw that her mother's look of shock surely mirrored her own. At that second, they both burst into side-splitting laughter, leaving Belle to stare in consternation.

ALL DAY SiNG AN SUPPER ON THE GROUND

Songs of praze an worship all day.
BiBLE Storys off-n-on
GAMz fer the littlns like:::
        Tote-sak races: Three-leged races: Egg tossin:
        Button-Button: Upset the frute baskit!

Lunchbox Soshel: Ladys! Decerate that pail prettier'n
anyones and stuff it with the tastiest vitals you kin make.
Pails will be sold off by me, Coopersmith. Wining bidder on
each lunchpail enjoys a noontime repast with the lady who
brung the pail!! Money from sell will go as prize for winer of
mens
FRUTE AND VEGA TABLE CONTEST!
BRING biggest, prettiest, Stranjest Pastor LeGrau will judge
and awarde PRIZE.

Supper'll be fixt by the ladys and on tables after evening
sing.

Bring yer mess kit and a kwilt to set on.

TWENTY-THREE

Lettie and Belle were up before dawn to scurry and struggle throughout the following days. They had come to accept that whatever winter preparations were to be made would be up to them and they worked harder for the knowing. When all the beans had been pulled and hung in the lean-to they started pulling up the cornstalks, filling the corncrib with the skinny sparsely kernelled ears. Thinking that she might not want to fight her way to the smokehouse or cowshed in the dead of winter to collect corn stalks for cow feed or fire starter, Lettie stacked the stalks against the south side of the house and prayed the deer wouldn't be so bold as to come near her campfire to nibble their way through the drying vegetation.

On the Friday afternoon before the harvest festival Lettie was hurrying to drag the last of the large hard-skinned squashes to the boulder pit. She had long ago taken all the animal hides from the walls inside the cowshed and hung them on the walls in the house for blocking out the wind; there were none left to cover the squashes against deep winter temperatures. She rushed up to her pallet in the loft and tossed down the Twenty-Year quilt then scooted down the rickety ladder. She grabbed the quilt and started for the back door then stopped, turned, and darted to the dark corner of the cabin where Papa kept his rifle.

The shotgun hung there, too, just above the rifle and Lettie changed her mind once again. She knew that pointing the shotgun in the general direction of something and pulling one of the triggers would get results of one kind or another so she hadn't thought to practice with it. But since she was taking the rifle....

She wrapped the weapons in the quilt lest Mama wake and see her leave the cabin then she hurried to the boulder pit. She spread the quilt over the top of the heaped up squashes and paused with a sigh as if saying good-by to an old friend. Somehow, using the quilt in such a manner made her as sad as nearly any of the horrible things that had happened in the last weeks.

Refusing to pine for the quilt, or anything else at this point, she dragged enough tree boughs over the top of the quilt to form a roof several layers thick. Then she touched her heart in a silent prayer. "This is the last big thing, God. It's in your hands now. We'll keep doing what we can but we shall need a lot of help."

Lettie sat to rest a moment on a large boulder still warm from the late September sun. She picked up the rifle and tried to hold it like she had seen Papa do. She sighted along the barrel at a bit of green quilt-patch peeping through the layer of boughs.

"Squeeze the trigger, don't pull it," Papa had cautioned when he fired the round that brought down the stag now hanging in the smokehouse. Lettie did neither. She knew that a bullet fired into this boulder pit would ricochet wildly and probably do some serious damage. And if there was any one thing she didn't need right now, it was damage—either to her own self or to her precious provisions. The rifle was loaded. She knew Papa kept it so. But what of later? After she'd learned to fire the thing, how was she to reload it? She'd just have to ask Dora.

She heard Belle's call and looked towards the house. Papa was coming up the path from the valley. She paused to consider the meaning of his visit then wondered why she thought it thus. As she sat beside the boughs she realized that she could see the homestead and the several paths leading to it but, unless she stood, she, herself, could not be seen from below. She couldn't have said how the knowledge might help her in her present situation except that Papa wouldn't see her hide the weapons beneath the boughs. How to get them back on their pegs without him seeing was a problem she didn't want to consider right now.

Lettie locked the chickens in their coop with plenty of water. She hated leaving Belle's big red hen outside but, search though she did, she'd been unable to find the bird's nest. She refused to accept that it might have fallen prey to something in the bush. There were just too many other bad things that had happened lately. Mama was no more than an empty shell; Papa was distant and cold, not speaking to them, not eating a supper, not milking Behayma or acknowledging the work that had been done by the girls. He hadn't seemed to notice the absence of the rifle and shotgun. She would accept that as a blessing.

She was bringing the docile Behayma from her shed when Mister Coopersmith arrived with his wagon. While she was tying the cow to its back rail Papa spread Mama's prettiest quilt on the wagon bed and tossed in a few of her onions for his entry in the vegetable contest. He climbed into the back with Mama and Belle so Lettie was forced to ride on the hard, wooden seat with Mister Coopersmith.

"*Coopersmith-Poopersmith, has he a given name,*" Lettie wondered? She scrunched as close to the handrail as she could to avoid contact with the man she found so repulsive. "*We thought his wife a loony, but it's 'im what is to blame!*" Her eyes widened in shock at the ditty that had sneaked unbidden into her thoughts. She wanted to share it with Belle—to giggle at the silliness of something, anything, like they might have done at the beginning of summer.

Instead, she rode in silence, letting her mind wander. She was worried about Belle. The girl had twice disappeared for quite a long period of time this week and refused to tell Lettie where she had been. Besides being worrisome, it was frustrating because it meant Lettie had to do Belle's chores as well as her own. She wondered if Belle hadn't been visiting Papa at some secret place.

Papa, too, was a concern. His anger with her she could explain but there was an underlying air of excitement she didn't understand. It was as if he was gloating about a deeply held secret. And secrets were something else that had come, strange and late, to this little family.

Lettie had packed a luncheon for the four of them but refused to participate in the Box Social. There would be no one at the festival with whom she would tolerate a private meal, but she had put forth a special effort for Mama and Belle. She'd started with a savory stew made from all the meat scraps in the cooler. While it cooled she'd made a batch of her flakiest biscuit dough and rolled it out in a thin layer. She cut rounds from the dough and on each one dropped a dollop of the stew then topped that with another circle over the filling and sealed it. These little tidbits she placed in a cast iron pot to bake in a bed of coals. Once baked and cooled, she poured a rich, thick gravy through a hole she'd cut into the top of each little pie before it baked.

"Now, Girlie, where's your lunch pail for the Box Social?" wheezed Mister Coopersmith. "My girls all packed lunches. Course, they's all three vying for the attention of that Charlton boy. He's a mite youngish for them but they's capable of bringing him along. Be nice to get'em to civilization where's they can all meet up with a blade or two. Them girls'er excitin' there's a fact. But they's no need you be worryin' about no lunch pail, Girlie. Your lunch partner already spoke up for you."

"I have brought a luncheon pail for the Social, Mister Coopersmith," piped Belle from the back. She had decorated the outside of a battered old lard-pail with her favorite blue beads then filched half a dozen of the cooled pastries from Lettie's basket and tucked them gently into the pail beside a jar of fresh milk.

Into the pail she had also wedged Mama's little hand-warmer—a palm-size ceramic Bible. Beautifully and delicately painted, it was hollow with a small hole in the top that held a cork stopper. On cold Sunday mornings Mama's servants would funnel warm water into the container and place it in the young lady's white rabbit-fur muff.

Today, Belle had filled it with cool water from the spring and hoped it would keep the milk chilled and the meat in the pasties from spoiling. She'd placed the pail on a square of calico, brought the corners to the top, and tied it into the neat bundle she now carried on her lap.

As if to bait the odious toad driving the wagon she continued, "I, too, seek the favor of Lumpkin Charlton as he is the only *young* single man in the valley. But I will play fairly. I promise I shall not divulge the contents of my pail."

Mister Coopersmith turned a dark shade of red but wisely held his tongue.

The scene was pure hustle-bustle; arriving wagons vied for parking spaces while passengers alit and scattered, vegetables were carted to a freshly raked dirt patch and displayed in their best light, food for the evening meal was hurried to the cooking compound where Misters Charlton and Bragg had built a shelter just for this occasion. Around this core of frenzied activity, brightly patterned quilts sprung like flowers on ground claimed for the vague attributes of shade, slope, or the proximity of friends.

Over all was an air of festivity; children finding new playmates, women renewing acquaintances, men shouting directions. Dust rose with the cacophony of groaning wagons, braying mules, and lowing cattle.

Lettie gripped the handrail, clamped her jaw, and grimaced at the scene before her. Her distaste of Mister Coopersmith made her want to be off the wagon as soon as she could safely alight but her dislike of crowds and noise kept her glued to the seat. *"The frying pan or the fire?"* she thought grimly.

"Jump, Lettie. Now!" the wind urged and, without question, she flung herself sideways and off the wagon. Her forward momentum carried her to the trunk of a huge oak tree where she leaned, panting, against its broad warm trunk. She looked at the wagon she'd just left to see Mama's expression as vacuous as it had come to be lately. Belle's look was one of surprise but Papa was vivid with anger. Mister Coopersmith was frantically trying to stop his mules but the surrounding traffic forced him forwards.

"*Papa's anger means it couldn't have been he who told me to jump. It certainly wouldn't have been Mister Poopersmith. Who then?*" She scanned the crowd and the area surrounding the ranch house. A slight autumn breeze caressed her cheek, flicked a lock of hair from her face and stilled her trembling heart. Mysteriously calmed, she turned, took a deep breath, and strolled towards the hubbub as serene as a queen.

Papa's jaw was clamped tightly shut and the veins in his neck stood rigid and purple. He untied Behayma from the wagon and dragged her towards the barn with no word to his family. Belle took her mother's hands to help the woman from the wagon. Lettie steadied her mother's bare feet then stood to accept the onions, Mama's parasol, and Belle's lunchbox from her sister. These she handed to Mama then caught the quilt and pillow Belle tossed down before jumping to the ground herself. Together the three women went in search of a shade tree under which they could spread the quilt for Mama.

"Why did you jump, Sister?"

"The tree told me to, Blue-Belle. At least, I guess it was the tree. Surely tweren't Papa nor Mister Poopersmith."

"*Tweren't* is not a word, Lettie. Please be mindful of your grammar," corrected her mother gently. With the wide-eyed girls in her wake, Mama wove her way to Lettie's oak tree. It was further from the center of activity—thus quieter—than most people favored. And though it was near the dusty road used by the arriving wagons, that soft autumn breeze blew the dust away from the women.

'Briela turned and faced her daughters. "Now. Belle, you shall tend me here. Letitia, Belle shall spread the quilt and make me comfortable; you will be safest in the kitchen. When asked by your father about his guns I implied that the man who came to call on you to help him find the Indians might have borrowed them. I have not seen that man in attendance but you do not want to be here when Dominic speaks with him and finds that to be an untruth. Go now. Quickly child. And Godspeed."

Startled and confused, Lettie gaped at her mother. Belle, too, seemed to have been struck dumb. "Go," sighed Gabriella, airily. "Hide while you can."

Lettie hesitated long enough to grab her mother in a brief breathless hug then turned and sped towards the cooking compound.

The cooking area was filled with chatting, laughing, sweaty women and Lettie reluctantly squeezed her way into a knot at the edge. She mindlessly picked up a brush to scrub dirt-encrusted gnarly potatoes when she saw Mister Coopersmith scanning the swarm of bodies. She slipped further into the midst and within minutes was stoking the fire in her own beloved cooking stove and sending someone's little boy for more wood. Here she resolved to stay, fire poker firmly in hand, until this horrible hubbub ended.

"Miss LeGrau, this is no place for the young women. Your sister is busy helping with the games for the little ones so I am compelled to seek your help. I must have a soprano to offset all the basses I have in my choir."

Lettie protested but Mister Charlton refused to accept her rejection. Taking her hand he led her to the low platform that had been set up for the singers and boosted her onto the stage. And here, standing next to

Papa, she found herself singing from the bottom of her very soul the songs of joy, of despair, of faith and triumph—the songs she'd learned from this man, this stranger, who stood beside her now. It seemed as if his bitterness evaporated with the music that wafted through the autumn air and the two were again sharing a private world just as they had when they sipped their morning coffee drinks under the overhang.

But the mood could not last. The food had been put on the stove to stew and brew and bake until suppertime. The little ones had raced and ran and tumbled themselves numb. It was time now for the Box Social luncheon.

More lunches had been brought than there were men to bid on them so it was incumbent on the men to buy and share more than one lunch pail. Papa knew that Lettie had brought food for the family so had no intention of spending hard cash to buy food made by another. Coopersmith bid a whopping five cents on the lunch pail of one of his daughters in hopes of driving up the price but he won the bid so thereafter reined in his recklessness.

Belle and Lettie sat with primly folded legs on Mama's best quilt, whispering and giggling about the lunch pails, their contents and decorations, the probable aspirations of the lunch maker and the lunch buyer. They had been reprimanded several times by Papa. This was, after all, a church function and demanded a reverence they were failing to display.

"Sister, stand with me," whispered Belle as she thrust her pail into Lettie's hand, "And please hold this whilst I tie my shoe." The bidding had just started on her lovely blue pail and she was showing uncharacteristic signs of nervousness. She knelt there, tying her shoe, leaving Lettie to stand beside the auctioneer holding the blue pail.

Mister Coopersmith was trying to get someone, anyone, to bid on the young girl's offering. It was, indeed, beautifully decorated but Belle was only a child and there were no bidders.

Lettie considered buying it herself but she had no silver. And had she a coin, would she, simply to save her sister some embarrassment, contribute it to the prize that was going to one of the men? She knew she would indeed do that for her sister.

"What is wrong with you, Blue-Belle?" hissed Lettie. "What is taking so long?"

"There's a knot in the strand. I almost have it," muttered her sister.

At that moment, from the back of the crowd, came a shout. It was the voice she had imagined urging her to jump. "One silver dollar for the blue lunch pail!"

A collective gasp went up from the attendees. Who would seriously offer a prince's ransom to have lunch with this white-haired child or be so cruel as to make the offer in jest? The gasp turned to a breathless silence as they watched the dark-haired man, sporting a patched buckskin shirt and a brightly colored silk scarf, stride to the front of the crowd, flip a silver coin towards the auctioneer, grab the lunch pail with one hand and Lettie's hand with the other, and retrace his steps with a not-quite reluctant Lettie in tow.

Lettie looked back only long enough to see Belle watching with a grin that would have wrapped all the way around her head had not God given her ears to stop it.

TWENTY-FOUR

Lane shoved the last of the gear into the back of the 'Burb and closed the tailgate. He gazed at his surroundings; at the river, the orchard, the dig site. It was still hot; hotter than it should be in late August. The hills were brown and the broad dry leaves of the sunflowers rattled in protest as he made his way through them towards where Jill sat sketching in the dying light.

"It's a flower," he stated, looking over her shoulder at her work.

"Um-m. But they'll be dying soon enough."

"Hello-o-o. Are you there?"

"I heard you! You said *it's aflower* and I said *they'll die soon.* What are you on about?"

Lane stood watching her for a puzzled moment then laughed. "Is *aflower* a word?"

"I don't know. You're the one who used it."

"So I did. But I didn't mean *aflower* as in *awash with flowers.* I meant to say your sketch looks like A flower—one flower."

"Hm-m. I don't see it."

"Squint your eyes. It's like one of those awful 3-D picture-within-a-picture posters they used to sell at the State Fair. May I?" he asked, taking her clipboard

198

from her. He turned it over and, on the back, used a permanent marker to draw lines as he talked.

"Here's the river, make it the top of the ground. From here, going up like a stem, is the creek. At the top of the creek, like a big blossom, is the Paterson farmhouse with its cluster of outbuildings. Down here, where the creek runs into the river—or the stem comes up from the ground, is this little tunnel. It would be that little stem thingy that sticks the leaf to the stem. At the end of that little stem thingy is your deer-leg den."

Jill looked at his sketch then towards the road.

"You won't see it from where you're sitting. The highway grade blocks your view; cuts right across the stem. But I can see it from up here—awesomely tall as I am. With the shadows lengthening it's even more obvious—kind of weird."

"I can see only as far as the road. When we get back to the 'Burb, if it isn't too dark, maybe I'll be able to see what you see.

"Why do they call this *The Leighton Place*?" she added.

"Long before this highway was built the Leightons put in the first apple orchard in the valley. Paterson is descended from them, but I don't know just how."

"If there is a cave here, he should know about it then, don't you think?"

"Beats me. If I recall correctly, the Leightons had no children so he's actually descended from a cousin of one of them. Though, he was born and bred here in the valley."

"It wouldn't have to be first-hand knowledge. The cave's too old...but family legends or something? And isn't that a funny expression...*born and bred*?

Shouldn't it be *bred and born*? Now, *born and raised*, I can see. That's the expression..."

"Jill, I'll discuss this with you for as long as you want to talk about it but only after we're in the 'Burb. The sun is down and the snakes will be coming out to hunt. Just walking through those dried sunflower leaves gives me the willies. The sound they make when they rub against each other sounds too much like a snake for my comfort." He shivered and added, "I don't even like talking about 'em!"

TWENTY-FIVE

Mules brayed, men shouted, wagons creaked, and chains rattled—a discordant melody over the slow steady beat of axes biting into pines. The little cabin was quickly taking shape on the northeast corner of Mister Charlton's oat field and Lettie was hauling buckets of mud and clay from the creek to mortar the chinks between the logs. She worked alone. It was well her bared feet remembered the path from the cabin to the clay bank and back again as neither her heart nor her mind could focus on her task.

Bucket after bucket of the icy cold goop went into the trough Ben had dug beside the path. Then Lettie would pull the back hem of her skirt between her legs, tuck it into the waist of her apron and step into the trough to thoroughly mix the brown mud with the grayish clay. Back into the buckets went the mortar and, after chinking as far as the mud would go, she'd trudge to the creek bank to refill the buckets and begin the process again.

Already she'd memorized Belle's short note. That had taken only one reading. Her walk to the creek and her kneading in the mortar trough had taken on a poetic cadence as her sister's words went round and round in her head.

She'd been as astonished as everyone when Ben appeared and bought Belle's luncheon pail—even more so when he led her to his horse, mounted, reached down for her arm and pulled her up behind him. The wild ride to the Indian's village, the welcoming embrace of Dora, the wedding gifts and food for the feast brought by Indians from surrounding villages had all been something out of Missus Coopersmith's fiction books and she waited in breathless anticipation for what surprise might come next. She'd rehearsed the teasing scold she would give Blue-Belle for surprising her so. And in a moment of quiet she'd had a flash of insight—the tiniest understanding of how her mother had come to love and marry someone with a background so different from her own.

Even now her heart thudded to the soles of her feet as she remembered just what did come next. How could so many things go so wrong? How could she have been so blind to the impending treachery? And had it really been only two days later that Mister Charlton had ridden so solemnly into Ben's village?

His words were so carefully chosen, his demeanor so serious, Lettie had first thought something terrible must have befallen his wife. As his words slowly dissipated the happy fog in which she was shrouded, her knees began to buckle and only Ben's strong grip held her upright.

When he saw LeGrau's wagon approaching his ranch the day after the church social, he explained, he'd assumed Dominic was coming to fetch his cooking stove and milk cow. Instead, Dom had asked for a place to camp for the night. He said he'd finally gotten rid of his burdensome daughter and sold the worthless homestead to Owen Stark. Now he could afford to take his once beautiful bride and their remaining, obedient, child and return to Ohio. Coopersmith, too, had had his fill of this God-forsaken land so would make the trek with them.

With that, Charlton handed Lettie the note Belle had slipped to Missus Charlton as she'd hugged her one last time.

Sister we are lost! Home is burned and prop'ty sold to Stark! Behayma and stove giv'n to Charltn. Papa taking us to fam farm in OHiO. Coopersmiths, too. UGH! --- Says taking Mama out of WashTerr is what YOU said he must do. He is so angry I am frightnd. For Mama, too. --- Do not worry for us. We cope, each in our own ways. We do so love you and work'd hard to arrange for Ben to come. PLEASE, PLEASE, PLEASE be Happy with him! Your very own Blue-Belle !
ps. . . Mama says she'd just as lief DIE as be a Yankee!

Lettie and Ben had rushed to the homestead with several of his friends. She'd wandered through the ashes in a daze, unable to comprehend the bitterness that could hide so deeply in a man's heart then erupt so violently. Ben looked grimly at the tracks of a horse and of many head of cattle that had milled about, trampling any trace of human habitation. "The one who is Evil has been here," he said sadly.

She'd heard a rustle in the brush by the path leading to the meadow and found the big red hen with her brood of five little chicks. After the Great Chicken Roundup, which would have been funny had the circumstances been different, she'd tied them in her apron and handed the bundle to Ben. The other hens might survive for a time but would never live through the snows of the coming winter. Perhaps, if she waited till dusk the rest would come home to roost and she could snare them?

She'd scampered up the boulder pile and found the squash cache intact. They'd fashioned a makeshift travois out of hurriedly hewn pine saplings and the twenty-year quilt then scurried to load as many of the squashes as it would carry. It wasn't much, but each morsel would help when the snows deepened and food grew scarce. Before they could get the last of them, Striking Horse signaled that a rider was coming up the path from the valley. Lettie grabbed the shotgun in one hand, the rifle in the other and melted into the forest with her new family.

Ben, with Lettie behind him, detoured to the Charlton ranch, closer to Ben's home than to the homestead, in search of more news. There Mister Charlton had explained about the prairie sickness; the malady that he was certain had killed Missus Coopersmith and turned Mama poorly. It was a wasting disease, he'd said. Folks just got sadder and sadder. Their will just seemed to shut down after facing hard times and they could no longer choose their own path of action; they could only react when others forced them to do so.

He was sure it was the prairie sickness that had turned Papa into the spiteful wretch of the past few months and he'd urged Lettie to remember all the times she and Papa had laughed together or shared an appreciation of any one of God's little miracles. Papa would get better once he arrived in Ohio, he'd said, because his family there could help him overcome the melancholy.

Then Charlton offered to let the newlyweds live on his property for the winter in exchange for work Ben could do on the farm. The decision would have to be made quickly, though. Calls for builders would have to go out and work begun on a shelter before the killing frosts heralded the onset of winter.

Ben would have been content to spend the winter in the tipi of Dora's family but sensed that arrangement would quickly wear on Lettie's solitary soul. So, leaving her there in the care of Missus Charlton, he rode to the Indians' village to again summon his friends. When he returned the next morning, neighboring homesteaders had already begun clearing space for a small structure.

Now, less than a week after the harvest festival, logs were being hewn, shaped, and stacked to form a windowless square of roughly ten feet on each side.

The butt ends of the logs were stacked at the front, the smaller ends to the back to create a natural slope for the roof. That roof, sloping from roughly eight feet high at the front to too-low-to-stand-upright at the back, would be made up of the outer edges of the smaller logs. The first would be placed crosswise at the back, the second overlapped that one in a manner similar to the cedar shakes on the ranch house. A third would follow. When the roof was complete, all the logs would be covered with animal hides then sod cut from the nearby meadow.

When Charlton and the men brought the cooking stove, ready to be moved into one corner of the shed Lettie was speechless with gratitude. It, along with her docile old friend Behayma, the big red hen with her chicks, the quilt, the blue beads and hand-warmer from the luncheon pail, and the hastily scribbled plea from her sister, were all that she had to remind her of her family—those things and Papa's weapons.

In the spring, Ben and Lettie would stake out a homestead somewhere nearby and this process of building and moving would be repeated, leaving Mister Charlton with a snug, only slightly used, new granary—for the use of which Lettie would always be grateful. So she mixed and chinked with care but let her mind wander where it would.

When Lumpkin Charlton came to help chink the cracks, Lettie was forced to come out of herself and interact with the young man. His quick retorts to her teasing made her realize how mindlessly boring her task had been and she began to banter with the boy about avoiding the back-breaking work of turning trees into logs by playing in the mud.

"I'll be in your debt now. When you build a home for you and a pretty young bride, I'll be duty bound to help you chink the cracks."

His uncharacteristic silence caused her to turn to him. The color had drained from his face and she thought his heart must surely have broken before her very eyes.

"Oh, Master Lumpkin, I am SO very sorry. I was not meaning to be cruel. I had no idea you would miss her so terribly. Please accept my word that she WILL be back. We will bring her back, you and I. We will write letters and make her miss us as we miss her. She'll not be able to stay away. I promise."

Once the cabin was occupied, Mister Charlton made a habit of stopping for tea and a pancake when he worked near the granary. He always brought news of near or far and both Lettie and Ben enjoyed his company and the discussions his opinions elicited.

He'd long ago read about a doctor back east, he said, who had studied the minds of a few Contrarians. The doctor thought those men who couldn't think straight were actually sick—overtaken by an illness no one had ever imagined but a handful of doctors was trying to understand. Mister Charlton believed the notion and argued anew that it was just such an illness that had taken Missus Coopersmith and had plagued Pastor LaGreu.

Lettie was skeptical and argued persuasively against this unheard of disease he called a mental illness, but only because she enjoyed the arguing. Truth be told, she appreciated being allowed to participate in the men's conversations though, in this small space, it would have been harder to keep her quiet than it was to let her speak her mind.

TWENTY-SIX

Ben's smithing skills had been in high demand since he'd moved onto Charlton's ranch. He traveled from ranch to farm, forest to vale, mending the few heavy implements for farming, logging, or mining that had found their way into the upper valley. Early on, the satisfaction of creating new parts, or repairing old ones, then watching a piece of dead equipment come alive was almost enough to ease his need to be with Lettie. He was seldom away for more than five or six days but lately he'd begun to feel the aching loneliness he'd first felt at cow camp those few years ago. His one abiding thought from the time he rode from home was to return to Lettie and the granary.

He had thought to find a section to homestead and build Lettie her own cabin come spring. But two spring seasons had come and gone and they still lived in that little hovel. Was he the only one to find that bothersome? Lettie seemed never to be bothered by anything. Maybe that was one of the things that made him love her so—that ability to hum and dance through the dark little lair and make it a beautiful palace. More than a palace, she made it a home—one he wanted never to leave.

When he was away Lettie spent her days cooking, sewing, and jawing with Charlton's missus, and now she was finding a degree of fame with her baking. Lately the messages from ranchers to Charlton saying they needed help from Ben, the smith, had an added postscript from their wives; *Bring a cake from the smith's wife* or *Bring some of Lettie's bread.* The last one has simply said, *Bring Lettie.*

Folks seemed now to plan on having one of Lettie's cakes at their special occasions and traffic in and out of the Charlton ranch had increased more than just a little bit. Extra callers made the gregarious Missus Charlton happy so, of course, Charlton was happy too. Ben smiled wryly, "Old Dog Kodiak, if we've learned nothing else from visiting all these valley folks, we've learned that if the womenfolk ain't happy, ain't no-o-o one gonna be happy. Let that be a lesson to us."

Ben was returning from Winthrop where he'd picked up chunks of iron hauled over from the coast on the last of the long train of freight wagons that would make it across this summer. This was meant to be a brief errand, nothing more than a shopping trip, but the storekeeper had pulled Ben aside and urged him to travel home by this particular route.

It was shorter, he'd said, though no faster because of the poor road with lots of twists and turns and the steepness of the grade up to the Wolf Creek camp—no more than a track, really. Still, he thought Ben would find it worth his time because the head of Wolf Creek was in a box canyon of sorts where one could run a few head of cattle or horses and not worry about them wandering off. He said a friend of his had staked a claim up there but had tapped out and was wanting only enough money to get back home. Ben could homestead the place AND own the mineral rights for pennies on the dollar.

Lander had been right about the trek being slow going. The wagon jostled and rocked so badly the dog chose to jump off and walk; the progress so slow he even had time to chase a few forest critters without losing sight of Ben and the wagon. The track was no more than the vague, seldom used path of a man leading a burro. Ben had no business trying to force his way through with a two-mule team and a wagonload of iron but there was no place to turn around now. He could only keep pushing ahead.

The path leveled onto a natural meadow just after sunset and Ben halted the tired mules. His mood was darker than the cloudless horizon and, like the sky above, was growing darker by the minute.

The trip down from this high plain would be much worse than the climb up, no matter whether he chose to retrace his climb and return to town or whether he bushwhacked his way forward and down to Charlton's ranch. The brakes of the heavily laden wagon wouldn't hold on a hill of any mentionable grade so he'd have to tie it off to keep it from overrunning the mules.

All that would have to wait till the morrow and daylight. Tonight would be one more night away from Lettie. He would have to content himself with this lush meadow in which to camp. Stars overhead, dried grasses for the mules, the wagon for a bed—what more could he ask?

As if in answer, Kodiak trotted up to his master, a freshly killed hare hanging from his mouth. Ben chuckled and patted the dog's head. "Okay dog, I'm being ungrateful. Let's get these mules watered. Then we'll build us a fire and, thanks to you, feed like kings escaping hoi-polloi.

"I love that word, don't you? I wonder where I heard it? It sounds so foreign it probably came from the Black Robes. And listen to me talking like I would know. But I should know bout all things foreign, shouldn't I dog? That's what I am—everything foreign. Black-hearted Frenchman for a father, Indian mother, Catholic schooling, Medicine-women training...who could be more foreign than I? And because everyone *could* claim me, no one does. Except my Lovely Lettie."

My Lettie isn't hoi-polloi,
She's beautiful and she's noble.
I'd give you all the common maids,
But I'd keep her at my table.

He continued to sing to the dog while he unhitched the mules and led them on a stringer around the meadow searching for the source of the water they could hear flowing fast and hard. At the edge of a cliff he stopped in wonder. Far below was the creek, twisting, turning, rattling its way through the narrow gorge. A few yards from his vantage point was the beginning of a path that switch-backed down to a meadow much smaller than the one on which he stood.

"Beggar. Billie. I reckon if you two are going to have water, you'll have to work a little longer for it." With that, he loosed the stringer and slapped Beggar's rump. The mules took to the trail and made their way towards the water with Kodiak close on their hocks. Ben set the brake on the wagon and threw his bedroll over his shoulder. He grabbed his grub sack, his rifle, and Kodiak's dead rabbit before following his companions to the bottom.

212

The rap, rap, rapping of the woodpecker woke him, surprisingly late. The sun's rays were already hitting the rim though they hadn't yet penetrated the deep narrow canyon where he'd camped. Apparently, neither had the heat of the past month. The field was awash with late-summer flowers and grasses. Butterflies lapped at a dewdrop then, intoxicated by the heady liqueur, fluttered and flitted to find another. Early birds swooped and sang overhead. He sat on his hammock and surveyed his surroundings, absorbing the harmony of the meadow.

He untied his hammock from between the cottonwoods, rolled his bed, and, leaving the mules hobbled beside the creek, set off to explore. Pasture, water, and canyon walls would do for grazing stock. Lodgepole pines, a perfect size for building material, encircled the meadow, and the flat field near the creek meant house and barn raisings could be started without much leveling work. The surrounding bluffs would protect a home from the gales that blew through these mountains in the winters and, like now, the scorching sun of August. Most importantly, there was peace here—a contentment he'd never before experienced. He began to understand what *home* might mean; what it could be like to find one's *place.*

When he returned to the mules he realized that, for the first time since marrying Lettie, he had spent more than just a few minutes without that gnawing need to be with her. Not that she hadn't been on his mind. He'd meandered back and forth through the canyon picturing where they would site the house, where the garden would grow, where they would build the forge. This was Eden, just waiting for Benjamin Adam to bring his Eve.

In his walking, he'd found a different way into and out of the canyon. Yesterday he'd somehow missed the fork that would have brought him here from town by a more direct route. He could have avoided the worst of that trip, but that knowledge wouldn't help him today. He doused the embers of his fire and took the hobbles off the mules then drove them towards the path—towards the upper meadow and the buckboard with the freight that still had to get to Charlton—towards Lettie and their soon-to-be old home.

He'd figured right. The trip to the ranch had been arduous for both the man and his beasts. Ben would tie the back axle of the buckboard to a tree then ease the mules down the hillside. When he ran out of slack in the rope he'd chock the wheels and climb back up the hill to untie the rope. Depending on the steepness of the hill, that distance ranged from a foot or two to fifteen or twenty. Sometimes, if the incline was more gradual, he would, himself, act as a brake, wrapping the rope around a tree and feeding it slowly as the mules stepped carefully through the piney woods. He'd given a brief thought to leaving the wagon and bringing help from the ranch but that would have required an explanation of his detour and he didn't want anyone to hear about Eden until he had shown it to Lettie.

Despite the heat and the difficulty, he'd grown wings. As if he'd become one of the butterflies flitting through his meadow, he hummed and bustled from tree to axle to mule and back again. He couldn't have said where the day had gone when he realized it was in nearly full-on darkness that he rode the buckboard up to the barn, nor could he have sworn he'd done more than a slap-dash job of rubbing down the mules and giving them extra grain though he'd always taken great care with them.

He'd sent Kodiak ahead to let Lettie know he was nearly home and she'd put a pan of biscuits into the oven beside the baking beans. Despite the heat, she built a fire in the stove every day so she could bake him a homecoming meal of one kind or another—and provide for her growing list of customers at the same time.

He burst through the door, swept her into an embrace and waltzed her around the dim room.

You have my heart, I've loved you for always.
Come take my hand, we'll share all our days.
In sunshine we'll dance through meadows of flowers.
In dark times we'll laugh in the light of the moon.

"My darling, Ben Adam. That's the prettiest one yet. What has loosed the poet in your soul this day?"

"I shall change your name to *Eve,* my Lovely Lettie, because today I found our Eden"

TWENTY-SEVEN

Within days Ben was driving the mules, ploughing through a small square in the meadow at Eden to level the ground for the cabin floor. Lettie followed, picking the largest of the stones from the freshly turned soil and tossing them towards the area where she hoped to someday have a garden wall.

"I think we should sleep here tonight."

"We didn't come prepared for that, Lovely Lettie."

"You always have your bedroll and your grub bag with coffee in it."

"What about supper? And breakfast? We can't do a day's work on just coffee."

The conversation was being carried on in short spurts as the two passed each other going in the opposite direction. The intervening periods of silence gave each a chance to ponder the comment made by the other on the previous pass. By dusk the two, hungry and exhausted, too tired to converse, were ready to load the plough back onto the wagon for the three-mile trek to the granary.

Ben unhitched the plough and led the harnessed mules towards the creek for water before hitching them to the wagon for the trip home. The most direct way to the water—the way they would walk from their cabin door—was heavy with currant bushes and willow trees. A man leading a mule could wend his way through the thicket without tromping and killing the shrubs. Two mules abreast made that impossible. Though it meant more work, he unhitched the team and led them, single-file to the creek.

He returned, laughing, to find Lettie sitting on the back of the wagon, swinging her feet and eating from the mound of fresh berries she'd picked and now held in her apron. He plumped two fresh fish onto the wagon bed beside her.

"The Misters Trout were too curious about the basket you'd put in the creek to hold the milk tin. They found their way in but couldn't find a way out."

Lettie untied the apron strings, placed her pickings carefully beside the trout and jumped to the ground. She laughed and twirled around the man and the mules with her arms outspread. "We are to have our first meal in Eden...trout and berries. You hobble the mules and make a spit for the fish. I'll start a fire."

"That'll make it too late getting home. That trail is treacherous in the dark."

"Home? My darling Ben, we *are* home!"

She clasped her hands and ran to face him. "From this moment on I shall sleep here every night."

Early on the second morning, John Bragg arrived with a wagonload of poles for fences, plank lumber for a real floor, tools, children, and food. Close on his heels came Charlton on another wagon—this one carrying the cook-stove.

Speechless, Lettie could do no more than gape. Tears tried to force their way to her cheeks but she fought them and won—briefly.

"When I saw you didn't return to the granary last night I figured you'd found your home. Knew you'd be wanting that stove first thing."

Laughing and crying, Lettie ran to the man and wrapped him in a warm embrace. Poignantly, she thought, *It should be Papa I am hugging, thanking for the cooking stove. Maybe, in a way, it is.*

Once again a forest sang the cacophonous song of the homesteaders—mules and oxen protesting the hard labor, harnesses and wagons creaking and groaning under heavy loads, and axes biting into the pines. As before, Lettie used her bare feet to stomp and trod in a mortar-trench, making plaster to fill the chinks between the squared, denuded logs.

The two Bragg girls were her helpers these days. More likely her charges, she reckoned; the Missus Bragg probably glad for a short respite from some of her child-rearing duties though these girls pitched in and stomped mortar as well as she. *Reminds me of me and Belle not so long ago.*

Young Lumpkin Charlton, now two years older than when they built the granary, could no longer help with the women's work. He'd be helping the men in the forest. She missed his company only because he never seemed to tire of hearing talk of Belle. Ben wasn't nearly so patient when Lettie repeated a story he'd already heard or when she spoke of wishing her sister here. Young Lumpkin wished it as fervently as she.

Most of the men camped in Eden while the work was ongoing. Charlton went home each night and each morning brought food for the crew. On the third day he also brought a bag of flour and Lettie's jar of bacon grease from the granary. The walls of the cabin were still no higher than Lettie's waist but, with all sides in place, two of the men could start building a floor. They seemed anxious to get on with that and Lettie laughed a little when she realized it was because they wanted to bring in the stove.

Ben, never one to complain, had once remarked that the men were "a little disappointed with Missus Charlton's vittles. Not that she doesn't make good grub, mind you. She just puts everything onto the hot part of the stove to get it started then goes off to do something else for a minute or few. That minute turns into too long and the food burns."

It was a Saturday, the fifth one in the month. Lettie had fed the workers a hearty breakfast of venison and gravy, biscuits and good strong coffee—liberally laced with heavy cream from Behayma's evening milk. In the last five days the men had built a cabin, a privy, a corral, and a cowshed spacious enough for Behayma to share with a flock of chickens as well as a mule and horse. She'd watched the walls go up for the barn and wondered if it wasn't bigger than the house she would be sharing with Ben. They'd brought Ben and Lettie's meager possessions from the Charlton ranch and moved them into the new cabin—almost twice the size of the granary.

Now the neighbors had packed up their tools and moved down the hill to the Charlton ranch to reunite with their families. After the hoe-down tonight and tomorrow's All-day-sing-and supper-on-the-ground, they'd return to their homes to take up the work that had been done by their wives and children in their absence.

"Iron Moccasin has a horse he would like to give to you. It's a fine stallion, out of Good Fortune. We could use it to start a nice herd."

"I'm not so able a rider as you. The stallions frighten me."

Ben laughed. "You do well enough on that young mule and he's as cantankerous a mount as can be found anywhere."

"I do *well enough* because he's following you and your mare. If I were to try to take him somewhere different he wouldn't budge. That's not the same as going too fast in a direction *I* don't want to go."

"Bragg says you can have that young black mare he calls Trilby if I fix up his manure spreader so it works right. Trouble of it is, she's a mare, right enough, but foals she'd throw wouldn't be helping the breed line. I can't see much sense in having a mare around if you can't use her to increase your herd."

Lettie let the mule walk on for several paces. When she spoke her voice quivered. "Like me?" she asked quietly.

Ben stopped his mare and dismounted, not hurrying but with purpose. He walked back to Lettie sitting patiently astride the mule, reached up and pulled her gently off to stand before him. He wrapped his arms around her and held her close. "That's not what I meant and you know it. God will give us children when He's ready and not a day sooner. Until then, you are all I need. And I do need you as I need breath itself. If something were ever to happen to you, God forbid, my life would be over.

"Besides, it is only just more than two years ago that we married."

"I know," answered Lettie. "Two years since Papa took Mamma and Belle away and sold his lovely farm. Two years since that awful man burned it to the ground. Two years since you have been my only happiness. And for you, I give thanks to God every single moment."

The roguish Merle Magruder had come all the way from his freight depot at Black Bear to play his fiddle for the dance. He'd hitched a wagon to a team of mules and brought as many of his lodgers as wanted to come along including the Braggs who followed in a smaller cart so as not to go all the way there and back alone. Excepting the fiddle, the dance music came from instruments fashioned out of whatever the settlers could imagine. Missus Bragg brought her washboard and kept the dancers stepping in a steady rhythm. When she tired, Missus Charlton thought to try it. With a few extra pit-a-pats here and there she soon had the washboard singing its own tune and the fiddler giving over to let her make the music. Missus Bragg refused to pick it up again. "I can only make it sound the beat others dance to, you make it do the dancing—and the singing as well."

Lander, the shopkeeper, brought a harmonica. He seemed to be competing with Magruder for the opportunity to play duets with the surprising Missus Charlton and her washboard. Magruder took the opportunity to dance, and flirt outrageously, with Lettie. Lumpkin Charlton, too, danced with Lettie but his conversation was centered on her sister.

The day had been a long one and the party, though lively, was short lived. Families were soon

222

retreating to their wagons and bedrolls. Lettie moved from family to family, thanking the wives for allowing their men folk to help at Eden, thanking the men for doing so.

Ben watched quietly from beside the bonfire. When Lettie came to stand beside him he handed her a cup of cold cider and smiled. "You look almost sad."

"I was wondering what it would be like to dress in such finery as Mister Magruder's lodger is wearing. The satin glows in the fire light and rustles mysteriously when she dances."

"And here I was, thinking that you are so radiant you don't need fancy dresses to attract attention. But, my darling, if you want silk, I shall work my fingers to stubbins to give you silk."

Lettie grinned and took his hands. "With the exception of baby gowns I've never had a new dress in my life. Everything I've worn has been remade from someone's cast-off garments. I wouldn't know what to do with finery. I'd probably catch the heel of my boot in the lace and fall on my face, ruining the lace, the dress, and my face.

"That raises other questions. What would I do with it when I wasn't wearing it? I have no space for something I could wear but once or twice a year. And would I have to start putting on airs?"

"You're too honest a woman for that. I do not believe airs would suit. On second thought, maybe they would. Just what are *airs*?"

"Now that I've mingled and watched a bit, I'd say it's having a fear of falling on one's face caused by the wearing of shoes without a sturdy heel, skirts with too much lace, and bodices that expose one's chest to the elements but not showing you're afraid."

Still laughing, she turned to him, anticipating a quick retort. He stood, rigid and cold, staring into the fire.

She knew he would tell her what had triggered this leap into another world—another time—only when he was ready. Prying and questioning would only send him deeper into that other place. She encircled him in a gentle hug and put her head on his chest, listening to the rapid pace of his heartbeat.

"There was a tiny painted picture...in...a box. I was very young. I thought when I saw it in the moonlight that it was a picture of Da. Next morning in daylight I could see the dark colors of her dress, the silhouette of a ship as the background. I thought the woman must have had less money for dress goods than we did. Good boots, maybe...tall lace-up ones with too sharp a heel for real work...but her skirts came only to the tops of them...like she didn't have enough money to buy cloth to make a real dress. And the blouse...bodice, you called it...came down very low, exposing more of her than Mam would have thought fitting. Her shawl was made of feathers...not enough to keep a body warm against an evening chill. Same with her hat...only a feather...angled off this-a-way. Couldn't say whether her look was defiant or brazen...certainly not sad or fearful. I know now that she was probably a dance-hall girl. There was writing on the back. I couldn't read it then but I've always remembered the picture the words made. It was *Ruby LeFleur-Kidd's Cove*."

"Where did you see this painting?"

He paused for a long moment before saying quietly, "In a box."

They stood, gaining and giving comfort, in the glow of the dying fire. She felt his sharp intake of breath as if he had made a sudden leap back into the present. He smiled down at her.

"I am beginning to question the wisdom of hiding you away in Eden. You are held in high regard by all of these folks. You should live in the middle of town where you can bake your wonderful breads and give advice and succor to all. Do you realize you have danced with nearly every man here?"

"Indeed, I do," laughed Lettie. "In fact, every one save one. And I'm nearly tuckered out! I have only enough energy for the last dance—with you!"

"I would only embarrass you. You do so well that which I cannot do at all."

"Please, Ben. All you have to do is put your arms around my waist and put your feet where the music is."

He did. And as they moved slowly across the ground in rhythm to the music of the last waltz, he sang—so softly only Lettie could hear.

> *Beautiful Lettie, I love you,*
> *Love you with all of my heart.*
> *Together we'll dwell in our Eden*
> *E'en Death will not keep us apart.*

"Ben-the-Smith! That's bordering on morbid!" she laughed.

> *'Struth what I sing you, dear Lettie.*
> *Please God, ne'er take thee from me*
> *I only want you to be happy*
> *And something here should rhyme with e-e-e.*

TWENTY-EIGHT

"You've been longer at your prayers this morning."

"There are many things for which I give thanks. My bounty grows daily." He smiled thoughtfully and continued, "I did not believe that a promise I made in a fit of spite would come back to haunt me as it has. I have, in a few short years, returned fourteen fat beeves to the Indian Agency. Tomorrow I take another one." He slipped past her and eased to the back of the cabin.

"You've taken extra ones every year. How long will you do so?"

"As long as God continues to show me kindness and mercy. Besides, we have more than enough for our needs."

"Would it not be better to take breeding stock so people can learn how to raise their own meat?"

"The one I take tomorrow has been bred. She is a good mama and will make a good lead cow for a new herd. Striking Horse will decide who shall have her."

She watched him remove the short cape he wore for his prayers and marveled at his serenity; at the peace he wore like his prayer-cape. She couldn't help comparing him to Papa whose prayers also had lengthened daily. When did her father reach the point

226

that he did nothing else? In the early years Mama said he was praying for guidance or courage—or both probably. When did he begin seeking escape? When did the love of his beautiful and dutiful wife and his children change in his mind from bounty to burden?

Was it really praying? Did Papa just have a bad case of the prairie sickness like Mama and Missus Coopersmith had? Was he so sad about his life that he could no longer think what to do? Could summon only enough will to go out, kneel before the huge boulder he called The Altar, and simply send his mind away?

But hadn't God told us to empty our minds when we came in prayer? Wouldn't Papa's empty mind make it easier for God to talk to him?

"The difference is in the accepting," Ben said softly.

Lettie's eyes widened and focused on her husband. It was the watching of him that had sent her mind atumble and she realized she'd stared, unseeing, the whole time he was changing into his work clothes.

"It frightens me that you can read my mind."

He smiled and moved to her side, pulling her to him. "It does me, too. I promise you I don't try to do it but when you're thinking of someone you love your thoughts shout to me. Maybe because you love so deeply those thoughts are more potent that others?"

She loosed herself from his embrace and gave the batter one more fold before tipping it into the pan and sliding the pan into the oven, leaving the door propped open with a small stick to regulate the heat.

She stepped around him and dipped water from the wooden bucket into the teakettle and put it on the stove to boil. They were all automatic movements and she did them with a puzzled frown. She'd made the tea and covered the pot with a cloth and placed it on the warming-oven door before she realized she'd failed to answer his question. And that he was standing patiently right where she'd left him, forcing her to step around him several times without seeing him.

"I'm so sorry," she whispered hugging him fervently. "I just can't imagine what's come over me." She plunked herself onto the little kitchen stool and ran her fingers through her dark hair.

He reached for the tea mugs that hung from pegs drilled into the log wall and spooned a dollop of top cream from the pitcher stored in a covered box on the windowless sill. He tipped half the spoon of cream into each cup then filled them with the hot tea. He reached her cup towards her and smiled.

"Here. I know you can't sit and talk. You must pace when you're trying to find an answer. Let's walk to the creek while we drink our tea and maybe we can solve your riddle together."

"I'll bring my gathering basket and pick fresh greens. We can check the robin's nest for little blue eggs and the hen yard for fat brown ones.

"And maybe the backwater for frogs," he teased latching the door securely behind him then patting his leg for Kodiak to follow.

⚜

"**What** did you mean when you said what you did about accepting?"

"When I said that, an hour or so ago now, you were busy with many things. Your hands were stirring cake batter (which is still in the oven, in case you've forgotten) and your thoughts were on your family. I would have been wasting my words if I had tried then to explain that *open* is not the same as *empty*. So, while your mind was not empty, neither was it open to receiving my explainings. You were right, though. Our

228

Gods—your God of Heaven and my Great God of All—want us to come to them with open minds and open hearts, ready to receive their directions or their answers to our questions.

"I have heard you say our Indian way of praying is ritualistic. But do you not see that your father's taking his Bible at the same time each morning then following the path to the boulder then kneeling before it and closing his eyes were all steps of a ritual he had created for himself? With each action he shed a bit of the ungodly that surrounded him. Each step along that dusty track brought him closer to being in a state in which he could accept the presence of God.

"When you say the prayer that thanks your God for your blessings—your food, your safety, your well-being—it is a different prayer than the one you say when you believe God is going to talk back to you.

Think about this. When you write a letter to Belle you first take a sheet of the paper from the chest; you open the stopper in the inkbottle and you clean the nib on the pen. All the while you are thinking of her. Then you write as if you are talking to her. You tell her what has made you happy or sad, you ask her to send you news of your mother. From the moment you make that decision to write a letter, nothing else is on your mind—not the baking, the housework, or the farm. Not even me. You are thinking only about Belle.

But you would prepare differently if you learned Belle was to come here to visit with you, to speak to you, to actually bring words for you to hear. You would make yourself ready to devote all your time and thoughts to her. You would tidy the house then do your chores and hitch a horse to the trap. You would put on your best dress and drive to the freight depot to await her arrival. And you would make that drive in great anticipation. All of that is the ritual of preparation.

"And when she arrived you would listen to every word she said. You would not be worrying about cakes in the oven or eggs in the hen house when she was speaking.

"So I believe that my people's ritual of prayer is the same as your preparing for a visit from someone you love. We cleanse ourselves in the sweat lodges and perfume our bodies with oils and herbs. We put on our prayer-capes and sing the songs and dance the dances to clear our minds of worldly things and let our God know we are preparing for a visit with Him—getting ourselves ready to listen to His words. I think it must be the same for the Black Robes. They light their candles, count their beads, and sing their chants. The chant means nothing to me but I believe that each word does a little more than the last one to push the clutter of daily life from their minds and hearts and move them closer to a receptive state."

Lettie stepped slowly along the shady path towards home, her gathering basket in one hand, Ben's hand in the other. "Is this the lesson Papa tried to teach your mam's people or was this something he should have been learning from them?"

Ben squeezed her hand gently. "I think your papa wanted everyone to try to *understand* his God. Our ceremonies help us *experience* ours."

"You still haven't explained the *accepting* part."

Ben sighed softly and again squeezed Lettie's hand. "I already said *open* is not the same as *empty*. I think when one wants to learn, one comes with an *open* mind and is prepared to accept God's counsel. I believe your Papa was, instead, trying to *empty* his mind; to forget about the past and not think of the

230

future. I think he wanted so badly to convert the Indians that he wouldn't let himself listen to what God wanted. He never stopped thinking of us as savages—never considered that we were created by the same god as he was.

So, I think God could have shot wisdom into your papa's mind with a bolt from Lightening and your papa would have refused to recognize or accept it. Your papa was not accepting that perhaps God wanted him to do something different—that maybe God's plan was to change your father's beliefs rather than ours. He was not praying, he was hiding. Maybe being with family in Ohio will bring him peace."

TWENTY-NINE

Since the time he'd come home to the granary to announce his discovery of Eden and found the room as hot as the oven and Lettie a wilted flower, he'd wanted to solve the problem of overheating the house every time she baked bread. Lettie wouldn't let him haul the stove outside even during the summer months and, though she'd tried, she couldn't master the art of baking over an open fire.

And now the ranchers' wives were more and more often asking why he hadn't brought his bride with him. He knew they wanted more than just her baked goods; they wanted her company. She was a bright and witty guest but could also bring news of other families who lived in the valley. Most of the ranches still lacked a cooking stove so Lettie couldn't bake while she was a visitor. He tried to find a way to explain, without making them think her a snob, that his wife was easily bored with visiting and stitchery and that she preferred to stay home doing the work she loved. He, too, enjoyed traveling in her company but he acceded to her wish to stay snug at Eden.

His hours in the saddle gave him plenty of time to ponder and the first item from his new forge was a portable oven. He hoped that being able to take an oven along would make Lettie an eager companion on his lonely journeys. Creativity possessed him like a demon and he heated and pounded and reheated the iron until he had created an exquisite little bundle that could be assembled and placed over an outdoor fire to become a baking oven used and envied throughout the valley.

Ben had taken half a dozen loaves of Lettie's sourdough bread to the store in Winthrop. She'd had orders for four but always sent extra so Lander would have some for his shelves. Ben suspected the storekeeper was charging his customers a darned-sight more for them than he was paying Lettie but even so, the shelf-loaves never lasted the day. Still, she enjoyed the baking, was good at it, and the credits to their account certainly helped when money from the sale of their beeves and horses dwindled, as it surely did for all of the ranchers from time to time.

From Winthrop he would travel south and east along the river to find a ranch owned by someone named Leighton. The man, like most who needed a smith, had written to Charlton asking about Ben's services. He'd reckoned he could use a repairman for the better part of a week though he hadn't been specific about his needs.

Ben thought it unfair to be so vague and had considered sending a message declining the offer of work. He didn't worry about Lettie. He knew she was self-sufficient and she liked the brief periods of solitude. He simply hated the emptiness in himself when he was away from her.

He rode his strangely spotted horse, a gift from Iron Moccasin, at an easy pace. He'd had no call to work this far south before but he'd been assured the

Leighton ranch was easy enough to find. The further he rode the more uneasy he grew. He wasn't being followed. At the first shiver of disquiet he'd slipped through a cottonwood grove and circled back to watch the river path just to make certain of that.

As he had done when he was first with Striker's band, he found himself watching the horizon, feeling as if he should know it but not recognizing why—not until he rode up to Leighton's farm. There, in the upper corner of the farmyard, grew a huge, glorious crab apple tree.

Ben sat his horse. He'd always practiced the Indian custom of staying mounted until invited to step down but at this moment he couldn't have moved if Leighton had been standing there begging him to do so. His heart was drumming its way through his chest wall. His lungs had surely burst because he could neither catch a breath nor let one go. His eyes were burning embers. His arms and legs were stone. As if by some hidden cue his horse whirled, nearly sending Ben into the dirt, and sped to the creek bank.

Ben took great deep gulps of air and gripped the saddle horn, trembling convulsively. His gut cramped and he slid from the horse to vomit violently onto the dry earth. Again he gulped the hot, dry air and forced his legs to take a step, then another.

When he was confident he could remount he did so and turned to ride slowly, deep in thought, back to the Leighton's farm. He had not once glanced at the spot, high up on the creek bank, where he knew there was enough of the Black-hearted Frenchman's treasure to dress Lettie in silks for the rest of her life.

Ben worked in numbness. Leighton's friendly chatter dwindled for lack of response and his wife's meals went back to the kitchen untasted. Darkness brought turmoil but not sleep.

He reckoned the Leighton's house was built directly over Mam's grave. He was appreciative that now no one could disturb her rest. And the Leightons were good people. They worked hard during the day and said their prayers at night. Mam would have liked them. They certainly deserved better than what he was giving them. His repairs to the machinery were good and right but people out here expected more from a traveler. They wanted news and company—confirmation of their existence and their worth from someone besides each other. Each dawn Ben would finally fall into a short fitful sleep after resolving to break through the numbness.

At dusk on the third day he forced himself to walk to the creek. As he'd learned to do so many years ago, he avoided the path, winding instead between the sage and the dried tsaltsaleken. At the creek's edge he scanned the far bank. Sarvisberry bushes still grew at the base but the upper rim had caved in, covering the opening to the den. Even he would have a hard time finding the narrow tunnel.

His gut began to wrench, his breath stopped, and sweat ran down his back; feelings he recognized from his childhood—the sense that Da was near. He turned quickly. On the horizon behind the Leighton's home a lone rider sat silhouetted against the darkening sky.

Ben walked back to the barn, again being careful to weave his way lightly through the vegetation. Under cover of the sturdy little structure he packed his gear, saddled his horse, and waited. At full darkness he slipped over to the wrap-around porch where the Leightons rocked gently on a hanging bench.

They'd watched his approach and offered him a glass of cool tea. Ben declined the invitation to sit and chat, offering instead his most humble apology. He must leave now, he'd said. He couldn't see his way clear to charge them for his work. Though he'd finished all they'd asked he knew he'd fallen short of their expectations.

"You leaving on account o' that rider that's been hanging around these past six, maybe eight days?"

"Know him?"

"Nope. Never talked to him. Far's I seen, he ain't been no closer'n that ridge top. Mattie says she's seen him down by the creek once or twice. Never got close enough to get a good look at 'im, though."

Ben took a deep breath and, for no known reason, responded to the old gentleman's query. "I suspect he used to be my father."

"You lived here once." It was a statement.

Ben nodded into the darkness and the old man continued as if he'd seen it. "Saw your reaction the day you rode in. Go. Know that we love this place. There's a presence here. She welcomes us each and every day."

"She?" Ben croaked quietly.

"Mattie says it's a she. On account of the fragrance, you know. Calls her Little Bearberry on account o' she smells like those flowers.

"We'll keep the fire in the forge going for a day or two," continued Leighton. "If you think that'll help."

"Don't put yourselves at risk. If that's him, he stops for no man, takes what he wants, makes no apology. And it's me that he wants."

The woman reached to the porch rail and picked up a small packet. "Here. You've not eaten more than a morsel since you arrived. Take this. It's just a piece of venison and a cold biscuit but it may get you by till you're somewhere safer. We'll care for the place... and all that's here."

Ben wanted to hug her, hug them both, but instead crossed himself in the fashion of the Black Robes and stretched his hand towards the two of them. Then he whirled and slipped through the darkness to the barn and his waiting ride.

THIRTY

He led his horse through the deepest of the shadows. His saddle was worn, soft and supple, but the leather against chaps would sound like a braying burro in a night as still as this. And by walking his horse he could place his feet carefully, feeling for deadfall that might snap and alert a follower. He, himself, could hear the footfall of a horse from a great distance and assumed Blackheart the Frenchman had trained himself to do just as well. He crept north and east, silently but with haste, his mind awhirl.

Should he simply ride up and confront the man? Surprise him as he slept? Most bully's were cowards and usually backed down from a fair fight. His mind knew that. But Ben was too close to this evil. Though all his gods were with him his heart would overrule his brain and he would cower before the devil who was his sire.

Where had the man been these past ten or so years? Had he wandered through the valley asking after Ben or had he followed leads beginning with the two inept scavengers who had lost him on the other side of The Great River?

Had Da sold the homestead or had he simply failed to prove his claim? Had he watched as wagons

240

loaded with lumber were deposited at his old place and the two-story stick house was being built over Mam's grave? He couldn't have seen the picture burned into the folds of the leather strap Ben had dropped into Mam's gathering basket. Ben didn't think even the alert and watchful Dora knew of the writing on that strap. But Da had tossed the basket, and any of Mam's things that were to hand, into the bier as well.

Now, with that map out of reach, only he and Dora knew the whereabouts of the den. Dora had been so much younger than he. She probably had less of an idea how to find the original homestead than he did. And, like him, she might have a vague idea of where the cave was but wouldn't know its exact spot. And even if she could find the cave, Dora didn't know about Da's treasure. Could that devil know of her escape from the bounty hunters? Had Da tracked Dora to Striker's village? Perhaps to save Dora, and Lettie of course, he could force himself to face the one he feared above all others.

Perhaps for them he could tell the man where his treasure was hidden; could explain that he had taken one tiny piece of it each time the man had beaten one of them. He would explain that he had hidden each piece with a prayer that, when Da found some of his treasure missing he'd bargain with Ben; bargain for the return of his treasure in exchange for peace. But the beatings were frequent and the pieces of treasure were not so numerous as to outlast the anger. Mam had died and Da had sold his children before the man would realize that one of them had taken his most valued possession. Ben wondered how long had it taken him to accept the truth—the treasure might never be found.

A mile or more upriver he mounted his horse and set off carefully towards the east. Several times he circled back to watch the path behind. He couldn't see a trailing rider. He reminded himself that he didn't know where his father had been and couldn't say what skills he'd picked up in the last ten years—didn't really know what skills the man had already known before he'd sold his children.

Ben let the mare pick her way along the path and he pondered the past. The idea of visiting the dead had always unnerved him but tonight, protected by the darkness and the solitude, he deliberately focused his thoughts on his mother and he was not afraid. For the first time since his confused and disoriented journey under the rawhide shroud, he celebrated her life and analyzed her death.

Sia had believed the valley would soon be home to more white settlers than it was now to her people. For this reason she insisted that her children learn to read the White Man's words and speak his language. She, herself, had spent two years with the Black Robes. It was they who had given her the Bible she used to teach him and Dora as much as she could.

She and her people had named him Squaku—Yellow Pine—but Da refused to call him anything but Moise. Ben didn't know what the name Moise meant but he was sure it was something not as good as Yellow Pine.

Ben had been named for his mother's father Skakuluk—Limber Pine—and he remembered his grandfather with fondness. Several times when Da had been about to beat him, Skakuluk came walking into the farmyard as if on a stroll through the scrub, though his village was many miles from the ranch. Da would mount his horse and ride away in a fury. Skakuluk would drink a cup of tea with the family then leave for home.

But Skakuluk had not come that time in the barn. That time when Ben had failed to hang the heavy horse harness quite properly. Da had roared and Ben tensed against the blow he knew would come.

He didn't remember that blow, though. Not specifically. He awoke, lying face down in the muck. The sun was low in the western sky. The rays glistened on something under a pile of rubble way to the back of the tack stall. He closed his eye that was closest to the dirt. No sparkly object glinted back. If Ben hadn't been lying just so, with his left eye just an inch off the muck, he'd never have seen the shine.

He waited, unmoving, for several minutes to make sure Da wasn't standing near just waiting for the boy to regain consciousness. When he heard no sounds, he pushed himself to his hands and knees; moved his head back and forth to clear the dizziness. When he could stand he slipped to the barn door and watched the farmyard. Da's horse was gone from the barn but Ben had wanted to be sure the man wasn't about. Then, piece-by-piece, he carefully moved the rubble.

Resting beneath the rocks and chunks of wood and old iron was a box wrapped loosely in fabric of some kind. The worn cloth had a small tear on one corner, exposing the tiniest golden edge. The box was the most beautiful object Ben had ever seen. It was glistening gold with blue and white and black stones set into the top and around the sides—sides which barely peeked out either side of the hand he placed over the top. He lifted the lid to find strange coins of nearly the same golden color. There was a picture of a woman inside but he had no idea who she was or what the writing on the back meant. He slipped a coin from the box, carefully closed the lid, and put it back exactly where he'd found it. Then he replaced the debris that had hidden it so well.

He was replacing the last of the rotten pieces of wood when he heard the soft footsteps of his mother approaching. He popped the coin in his mouth. He used his tongue to hold the coin against his cheek while she bathed his bruises with herbs. When she insisted on looking into his mouth to see why his speech was slurred so, he swallowed the coin. It was several days before he retrieved the coin and hid it beneath a small stone in the floor of the den they had dug. Eventually, even the beautiful box and the picture had been wrapped in hides and buried in that root cellar.

Old Skakuluk had gone on his starwalk by the time Ben had found Dora. He was sorry about that. Perhaps he could have summoned the courage to discuss Mam's passing with his grandfather.

Ben knew Mam had a close bond with her sister, Tsaltsaleken. If one wished for her, the other would appear and he realized now that the thinking trick had likely been a gift handed down from their father. But his aunt hadn't visited his mother during her last sickness. Tsaltsaleken could have used her curing ways to help Mam but she had not come. He blamed her absence, and so she herself, for his mother's death and he'd shunned the woman since coming to live in Striker's village.

Ben's horse stopped. Ben waited, curious and silent. The air had changed. There was no breeze, no breaking dawn. He started to dismount but a hand stayed his foot in the stirrup though no one stood beside him. He heard the rider, coming quietly but confidently from back along the trail. Ben reached for the scabbard to pull his rifle but the cool hand pressed his wrist.

He saw the rider, a large-bore rifle at the ready, hurrying towards him. He saw a look of puzzlement, as if the man had seen his quarry then inexplicably lost it. Ben saw him as if through the bough of a tree but he was recognizable just the same. Panic-stricken, he would have plunged towards the man in an onslaught of fear and rage but that hand rested firmly on his thigh and he couldn't move.

The path ahead widened onto the foothills from the high country. The pines abruptly gave way to shrubs and sage and from that point one would be able see a rider a great distance ahead. Ben watched the man spur his horse into a gallop as if certain to catch his prey there but he stopped, stood in his stirrups, scanned the open country, then spun and rode back just as fast. He circled in big loops always to come, cursing and sputtering, to mill around within sight and sound of his son.

Confused, Ben was certain the man had looked directly at him more than once. He blinked to clear away the pine boughs but blinking didn't help. He dared not move to wipe the branches away from his face, his hat, or wherever it was they had collected. He remembered Dora's story of the Sanctuary Tree, the one he'd always thought the figment of an eight-year-old girl's imagination. Was this the work of Lettie's God? Of his own? Both?

The irate rider spurred his horse back the way he had come. This time he did not loop back but continued at a dangerous pace until he was well out of Ben's hearing.

Ben blinked a slow thank you to who or what had saved him and when he opened his eyes the tree boughs no longer blurred his vision. The staying hand had gone from his leg and, without urging, his mare picked up her pace as if she'd never stopped. He worried briefly that the man was returning to the Leighton ranch to harm the elderly couple but the hand rested for a moment on his back as if to give him peace.

He kicked the horse into a slow trot. He wanted desperately to fly with all speed to the village but flying feet stir up dust and he didn't want to signal his presence to anyone with a large-bore rifle. He zig-zagged slightly between the taller brush but held a mostly straight course towards Tsaltsaleken to warn her of the evil that had returned to their home lands.

After that he would accept any help offered in order to go unseen from Tsaltsaleken to Dora and then on to Eden and Lettie.

247

THIRTY-ONE

His talk with Tsaltsaleken took longer than the one he'd practiced in his mind. He'd dismounted when invited to do so and followed her into her home. He sat cross-legged before her fire and waited for the tea she'd offered.

"You bring troubling news."

He nodded once. "But, I have wronged you and I must first apologize for my bad judgment."

Wisely, she waited for him to continue.

"I have always thought you did not come when my mother called you and so my mother died. I have just this morning seen that my mother could not call you; that the medicine my father was giving her to ease her pains was clouding her mind and not letting her send for you. I should have been a better son. Knowing you *would* have come if you'd been called, I should have run to bring you to her. I am so very sorry to you both for my stupidity...my lack of faith in you."

"Do you know what was your Mam's sickness?"

"I didn't then. Now I think it had something to do with childbirth."

"With child death." The woman spat the last word. She chewed on her tea leaves for a dark moment before she continued.

"We all love you, Squaku—you and your sister. But your mother should not have had a child, definitely not two, and all, including your Da, knew that a third would kill her. But your Da would not control his appetite. Many times I gave her the expelling tonic and saved her life. Yes, I could have saved her this time if I had been called many months before. But it was winter and your mam thought she had that White Man's sickness he calls by the name *the fluensa* or some such. By the time she realized the truth, the expelling tonic could not help her.

"Do not feel guilty for not running for me. Your Da was putting the drops into all of you. Skakuluk saw him in a vision putting it into your water pail. He hurried there to warn you but all were gone. He watched for many days. Then your Da rode into the barn and when he came out he was in a rage. He was searching for something. He tore everything down and burned it piece by piece—the house, the barn, the chicken pen, fence posts even...all into the fire. Skakuluk watched until your Da rode away. It had taken him three whole days to burn everything. He left nothing but embers and ashes; no trace of himself, of Sia, of Squaku or Kanit'sa."

She sighed deeply. As if an afterthought, she added, "Your Da did not go to the root cellar."

Ben eyed the woman, remembering the flower she'd drawn for him on the small strip of hide, but he dared not interrupt her speech.

"Skakuluk walked here and walked there and finally found your Mam's grave. He prayed with her while the fire died. For two more days it burned over her and she was happy for it. She said it was a cleansing fire. Between her and the heavens now there was nothing of the devil who had claimed her. She said it burned so long and so hot it melted the doors to Heaven. They cannot close now against her. She is free to come and go, as she is needed."

"The people who live there now feel her presence. She pleases them. I suppose that means they please her."

"She is a happy spirit. She was especially glad for the things your Da sent with her, though they were sent in anger and hate.

"Now Squaku, what of your news?"

"When Da took us from the ranch, Kanit'sa and I were shoved into the back of the wagon under a blanket. And it was dark. We didn't know where we were going or where we'd been. I have been certain all the years since then that the ranch was close by but had no notion how to find it.

"Last week I was called to make repairs at a ranch now owned by Hiram Leighton. His wife is called Mattie but that's not important. When I rode up to the barn I saw Mam's crab apple tree. Seeing that tree shocked me beyond imagination.

"After a few days of working I went down to the creek to see if the...root cellar...was still there. I don't know why I chose that particular day to go check, but when I turned to go back to the barn I saw the Frenchman on a horse up on the bluff watching me. I left Leighton's place as soon as it was dark. He said he would keep the forge burning so Da wouldn't know I was gone. I guess that didn't work because the devil was right behind me when I broke pine cover on the pass."

"How did you escape?"

"I don't know...as a rational man. It was as if the biggest tree in all the world covered me with her boughs and he couldn't see through them. It reminded me of Dora's...Kanit'sa's story of the tree that saved her from the bounty hunters. I just don't know how he

250

couldn't see me but I hope and pray that he didn't go back to visit harm on those good folks."

"Young Squaku...he had already killed them. And, as is his custom, put fire to their loving home."

THIRTY-TWO

The peal of anguish echoed through the vale, screaming from canyon wall to tree trunk and back again—a wave of darkness enshrouding the landscape. It rang from his throat, from his chest, from his bowels. Only the desire to tear away after the killer, one he had once called Da, kept him on his feet.

Tsaltsaleken, in uncharacteristic vigor stood toe-to-toe with the angry whirlwind before her and, shout-to-shout, insisted his first duties were to warn his sister and protect his wife. "Your Da is a White Man," she spat. "Let the White Man deal with him."

Ben looked around and, even in his grief, realized what his aunt and her family already knew. The one without a soul would ride here next. The people must be away before he did so.

Tsaltsaleken's village was a small one. The young men had grown old and had watched as their own young men had gone to larger villages. Those few remaining families had collected their rifles, most as aged and decrepit as they themselves, mounted their horses and collected their five or six head of cattle for the drive north to Striking Horse's village. They milled patiently, quietly, at the path.

"Will you ride with me?" Ben offered contritely.

Tsaltsaleken smiled at the image of herself on the back of Ben's spotted horse. "No, child. You must go fast. I can walk as fast as the cows I follow. We will be with your sister by nightfall."

Ben had acquiesced and ridden north in a frenzy to find his sister and her family. It was late summer. The women would be out gathering the berries and grass seeds they mixed with dried meats for winter food. They'd be defenseless against a marauder. Tsaltsaleken had been right. They must be warned.

Runners scattered to each of the harvesting places to call back the women. Ben waited and worried in Dora's tipi until, late in the afternoon, the women had cached their pickings and all had returned in haste to their homes. When a rider came in to say Tsaltsaleken and her small band, joined now be some of Striking Horse's men, were within sight of the village, Ben and two riders rushed towards the Charlton ranch to warn again of murder and madness.

Locals knew the road to Eden went through Charlton's land so men wanting to hire him still contacted him through Charlton. That meant Da might not know about Eden and Lettie yet. Ben would do his best to keep it that way. He'd stay with Charlton until dark then walk the few miles to Eden. Da might be watching for Ben to ride for home. He might not be expecting him to walk.

A rattlesnake slithered across the path. The horse would have continued at her gallop but Ben instinctively jerked at the reins. The horse, startled, sidestepped and nearly threw her rider. At that moment a bullet zinged past Ben's ear. His companions flew from their mounts and darted into the trees. Ben was but a short second behind. Before they could regroup, more shots rang out—this time from the direction of the ranch. The three could only stay hidden in the trees and wait until the sniper had been driven off and Charlton helloed for Ben.

Charlton and his men led the three Indian horses towards Ben and his friends. "I'd say this was your lucky day, son."

"Only just and just so far," concurred Ben. "But I'll have to thank you later. Right now I have to get to Lettie."

"Lettie's here...and your dog...at the ranch with the Missus. Sent men out to get'em soon's we heard about the Leightons, may they rest in peace."

"Amen. How did you hear?"

"Apple pickers looking for work. Saw the smoke. Got there just as the Missus was passing. Too late for Hiram, though. She told them to warn you and the law. There's posters going up all over the valley by now. We'll have him soon enough, son."

"No, not soon enough."

"Lettie said you'd go to the Indians first—to warn them and to lead that devil away from your Eden. We were on our way to give you an escort. You'd just come into view when we saw you flinch right when we heard the shot. Thought for sure you'd been hit."

Ben remounted his horse then looked back along the trail. "Never thought I'd be thanking a rattlesnake for saving my life."

THIRTY-THREE

Lettie sat with her back against the side of the barn and watched the eagles glide overhead. They were looking to nest and though they nested on the same crag year after year, they were careful to survey the surrounding area before setting to the work of repairing and reinforcing the previous nest. With reverence she took the letters from her pocket. She didn't need to unfold them to know what was inside. She'd long ago memorized every word, but the feel of the paper, the look of the handwriting, the smudges of haste, amplified their sanctity—turned them into blood and bone.

She'd shared them with Ben, each as it was received. But his interest was in the present, in the here and the now. He didn't understand her need to read and re-read—indeed, memorize—every word in each letter. In a moment of frustration she had once blurted, "You've never been separated from your sister so you wouldn't know how it feels."

He'd turned and left the cabin without a word. Lettie had no idea where he'd gone or why he'd stormed out, she only knew that he hadn't returned by milking time so went to milk the cow herself. That was when she found him, lying so deathly still there in the horse paddock.

256

Now she unfolded the short note Mister Charlton had delivered to the Indian encampment that Monday morning so long ago. Fresh teardrops splattered to the paper.

Kodiak hobbled over to her and put his head in her lap. She refolded the letters then ruffled the fur behind the dog's ear. "You're a funny old dog with a funny old name. He's never told me where he found you or why he named you thus. He's made it pretty clear, though, that he thinks as much of you as he does of me. I wonder how you came to mean so much. I wonder about a lot of things that are in his past. Were you there? Would you tell me if you could? No, you're too like him. But that's okay. We love him for who and what he is now, don't we dog."

The old dog sighed and closed his eyes. Lettie knew that if Ben were awake and about, the dog would be beside him so she opened the second of her letters, the one that had come more than two years after Belle had been spirited away to Ohio.

My Darling Sister – I miss you so incredibly. We are living near the town of Pettyjohn. Everyone knows us here so if you send a letter general delivery, I will receive it. I do so wish to hear of you and Ben. I am certain beyond doubt that you are deliriously happy. You prob'ly have little ones by now—well mannered and stalwart because you were ever a better momma than Mama could be.

Mama is somewhat improved. She attends church regularly and is stronger by the day though the sadness lingers. Papa is a changed man. He is robust and hearty and seems to love this small farm, the dust of which he was once in such a hurry to leave behind. Even in his happiest moments, howsomever, he refuses to hear your name spoken. He would be upset beyond belief if he were to learn of my sending this letter. (I have only this eventide learned that there are three wagons passing through the town on their way to the Oregon Territory. They resume their journey at daybreak on the morrow. I send this letter in their care to Mr Charlton, ever hopeful that he will be able to get it to you.) I am vexed that I must, once again, dash off a missive to you in this hurried manner. Know that we love you and wish you could again be with us but are desirous of your own happiness as well.

As ever, your very own Blue-Belle.

post script: *Mama wonders if that man who bought Papa's place, Owen Stark as I recall, could be Grandpapa's business partner who was supposed to follow her and Papa to Panama and give them Grandpapa's treasure. She'd never <u>seen</u> the business associate but only heard his voice when he was in the Library with Grandpapa. She thinks her treasure could be somewhere in your valley and wonders why the man didn't give it to her long ago.*

*Poor Mama! Ever the silly one. She reasons the man was keeping it (and her) safe all these years. The thought of a protector being near is the only thing that kept her going all that time. (Well, I say! No thanks to you and me for all we did???) (<u>**I**</u> think he was wanting to do away with poor Papa and have the treasure <u>and</u> the Beauty <u>**AND**</u> the wealth she would inherit from Grandpapa!)*

Look for a gleaming golden casket that is about four fingers in height, maybe six fingers acrost, and might be eight fingers in length. It has an emblem on top that could be a family crest of white and blue and a ribbon pattern all around near the bottom that is white and blue and black. And, I think what Mama calls a "finger" is probably what the schoolmaster would call an "inch". "Don't tell Papa", she says. .... B-B

Memories of the frenzied days that followed Ben's injury still brought trembling hands and a racing heart. Lettie stroked the old dog's head and bid them come—as if remembering would make them less painful. She could still feel the varied textures that made up the Twenty-Year quilt she'd used to wrap him in so she could drag him to the cabin; the warmed stones she'd placed at his feet and on his heart; the frantic ride through the icy blizzard to reach the Indian village. She'd thought it an answer to prayer when she met the Army Surgeon waiting at Brewster for the Ferry to carry his detachment across the Columbia River. Though he rode back with her, he couldn't help Ben and his prognosis was grim but he did agree to find Dora and send her to them.

Instead it was Tsaltsaleken, Sunflower, who fought her way through the winter snow to reach the beloved son of her long-dead sister; Tsaltsaleken, the Healer in her village, who saved Ben's life and stayed to be mother to him and to Lettie. It was Tsaltsaleken who taught Lettie to use herbs to ease Ben's pain, massages to strengthen his muscles, and chants to calm his mind. It was Tsaltsaleken who stayed at his bedside so that Lettie could take over the farm work he had done in the past.

It had taken more than a year for Ben to regain a bit of mobility. With the summer sun shinning through the open door, he had, painfully and determinedly, forced himself into a sitting position on the edge of the bed. Each day he'd pulled and pushed and strained to get further, do more. He used their meager furnishings for support as he moved slowly around the room. It was only when he went outside that he accepted help from his wife or his aunt.

Months after his first, surprising, effort to sit on the bed, he'd made his way to his workshop and forge. There he fashioned a sturdy wooden chair and bolted rollers on the legs. He wasn't pleased with the results of his wheeled-chair but it made his moving through the workshop a little less painful. When Mister Charlton called on the next of his regular visits, Ben had a shopping list ready. Topmost on that list was a set of two larger wheels with which to modify his wheeled-chair.

The months dragged into years and Ben's good humor was being stretched thinner and thinner. With his limited mobility, he found his smithing skills limited now to making small tools for gardens, kitchens, and nurseries. Ranchers and stockmen would, without a second thought, overpay for equipment for their spreads, but wouldn't pay a fair price for garden hoes, soup ladles, or baby rattles—items used by their wives and children. Ben's fat cattle and the blooded horses had all been sold, as much to ease Lettie's workload as for the supplies their money bought.

My Dearest Sister – This letter brings sad tidings. Our Papa, Dominic Milton LeGrau, has <u>gone to be with his maker</u>. Doctor said he died of stroke but I will always believe it was remorse for the way he behaved towards you that carried him off. Mama is mourning but holding up remarkably well. She is more <u>beautiful</u> in her widow's weeds than I have <u>ever</u> seen her. Her brother has come from Charleston to be with her and I believe I actually heard her laughing yesterday! Oh, Sister, I do so wish you were here to counsel me.

Wednesday – Oh, Sister. Papa has been in the ground no more than a month and already Mama is selling the farm! We are going to Charleston to live with her mother in the big white house. Granmama can no longer afford to keep servants since that war of Northern Aggression! Our Uncle Gaston tells terrible tales of scoundrels he calls Carpetbaggers (and tells me I am not to use unladylike terms such as scoundrel and Carpetbagger). We will be going by TRAIN! and I am told that trains run all the way to the western ocean now and letters can go more quickly from Charleston to the Oregon Terr and then on to Mr Charlton with whom I am, once again, entrusting this letter.

What of young (no longer!) Lumpkin Charlton? I would not be surprised to learn he has grown from a fine youth to a handsome man. Mama says I shall learn to DANCE! and shall have suitors. I so wish you could be here but am ever so certain you are still as happy with your Ben as one woman is entitled to be! I would take this letter with me on the train and write you every detail but the sad news of Papa's passing makes me send it with Uncle Gaston to be POSTED!

PLEASE, PLEASE write to us Dearest Sister, in the care of Mrs Honorine Eadrich in Charleston, South Carolina.

As ever, your very own Blue-Belle

post script: *Mr Poopersmith wanted to buy our farm but Mama said Papa thought him a waster so she could not trust him to work hard and bring in enough profit to make payments to us.*

Just think of Papa admitting his mistake in bringing that man to Ohio! What if you had married him instead of your Ben! .... B-B

Lettie was saddened by her father's passing. She'd long ago come to realize that carrying a grudge tied her to the hurtful things he'd done and kept her from appreciating the joy in the rest of them. She'd made peace with his memory and harbored neither bitterness nor regret towards him. When she first read the letter she realized she'd never known his second name and she pondered the co-mingling of cultures. Such a strong English second name bespoke a mixed heritage and she wondered if an experience in his past, brought on by that mixing, was the cause of his unyielding anger at her marrying Ben—a man Papa thought to be an Indian. Would he have been so opposed had he known that Ben, like Papa himself, was half French?

She was roused from her reverie by the squeaking wheels of Ben's wooden chair.

THIRTY-FOUR

Lettie supplied bread and cakes to Lander's store in exchange for the flour and sugar to make the next batch. Eggs, cream, and butter came from her own farmyard, but her own supplies—beans and coffee—cost extra and the little family was fast running out of reserves to pay for those things. It was Tsaltsaleken who first suggested that Lettie pack up the little oven Ben had made and take her baking talents to the hungry miners. No one thought it a good idea, especially Lettie who argued that being away from Eden would leave too much work undone; too much to catch up on in the fall. All reasoned, however, that it would be a means to keep them fed until Ben could again work for the ranchers.

The first trip up to Slate Creek Coulee was the easiest. Lettie saddled Trilby, loaded her gear and bedroll, and spent the next three days climbing into the high country. On reaching the mine complex she went directly to the office of the overseer and handed him a loaf of bread. When she left his office, it was with the promise of a cabin of her own, wages from the company, and a percentage of what the miners paid for a loaf of fresh-baked bread. The company would furnish the ingredients as well as transport the stores, and Lettie, to and from the mine.

With a handshake and a wave, Lettie turned her horse and headed for home. It was the last time she would ride from the mines. Thereafter, she rode the freight wagons up the pass in the spring, mostly to inventory her supplies and make sure they made it to the mine, but by the end of the short summer, she was ready to leave before the miners were. She simply set off on foot through the mountains.

Just near their home, Wolf Creek disappeared. It ran through the bottom of a small rocky pit at creek-side and reappeared several yards further downstream. With the exception of that short stretch, the entire creek wrapped herself in ice for Christmas—a lustrous opaque boa shimmering along the cliff base—and remained cloaked and sealed throughout the rest of the winter. Water bubbled and sang inside the pit however, splashing droplets of creek water onto the walls of frigid rock.

Ben had long ago chiseled at a roundish stone so it nearly plugged the narrow opening to the pit, extending the life of the ice that formed inside and protecting the stores they cached there through the early weeks of the brief hot spell that was summer. To her dismay however, Lettie had found that Tsaltsaleken couldn't move the cumbersome stone without help and by the time she, herself, returned from the mines, the supplies left inside the niche were no colder than the glacier-fed creek water below. She'd carried the rotting meat well away from Eden and left it for the bears.

Each spring since that time, Tsaltsaleken had taken any remaining provisions with her when she went to visit her people prior to Lettie's leaving. She traded the last of Lettie's frozen beef and venison for smoked fish and dried berries to feed herself and Ben during Lettie's absence. Should he develop a hankering for fresh meat, Tsaltsaleken was adept at butchering chickens and catching fish. However, he ate little but soup since his accident so the two were content to do without red meat until Lettie returned and could kill a stag for winter meat.

It was very like a spring storm; blustery showers between bursts of bright sunshine. A double rainbow preceded her as she meandered towards home. The brighter one touched the willows that bordered the stream, blazing the way just ahead and out of reach. The autumn foliage, gold and orange and red, received the sprinkling of rainbow dust and continued to sparkle long after that which had blessed it had moved on.

She knew these willows; had watched their bases broaden, their branches stretch to the stars. *Each tree is like a society*, she mused. *As the leaves contribute to the life of the tree, so do we give our little bit then move on to make way for new contributors. Just as the decaying leaves provide food for the roots, the teachings and values we leave behind when we fall provide a foundation on which our offspring can build.*

She had returned only yesterday and was reacquainting herself with Eden and all that made it a home. She'd checked on the ice cave and reckoned it wasn't cold enough yet to preserve meat. She'd have to wait several weeks before bringing down a deer. She'd picked out two new fetishes Tsaltsaleken had hung in the woods. Either she was learning to spot them or these were easier to see than were the first ones the woman had hidden. Lettie never did see those two—only knew of their presence when Tsaltsaleken told her what she'd done while expressing her belief that visible symbols were both protective and comforting.

She halted abruptly. Standing motionless she willed a sound to reach her but even the leaves had stopped their rustling. Had she heard the footfall of a horse being ridden stealthily through the woods or was it the sudden and profound silence that brought her up short? She couldn't say what had alerted her to danger—couldn't even say what that danger might be but she dropped her armload of dry cattail stems and sprinted for home and for Ben.

She recognized the man who had bought their homestead and burned Papa's lovely cabin; the same man who had killed the Leightons and burned their home; the very man who had been absent from these parts since that time nearly five years ago.

Her bullet struck the ground between his feet, sending dust and bits of boulder into the air to settle on his dry, cracked leather boots. Lettie had always thought you could tell a lot about a person by how they took care of their boots. If she'd known nothing of this man's past she'd have said he was a slovenly, lazy, no-hoper.

He eased his head around looking for the source of the shot. Seeing it had come from her, the question in his glance turned into a leer.

"So the little camp cookie's already back from the mines. Or should I say 'miners'?"

"You move wrong and the next one'll be high enough you won't be able to say naught but in squeaks," she said with chilling certainty.

"What say you miss?" he sneered.

"Okay, go ahead...just say I do," she replied calmly with a shrug of one shoulder. "Just say you're gut-shot. You'll die sure enough. Probably not today, though. Maybe not even tomorrow. Won't be fast.

266

Won't be easy. And, sure as there's a Hell, it won't be fun. But it will be.

"Now, what say you get on that horse and get off our farm? And while you ride, while you're telling yourself you won't come back, ponder this. I have not missed what I aimed for in a very...long...time."

The man hesitated. There was only one thing he had bothered to remember about women. Those who can take care of themselves don't push their luck to the last round because they no longer have anything to prove. They know—as the woman standing before him knew. Still leering, he mounted his horse then turned as if to speak. Lettie fired another round, this time close over the rump of the scraggly horse. The frightened animal lunged towards the forest, the rider grasping wildly for a grip on the saddle. After such a fright, the mount would not readily come to these woods again.

She turned a questioning gaze to Ben. He turned his face, refusing to look at her, and she studied him in silence. Under his red lap robe was Papa's shotgun. Each barrel had been sawn to a length that would lie hidden beneath the blanket and each was packed heavy with powder and shot. This man she loved was neither as subtle nor as patient as she yet he had not fired to protect himself.

Tsaltsaleken, returning from a foraging walk to the creek for peppery cress had seen the stranger and, with a gasp, stepped behind a willow. Ghostlike, she had become one with the grove. Trembling, she prayed for strength, for courage, and for wisdom. When the horse had carried the man beyond the reach of her family she hurried to the cabin and, with a look, drew Lettie into the kitchen.

They stood side-by-side at the makeshift window and looked out on Ben sitting with his face to

267

the woods where the rider had gone. Something had gone out of him now. Something tangible. More than ever before they saw dejection in his form—a transformation from the positive to the dispirited. He slumped on the wheeled wooden chair.

As they mourned for the newly-dead spirit of the young man, Tsaltsaleken told Lettie about the life of Moise Stark. Told of the beatings and the death of his mother, Sia; the sale of Ben and his sister, Dora whom the Indians called Kanit'sa. All this at the hands of the man who had ridden through the forest to find them this day. She told of Ben's escape, his time with the Black Robes, and his quest to find his sister. She told of his rescue by Striker, the leader of the band to which she, Tsaltsaleken, was related.

Lettie made no effort to wipe away the tears, to stop their falling, even. "I knew Kanit'sa was his sister. I guess, because she and Striking Horse seemed so compatible I thought she had gone to him as an adult, as I had gone to Ben.

"I did this to him."

Tsaltsaleken turned her soft gaze to Lettie and the younger woman continued.

"We were disagreeing. I wanted to read again a letter I'd received from my own sister. He was tired of hearing it. I accused him of being uncaring, of not knowing how it feels to be separated from a sister. That's when he went out. In one careless remark I destroyed a man's life."

"No," Tsaltsaleken said. "He had chosen to keep his past from you. He chose to chase the horse around the corral. He chose to live through the dark days that followed. Each of us has the final choice of a path, but we must be mindful of the stones others are trying to avoid on their chosen way.

268

"His mother has protected him many times in his search for peace. Perhaps he thought she would again. Perhaps, with the appearance of this evil one, he has come to believe there can be no peace for him. Perhaps he is afraid that when the bad one passes, that evil spirit will come to live in the son.

"We cannot know what it would take to make him kill a man. He probably doesn't know. He has already much justification for killing that one. We can only love him for what he is at this moment not for what he might have been or what he might have done."

Darkness was threatening when the women left the quiet of the kitchen to bring the crippled man inside to rest.

They helped him to his bed and tucked the red woolen blanket around his legs. While his aunt tried coaxing a few sips of rich chicken broth into him, Lettie sped to the barn to finish the evening chores before full-on darkness made the tasks difficult, though not entirely impossible.

The mare would need a bit of grain now with the onset of winter; the cow and the newly-weaned heifer, a heavier forkful of hay. In the quiet solitude of the dilapidated barn she breathed deeply of the scent of the sweet-feed and the newly scythed meadow grass.

The cows snuffled through the hay, cornering choice bits of dried flowers and seeds against the sides of the manger where they could be more easily taken up on long wet sandpaper tongues. Likewise, Trilby chased her grain around the bottom of the old bucket then munched and crunched through the coarse nuggets. They bumped against each other and into the walls; they huffed and snorted and stomped their hooves. Wind whistled through the cracks and now rain drummed on the roof. In the peace induced by the symphony in the cow shed, she prayed to understand what had happened in the storm-swept yard that afternoon.

Ben's had been a life of surmounting and conquering Evil; a life defined and controlled by his rigorous childhood, the death of his mother, his long and frustrating search for Dora. His true identity had not been fully born until he had married Lettie. Only then could he begin to grow into the role of provider, lover, and companion. And as long as he could force the memories of his childhood into the deep recesses of his mind, he could summon the wit, the intelligence, and the passion to make the best of everything.

Now, the reappearance of that Evil forced him to accept his dependence, even his own mortality; forced him to admit that, just like in his earliest memories, he could not live by his own productivity but would have to rely on another person to direct and protect him; forced him to acknowledge that, after all he had been through, there again was that same Evil to surmount and conquer. This battle might prove too much for the young man to bear—alone, certainly. But could not the two of them bear it together?

Or had Ben, like she had done so long ago, simply forgiven his father for all the evil he had inflicted on the boy? In that moment when he could have, indeed *should* have, fired his shotgun, had he realized that taking the life of the man who caused such grievous pain and sadness would not have erased that agony?

She wished she could have, at some time in her adult life, had a discussion with her father about degrees of sin and personal forgiveness. Her father's sin, she believed, was one of confused and misdirected good intentions and she could forgive him for the hurt it caused her. But Owen Starks's sins were those of malice; of mindless vicious evil. He could be forgiven again and again by everyone and anyone but would continue to destroy and brutalize, committing the same sins again and again. Like a mad wolf, he didn't need to be forgiven—he needed to be stopped. Hadn't Solomon written that there was a time to kill?

Tsaltsaleken stepped into the barn and coughed softly to interrupt Lettie's thoughts.

"I go to my people tomorrow so I bring this to you. When he was a child, Squaku asked me to burn an image onto a strip of tanned hide. It was a map to the root cellar at the creek that ran through the homestead. He wanted to put it in a secret place in case something happened to him. He wanted me to know where the root cellar could be found. When his Mam died he brought it from its hiding place to tie it to her wrist before she was buried so that she would always be able to find her way back there. But there was no time. His Da bound her shroud too tightly and put her into the ground too soon.

"Squaku hid the strap in her sewing basket intending to fetch it later to put with her special things that would go into the sacred fire at the ceremony in which our people would sing her to her starwalk. But their Da tossed the basket into the grave with Sia. Even now the boy thinks it is as he first wanted—the map is with his mother. He believes that is how she has been able to find her way back to help him so many times. But she has not needed a fetish or a map. She has a mother's love."

The old woman smiled ruefully, shook her head sadly and continued. "His sister saw him slip something into the basket and, as quickly as he had done, sneaked it out again. She didn't know what it was and intended to put it back but then their Da slammed through the door, gathered everything of Sia's that he could carry, and took it out to toss into her grave. Kanit'sa wasn't able to get the map back into the basket but she knew the drawing was my work and brought it to me. I have kept it for him.

"I give this to you. He has not told me what was so important in that root cellar. He will not ever be well enough to fetch it. But maybe you can someday honor him by finding his treasure. Please remember, it is of such great value his Da has killed for it...more times than one."

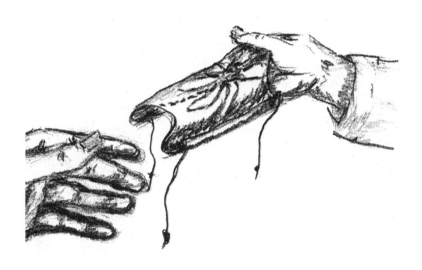

THIRTY-FIVE

Striking Horse, astride another of the horses descended from Iron Moccasin's lucky horse, sat quietly at the door. Lettie, beaming with delight at seeing him there, pulled the door open wide. She froze in dread. The face of her husband's brother-in-law told of deep sorrow.

"Please come in," she said softly. She stood aside to let him stoop into the room. Then she followed him to her husband's bedside.

While Striking Horse sat with Ben, Lettie penned a letter for the man to take to Charlton for posting.

Sister – Striking Horse brings sad news of great grief. Our wonderful aunt / our nurse and our rock – our ANCHOR / the one who has mothered us, taught us, and held us together has been taken from us. Striking Horse says only that she died on her way to visit her family. She was very old but in good health so I wonder if there is something he fails to tell us out of fear for Ben's wellbeing. (That <u>worrisome</u> Mr Stark has come back to the valley after a long absence and it has changed my Ben for the worse.

And if <u>THAT</u> is the man with Mama's treasure we surely will never see it.) - - - Much has changed in this year since I've written and I have the urge to tell you EVERYthing I have left unsaid. - - - First, and MOST important, Mr Lumpkin Charlton has grown into a fine man. Many families have moved into the valley of late, some with young women who have set their hopes on being Mrs Charlton, but he is still fixated on you and lives in hope you will return to us—as do I, my precious one. - - - Striking Horse is visitng with Ben still, trying to cheer him, I know. As I write they are remembering the time Striking Horse met Dora (how he found her 'neath the tree - how she followed him home and would surely have followed him to the Sacred Fireside had not Tsaltsaleken - there to tell her kin of Sia's death and the children's disappearance - prevented her doing so). Striking Horse is trying to be amusing but my Ben finds little to make him laugh these days. - - - My Ben is now telling of the time HE first met Striking Horse and of being so frightened by Striker. He thought Striker a witch because of the way the man studied him. Then he learned that Striker saw the resemblance between Nahtahk's toymaker, who called himself Ben, and the girl Striker called Kanit'sa (daughter!). - - - And now, Sister!!! A WONderful thought has just come to me!!! YOU can come to help me with my Ben!!! You, yourself, have said the trains go all the way to the west coast. Please, please, please ... take a train to San Francisco, then a packet boat to Seattle. If you leave in time, you can ride on the FIRST freight wagon from Everett to Black Bear in July. The station-master, Merle Magruder, will bring you here to EDEN as I must, on that same freighter, go to the mines because that is the freighter on which the first *of the miners will arrive. Howsomever, I return in late August or early Sept. - - - I fear this will be my last venture to Slate Creek. My Ben suffers so when I am away and ... I think his (Condition) makes him worry about my being near other men, though I have always loved only him. - - - I must bring everything with me when I leave Slate Creek this time. My bedroll, my baking pans, and my beloved oven. - - - I have no funds to send to you for fare but if you could find someone to lend it, I will repay the benefactor (with interest and warm gratitude) when I return from the mines in August. If we have had no word of you, we will await your arrival at Black Bear. - - - I LOVE you so much and wish you safe travels and an adventure or two of your own. Ever and ever, Your Lettie*

THIRTY-SIX

Lettie stopped the little cart at the front door and Dora jumped from her seat to the ground.

"Do you need help unloading, Sister," she asked?

Lettie shook her head and smiled, "No, I can handle the grain bags. Go in to him quickly. He's been anxious about your coming.

"Wait, " she called. "He has changed since you saw him last fall. The...your father's return, the death of Tsaltsaleken...this especially cold and long winter that kept us both inside for too many weeks. They've taken their toll on him. Don't be shocked by what you see."

Dora nodded somberly then turned to the house. Lettie clucked Trilby into motion. She'd hurried the little mare more than she usually did and now both were glad to see the dark cool interior of the barn. She unloaded the sacks of grain into the barrel then backed the cart into the empty stall reserved for it. She unhitched the horse, giving her extra grain in her ration, and rubbed her quickly with a burlap bag. She would take time to thoroughly groom the horse after she had checked on Ben. He would chide her for doing such a slap-dash job as she had just done but would be furious if she had left the mare wet and hungry even for just long enough to check on his condition. "Well, as Papa would have said, *A bit is better than a bob—by half a pence anyway.*"

Before leaving for town she had put beans in the pot on the back of the stove to simmer slowly and now grabbed an onion from the braid that hung in a dry corner of the log barn. The bacon would fry quickly and the bread was fresh just yesterday. The meal would be quick and easy today.

She helloed a greeting at the closed door then stepped to the washbasin that rested atop a narrow table on the porch. She splashed cold water on her face and, after rubbing it briskly with a small towel, picked up her onion and entered the little one-room house.

Ben reclined on the bed, his back against the wall beside the one window on the north side of the house. Light streamed over his right shoulder onto the book he had been reading when his sister arrived. He smiled at Lettie from across the room and she knew without dwelling on the thought that it was the first smile she'd seen all the winter long.

The spring rain had kept them inside longer than usual this morning. One cup of tea led to another as the three of them sat wrapped in wool blankets and gossiped about changes in the village, family, and events on the little farm. "I must leave you two to visit," smiled Lettie as she reached for her work boots. "I have brush to dig and layer while the ground is still wet. Your aunt would surely scold me if I were to leave before I have finished the east garden."

"I will help you, Sister," offered Dora rising to follow Lettie.

"Oh, no. I would rather you stayed in here with your brother. He loves your company.

"Darling, if it weren't raining we could all go and you could sit on the watching stage and watch us instead of watching for crows or deer." She leaned over and kissed his cheek before sitting on the edge of the bed to lace her boots.

She closed the door softly behind her and started across the bare earth towards the barn to retrieve her ax and grub-hoe. Movement from the corral caught her eye and she turned to stare aghast at Ben's beloved Kodiak. Oblivious to his surroundings he was playing a game of catch-the-rooster with the protector of her flock. Up into the air he threw the bird and caught him before he hit the ground. He shook the bird vigorously then flung him back into the air. He romped through the corral with the lifeless bird bobbling grotesquely from his muzzle then stopped and flung him into the air once again.

Black iridescent feathers littered the ground. With the exception of a few tiny pin-feathers around his eye sockets, not a single one remained attached to the dead rooster. Lettie's heart stopped. She knew the ways to cure a dog of killing chickens were few. The most drastic was simply to kill the dog. The second-best method was to tie the chicken carcass securely to the dog's neck until it rotted off. Either way, Ben would be deprived of a beloved, indispensable companion. She spat a sharp "YA" at the dog and he dropped the rooster then sat on his haunches and smiled at her, ever so proud of the game he had invented. Lettie grabbed the dog's ruff then picked up the carcass by its feet and began to beat the dog with it.

"Do you realize what you've done," she chastened? "I'm going to have to shoot you now. He won't do it. We can't let you kill our livestock. I can't have you dragging around a stinking rotting bird carcass."

With each blow she chided the dog for his actions. Several times she dropped the bird but picked it up again by a wing or it's head, one leg, or two. When she thought the dog realized this was not a game he should have been playing, she pitched the dead bird into a water puddle and dragged the dog to a stall in the barn. He could, should he choose, wriggle between the planks but he knew he was being punished so would stay where he'd been put.

Her mind was racing as fast as her heart. She grabbed her spade and strode out to the garden area to dig a hole to bury the dog. She'd butcher the chicken for dinner though the meat would be badly bruised. She'd found a chokecherry bush down by the creek last week and thought to transplant it closer to the house. She would dig the dog's grave large enough to hold both the chokecherry's rootball and the dog.

Her digging was spurred by anger, frustration, and sadness. Ben loved that dog but, more importantly, he needed the dog—relied on it for companionship, love, amusement, protection. The rain had stopped by the time she decided the hole was deep enough. She wanted to get the dog buried before Dora decided to take her up on her suggestion to bring Ben out to the watching platform. She heeled her spade into the mud and turned towards the barn.

The rooster stood, weaving like a drunken miner, chicken-knee deep in the puddle of water. She watched him take a step, shake his featherless wings as if to steady himself with the bare spindles, then take another halting step forward. He tried to navigate the slope that had caused the water to collect there in that spot but fell instead onto his broad featherless breast. He marshaled his strength and staggered to his feet to, again, repeat the whole process. Horrified, Lettie stood rooted to the earth.

Sprinting to the usually aggressive bird she circled him to grab him from behind. Instead, he spun on one wobbly foot to face her. The one open eye dared her to come closer. She again maneuvered to come at him from behind but again, he wobbled around to glare at her as if she herself had robbed him of his beauty, his power. Mindful of the spurs he was always so quick to use against an opponent she feinted right, jumped left and grabbed him with both hands, palms over the muscular wings, fingers over his struggling thighs and across his breast.

He screamed like the mountain lions that haunted the forest and, startled, she yelped and instinctively thrust him away. Then the whole dance started anew. The second time she grabbed him she was prepared for that raucous scream and managed to keep him in a firm grip. A quick examination showed that the dog had managed to totally denude the rooster of feathers without breaking any skin whatsoever.

She rushed into the barn and pitched him into a barrel as she hurried past. She grabbed several of the gunnysacks hanging on the back wall and hurried back to the rooster, now strutting around in the barrel and trying to crow his, "So there!"s. Lettie looked around at the meager furnishings in the barn. "More of a wind-break," she said to the rooster. "And not much of one, at that—roof full of leaks and walls full of cracks. Guess it's good for shade in the summer. Not much I can do about all that right now. Best just focus on keeping you alive so you can help keep us supplied with chicks."

While she muttered to the rooster, she began to transfer the grain from its barrel into the toolbox of the large farm wagon. They had no draft horses to pull the wagon now so it sat empty and weathered. Trilby could handle the hack but the wagon was too heavy for one lone horse.

She had used the wagon only once since Ben's hurt. That was when she'd borrowed Charlton's team and carted a piece of equipment Ben had made down to the Charlton ranch. She'd wanted to sell the wagon to the homesteader along with the machine he'd ordered but he refused to buy it, arguing instead that Ben would need it again some day for hauling newly built machines to neighboring ranches.

Charlton did consent to borrow the wagon each summer to help with his haying. Leading his wagon team behind his saddle horse he'd ride up early of a morning, chat with Ben a spell then ride away in the wagon, leading his saddle horse along with one of Ben's cows and the yearling calf. He reversed the process several weeks later, bringing the wagon home with his saddle horse and the cow, now bred to Charlton's bull, tied behind. The wagon would be filled with the meat of the calf, a few bales of grass hay, any supplies Lettie had neglected to purchase on her trip from the mines, and always, a new blank book for her writings.

After he put away the wagon and brushed his team, he'd chat with Ben then ride for home by moonlight. The spring calf, having spent the time without its mother, would be weaned now and would forage with the rest of the stock until the next year when it would be the one going to market. The newly bred cow would calve in late spring and suckle her young one throughout the summer—a necessary convenience since Tsaltsaleken refused to even consider milking the cow. Ben refused all recompense for the use of the wagon and Lettie never spoke of the extra barrel of grain in the storeroom or of the two or three hams—from the wild boars that roamed the forest—that had been shoved unnoticed into the ice cave.

So intent was she on worrying about how far she could stretch two or three hams in the absence of a flock of chickens she failed to hear the footsteps approaching the barn. When the dim shadow stretched across the floor she spun with a gasp to face her stern-faced sister-in-law.

"Squaku says bring Rooster inside. Nights are still cold. He will die without feathers."

"Oh my," whispered the horrified Lettie. "He saw?"

Dora nodded curtly. She started to speak but the word came out as a sputter and she doubled over with laughter. She pointed to the rooster and again tried to speak but could form no words. She pointed to Lettie with the same result.

Lettie heard the squeak of the wheels on Ben's wooden chair and looked around to find that he had managed to maneuver himself into the doorway of the little barn. He smiled crookedly at her, as if laughter, so long unpracticed, wouldn't—couldn't—surface. He leaned to look into the barrel at the naked, irate rooster. The bird squawked at him in complaint, or defiance, and then, Ben too, was laughing. Lettie looked askance at the two then began to see what they had seen from inside the cabin.

THIRTY-SEVEN

Her parents would have been celebrating Easter about now. They would have bought a spring lamb for a ritual meal, but she could not—there were no sheep here. Since the coming of the cattle barons, shepherds and their sheep were sought and slaughtered in much the same way Tsaltsaleken's family had been since Army troops had accompanied the first homesteaders into the area.

In previous years she had used the last ham from the ice cave for the Easter meal. This spring however, Lettie wanted to save it. She had it all planned—set in her mind—cemented with anticipation and colored with joy.

After Lettie left for Slate Creek, Belle would boil every last morsel of meat from the bone and give the spent bone to Kodiak. When the last bits of ham had been eaten Ben would tell Belle how to set the fish weirs and how to kill and dress a chicken.

She knew the younger woman wouldn't be able to snare a grouse and, in one dark moment, wondered if her sister would even be able to catch and clean the trout that sometimes threatened to choke the creek with their abundance. She reckoned Belle could buy a few cuts of beef from Mister Charlton.

She broke an egg into her cupped palm and let the whites slide through her fingers into a cracked bowl then dropped the yolk into the batter for the rich Easter cakes. Easter was supposed to be a celebration of Spring; of new life bravely forcing its way through softening snows and of mature beings welcoming another cycle. For Lettie it was also an excuse to make a feast using the last of the winter provisions in order to have room for fresh ones. It was why she always used the last ham for the Easter meal; and the last gnarly spuds from the root barrel Ben had buried out by the barn. The last of the honey went into the cake; Mister Charlton would soon be raiding his hives in order to drive the bees to make more. The last of the eggs, too, before she let the hens keep their cackle berries to set their clutches.

This was the last of the wheat flour. Winter temperatures kept the mealy bugs in check but they'd soon be swarming into the cupboards looking for food. She was repulsed by the idea of cooking with bug-infested flour but wouldn't throw food away—couldn't afford to. Tsaltsaleken had put herbs in the flour bin to repel the bugs but Belle wouldn't know which ones to use. Lettie thought it best to leave none here to draw the bugs.

Belle could live without flour; could make do with cuts of beef from the Charlton ranch, especially if it meant a visit from young Lumpkin Charlton. But what of him? Would he find it a bother to be the teamster bringing food to his crippled neighbor? Not if Belle had grown into the beauty Lettie had always predicted she would.

That raised another worry. Belle had always favored her mother's ways. Fun and frivolity were her favorite words. Would she be able to cope with the solitude here? Could she stand the rigors of life in

Eden or would she, like her mother, be one of God's beautiful lilies and wilt in the heat of the struggle?

And how would Ben take to having a young swain hanging around? Mister Charlton had once sent his son to deliver several bales of hay for the cow. Ben had not been pleased to see him. Lettie recognized that Ben's condition made him feel vulnerable and that the feeling was exacerbated when he saw the youthful, handsome, healthy, man in the proximity of his young and vibrant wife. Lettie made just such a point to Mister Charlton and Lumpkin had never again been sent on an errand to the smith's. Lately though, Ben had begun to show signs of annoyance when even old Mister Charlton came around. Understanding his feelings, the two were careful to behave with the utmost decorum, but Lettie worried for Ben's mental state.

She loved the early mornings; the stillness of the pre-dawn, the crispness of the air, the whispered promise of the coming day. Since Ben's injury she'd established this routine of lying here in the warmth of the nightclothes and analyzing her morning dream—not in great detail but a simple remembering and pondering. Then, still in silence, she gave thanks for her blessings, naming each one so none would be forgotten. Her Blessings prayer would always flow into her plan for the day and lead to her humble petition for God's favor on her work. Finally, and most earnestly, she prayed for His mercy on her Ben.

Still in a state of contemplation she slipped from beneath the old quilt and pulled on her oft-patched slippers. Belle had knitted them for her before Papa moved the family back to Ohio and her heart ached each time she wore another hole in the sole. Still, Belle would be disappointed if she thought Lettie didn't wear them, no matter how honorable the reason.

Quietly, so as not to wake her sleeping husband, she moved across the one-room cabin and rekindled the fire that, every morning, was nearly-but-not-quite cold. By the light of the open stove-door she began her day. Today felt different; indeed, would be different. She stood before the stove and examined the little room, feeling for the briefest moment like she was seeing it for the last time though she knew she would be back in just a few weeks—six probably, eight at most.

Behind the bed hung the brightly colored rug Tsaltsaleken had woven and nailed to the logs to protect the invalid from the wind that blew through the broken chinks. Across the room was the little cot where the woman had slept. Lettie had started using the cot herself on nights when Ben was taken with his nightmares—more and more frequently now. Beside the stove were the pegs where she hung her wet gear when she came in from doing chores.

Above the little bench where she kept the water pail and the washbasin were smaller pegs where she hung the enamel cups and her washing-up linens. The oven door, kept slightly ajar, barely hid her heavily greased cast iron frying pan and her stew pot, both of which doubled as bread pans, now clean and resting upside down on the rack.

Ben had built a miniscule table and two matching chairs. Small as they were, they filled one corner of the little cabin. When Tsaltsaleken came to live with them he had insisted on building a third chair. Before he could finish it he grew frustrated with his restricted mobility and now, as a table of sorts, it sat beside their bed holding her Bible and a beeswax candle—given to them as a Christmas gift by Lumpkin Charlton and the only luxury item in their home. On the bed, covering him against the chill of the morning, was spread Ben's red blanket. Woven of finer threads than the rug that hung above it, it was almost cuddly in comparison. Cured hides of the yearlings and the stags she had shot were spread on the floor for added warmth.

Lettie shook herself from her daze and poured fresh water into the coffee pot then put it on the stove to heat. By the time she had traded her night shirt for a bulky woolen pullover, an old pair of Ben's trousers, and several pairs of holey stockings, the water would be near to boiling and she could drop in a few spoons of ground coffee and move the pot to the back of the stove, there to steep while she laced the funny boots Ben had made.

He had used several layers of deer hide for the soles, being sure they were thick enough to protect her feet from the small stones that littered the countryside. The top of the foot was left uncovered save for her thick woolen socks. Three wide strips of tanned hide were affixed securely to the sides and heel of the sole of the boot and reached nearly to her knee. These were held around her legs by long lashings.

When he was living with the Black Robes, Ben had seen a sketch of a similar boot in a book about a place he called Ancient Greece. They called their boots *buskins* and he thought them ideal for the cold dry winters here on the home place. The open toe, top, and front made them different from the shorter moccasins their aunt wore.

Before they set out for Black Bear she would slather them with bear grease and hang them on a peg behind the stove. She had no use for them at Slate Creek. The coulee stayed wet and muddy from the time the winter's ice started to thaw until the temperatures dropped below freezing again in late summer—long after Lettie had left for home.

Lettie poured milk into her mug, making sure to get plenty of the cream that had risen to the top of the pitcher. She topped off the mug with the strong, hot coffee and drank the beverage in one go. Though she usually had a cold biscuit and a boiled egg to go with it, today the coffee would be breakfast until Ben woke.

Any of their stores that would last a couple of weeks—allowing extra time for them to reach Black Bear then Ben to return with Belle—had been sealed in her few, precious, glass jars and cached in the root barrel. She'd also rolled her little soft-sided notebooks and stuffed them into the largest of the glass jars. Then she'd dipped the edges of the lid in the melted wax of the candle to seal it. She'd paused, wondering why she was being so careful with something that wouldn't sustain life but she put them lovingly into the barrel anyway. The two blank books she planned to take to the Coulee were already stuffed into her bag.

Any perishables Ben might savor, like the coffee and the butter, she had put into a basket to take on the journey to Black Bear. Everything else had already been fed to the chickens. Now she must collect her three little hens and rooster and put them into a tote-sack before the coming dawn wakened them.

Charlton would be coming soon to take the cow, the chickens, and Kodiak to his ranch until Belle returned with Ben. Lettie thought of all the summers Tsaltsaleken had cared for Ben and their little homestead and said an additional prayer to ease the old woman's journey on her starwalk. When he arrived, Charlton would help her harness Trilby, then he would help Ben to the little cart, place him just so on the pillows, wedge the warming brick beneath his feet, and tuck the quilts around him. Ben would grouse about the help but all of them knew he was no longer able to mount the wagon without it, even with the use of his sling.

It would be a painful ride, no getting around that, but one Ben chose to undertake. He was as certain as Lettie that Belle would arrive to help and he wanted to await her arrival at Black Bear with Lettie rather than accept again the offer of temporary lodging from Charlton. The absence of word confirming Belle's acquiescence puzzled no one. She would have sent a return letter only if she had been unable to be there. But no letter had reached this remote cabin in Eden.

Lettie pulled on her calfskin cap and stepped out into the cold rain of a High-Cascades Spring. She scanned the horizon, silently praying that Belle would arrive safely on the freight wagon.

THIRTY-EIGHT

Yesterday Lettie had wrapped her six flat pieces of iron—the oven's sides, top, and bottom—in a greased tarpaulin, then in deerhide, and secured the package with an old section of drag chain salvaged from the mill's dump. She dragged the bundle up the muddy track that ran through the settlement and left it with Levi, the Dutchman. He would put it on the freight wagons headed for Black Bear the following week. She would retrieve it from the depot when next she went to town though she'd not be in a hurry for it. She didn't use it when she was in Eden and, with Ben's injury, would have no reason to be leaving there for more than a trip to Winthrop for supplies.

She tucked the little connecting pin inside the bolster with the oven legs, lest the small pieces get lost in the chaos created by dozens of miners abandoning the canyon for the winter. In the flickering glow of the bear-grease candle, she tamped her bedroll firmly into her pack, hoisted the burden high onto her back and slowly scanned the shadowy interior of the shack. It had been a secure little cloister. She would miss it.

With a sharp intake of breath she stepped to the door, blew gently towards the candle flame, and was striding up the makeshift road before the wisp of smoke had wafted to the eaves. The once muddy track was now surfaced with welts and weals of ice crystals that scrunched as she strode with confidence towards the upper reaches of the disjointed settlement, certain that the firmer ground would make the going easier.

Levi came out of his cabin to say a final farewell. "Gonna snow, Lettie. Wait for the freighters."

"You know what they say, Levi. The only people who try to predict the weather in The Coulee are newcomers or fools."

He grinned. "Struth. That's 'cause the only people in The Coulee are newcomers or fools."

The company's freight wagons would be coming soon to transport the bulk of the miners out to Winthrop. A few would stay, holed up in their little shanties for weeks on end while the wind and snow swirled outside, but most, like Lettie, would leave until the following spring.

She couldn't wait for the freighters, though. Ben would be waiting at the depot.

"Snow ain't due for another month," she had argued. "And even if it starts today, I'll be heading downhill before it gets to me. I'll bet my reputation on that."

"You're betting your *life* on that, Lettie," Levi had responded soberly.

"Ha! You're turning into an old woman, Levi. You get to Black Bear next week and there'll be a fresh apple cake from me waiting there for you. Best go back inside before you take a chill!" Lettie waved the bewhiskered Dutchman back to his stoop then marched up the frozen incline with a laugh. Levi watched from his doorway until she'd disappeared around the first switchback. He had not laughed.

A steep three-mile climb would take her to the top of Silver Ridge, one of the wracked and weathered walls that defined the crest of these North Cascades. From the summit, the trail hugged the cliff down through Rattlesnake Canyon—a path so narrow and with such sharp switchbacks the mules couldn't use it. One misstep and she'd have plummeted over a precipice of such magnitude even the scavengers wouldn't have been able to get to her remains. Once past that part however, the hike became almost easy.

The trail dropped down through a high pasture and it hadn't been so very long ago that she'd realized it was the meadow in which she and Blue-Belle had been picnicking the day Papa sent Mister Poopersmith out to call on her that first time. And the old hermit's hut at Lost Tree Spring had been the site of Mama's Western Mansion. Would Papa have been disappointed by the degradation?

Just below the old hermit's hut she would pick up the wagon road that led down to the freight depot at Black Bear.

She thought about her beloved sister and wondered where she might be. All summer she had prayed that Belle would show up at Black Bear, but every teamster on every freight wagon shook his head sadly in response to her inquiries. No woman had ridden the train of freight wagons across from the coast, young, blond, or otherwise. And her Ben, they assured her, still waited at the Depot.

"You stay where you are now little Blue-Belle, and be safe," she said into the wind. "No need now to be coming along here and worrying about me and my Ben. We'll be fine. You go some place nice and refined. Pray God, keep you away from this brutal life and maybe help *you* to find that Sanctuary Tree if ever you have a need for it."

The snow did come—earlier by a month than anyone but Levi had expected. The icy pellets stung her cheeks; peppered her eyelids. Pressing into the gale she willed her feet to move. Her legs ached. How long had it been since she'd last felt solid ground beneath her feet? When had she last moved forward without sinking to her knees in the heavy snow? Her burden slowed her progress but she dared not stash it, dared not risk losing so much.

She tugged at the lashings that girdled her waist and looped across her shoulders then circled her brow. She'd made them herself. Tsaltsaleken had shown her how to tan the hides, carefully cut ribbons from the new, stiff leather, and then work the thin strips until they were as supple as silk. She'd strung her favorite blue beads—Belle's blue beads from her Box Social lunch pail—onto the cords and braided great lengths of them to make the lashings for her pack.

Last night the miners had thrown a farewell party. They all knew about her Ben and many had slipped her an extra little grain of gold during the frolic. "For your Ben," they'd said.

She'd fallen onto her rope-bottomed bunk for the last time—tired but content with the certainty that by the next nightfall she would be sleeping in the arms of her beloved husband. He'd be waiting at Black Bear, worrying until he saw her come trudging down the corduroy road.

"Can't see an inch ahead o' me," she muttered into the hood of her long heavy cape of elk hide. "No landmarks. No chance I'd ever find its hidey hole again if I was to shuck this pack."

She squinted into the gale and forced herself to focus on Ben. Big Burley Ben-The-Blacksmith, he'd been. She focused on the early days when he would burst into their cabin, swoop her up in his massive arms and dance her, laughing, around the room while he sang a new verse to his made-up song about how much he loved her today.

She thought of their last good-bye; that night under the lean-to beside Magruder's hide-covered log hovel. She was resting in his arms when he began to sing. It had been so long since he'd done so she thought for a moment she'd fallen asleep and was dreaming.

Lettie, you leave me tomorrow.
My darling I'll ache for your touch
I'm lonely without you already
I love you and miss you so much.

Lettie had stopped him then. Though she'd always loved it when he sang to her, she couldn't take anymore of it now.

"I've not been fair to you, Lettie. I've always said I don't have an Eden without my Eve but I've come to realize that Eve deserves an Adam and I have failed you. That day my father rode into Eden, my whole world died. The sky was no longer blue, the grass wasn't green. I even think that, for a time, you were no longer beautiful. I'd been tumbled right out of the Garden and I wandered in a gray fog, thinking I could never find my way back.

"Then that ridiculous incident with the rooster started me thinking. Maybe I was like that old bird. 'Bout the time I started getting cocky and crowing about my goodness or cleverness or wealth, God came along and shook me loopy; pulled out my feathers and set my senses whirling; left me just alive enough to know I could survive."

296

"And when God tries to rescue us we scream and run away," Lettie smiled, remembering the way the rooster had screeched in her clutch.

"I will do more than survive this time, Lettie. I will thrive. I will be stronger and better than before. I don't know what it might be but, the way I figure it, God is turning me into something sturdy and sound and enduring: something better than the foolish bird I used to be.

"I've realized that I don't want to come to the end of my life without ever knowing who I was meant to be. Maybe it's just a wiser rooster, maybe the hawk winging over our canyon walls, maybe the eagle soaring over all of that.

"I know I have given you every right and reason to leave and never come back. And if you do, I'll understand. But when, if, you come home this time, I'll be back at my prayers with an open mind and a willing heart; back in the workshop, making something—anything—God directs me to make. Just know that it will be something that will make our Eden a garden again."

If you don't return Darling Lettie
From moiling and toiling for gold.
I'll wait here, bound to this hovel
But my heart will e'er go where you go.

He'd wiped her tears with his once-callused hands and shushed her to a fitful sleep.

Belle wasn't on the freight wagon that arrived that morning but there was another due tomorrow and another a few days after that. They'd be coming regularly for a few weeks and Lettie knew Belle would be on one of them. She'd tucked his red woolen blanket around her husband and this time it was she who wiped the tears from his eyes. She'd kissed him softly then left him to wait for her sister.

The first snowflakes had been like dander dancing on the wind; tiny specks cavorting capriciously in front of her, drawing her forward. So tiny she didn't think of turning back, of looking for a place to stash her pack. When she realized the ground had turned white, thoughts of a winter without the provisions her gold would buy drove her to walk faster.

She was past the most treacherous part of the hike, past the cliffs and rock walls. Surely the hermit's hut was just steps ahead. Might she stop there for just a moment if she should stumble on it? Would she be safer inside a shelter with the maniacal killer than out in this snow?

Dora and Ben had told her stories about giant trees they'd called Sanctuary Trees. Trees that had branches that swept the ground and acted as a barrier to the cold and the wind and evil. She could use sanctuary now—somewhere to stash this heavy pack—somewhere to rest—somewhere to wait for the storm to pass. She wished Ben were here to guide her. She realized she couldn't see *any* trees. Maybe that meant she was on the trail after all. If she had strayed from it she'd have collided almost immediately with one of the crusty little jack pines that dotted these hills. With that realization she gained new energy and sneered at her fear.

As reported to Lettie by the teamsters, Ben was, indeed, still waiting for Belle at Black Bear. He had met every freight wagon excepting the one that came the day after Lettie left. That one had come in late in the night and Ben had already gone to bed. Magruder had seen no sense in disturbing the invalid's sleep.

Ben, as promised, worked at strengthening his legs and back. He tried to prove a welcome guest by helping Magruder around the depot. Sometimes that help was with the mules but he found that tiring. Most often, therefore, the help was in the form of companionship to the stationmaster—playing cards or simply jawing when the nights were long and Magruder needed company. On those nights, Magruder argued that Belle was never coming but Ben knew otherwise. He often insisted that Belle was in the area; he could feel her presence. Magruder would curse and rail then take his whiskey to his room to drink himself into a stupor.

Before Magruder rose in the mornings, Ben hobbled into one of the dark tack rooms. Sitting down or rising up was still difficult to do alone; kneeling was impossible. Ben prayed in a prone position in the back of Magruder's farm wagon. Here, amidst the smell of the leather and wood and mule sweat, he would begin to clear his mind. It was here that he came to the certainty that Belle was near and it was here that he saw his lovely Lettie struggling through the snow.

He knew that Magruder would be no help. The man had polished off a full bottle of whiskey the night before and couldn't be roused until midday. With agonizing slowness he made his way to the door to whistle for Trilby. He was shocked to see the blizzard-like snow falling. He couldn't mount a horse. While the farm wagon was heavy for Lettie's little mare and the harness too big, they would have to do.

Ben led the harnessed and nervous mare through the corral gate and locked it securely behind them. He hobbled to the back of the wagon and draped himself into the back. Then he pulled and crawled and scooted until he was kneeling behind the seat. He clucked the horse into a trot up the steep, slippery track and then flicked her into a run. Trilby eagerly did as she was bid. Together, the two would reach their Lettie.

A bough brushed her face; then tangled her feet. Now she *had* strayed. But not so very far yet. Ben could find her here. Spent, she sunk to her knees and pushed through wind-whipped branches into a deep, profound silence. She would rest here in this haven for a bit. Just until Ben came. She pulled the pack from her shoulders and worked it beneath a cusp of gnarled roots then turned and huddled against the broad trunk, her back wedged snugly into a wide cleft. Heady from the aromatic stillness, she closed her eyes and listened to the wind softly crooning a new verse to Ben's made-up song about how much he loved her today. And her mare came to her, nuzzling her face and nickering softly. Lettie smiled with contentment. It was sweet, blaze-faced little Trilby, pulling the cart that would carry them home.

THIRTY-NINE

Her story came slowly though her words were no more than affirmation of what was apparent. She was afraid to speak of the Evil so spoke first of other things. A victim of rape would be forced out of the community where Mama and Gran'mama lived—cut from the social circle because they were no longer fit for wifedom no matter the evil of the perpetrator nor the virtue of the woman; no matter the unworthiness of the future husband, even.

But she had been married to the man—had papers to prove it though those papers were now buried beneath the boulder against which he had slammed her head so many times.

The older woman kept trying to spoon broth into her mouth and, although she hadn't eaten for how many days, Belle swallowed only to keep from dribbling. The three men in the room listened, their faces cold and hard. They averted their eyes from the tiny shape that trembled beneath the patchwork quilt.

An Indian woman, not much older than Lettie would have been, tumbled into the alcove bringing the scent of the outdoors. She strode across the room as if she'd been invited and placed a deerhide pouch on the floor beside the bed then turned and went back through the main room and out the door. She returned immediately with a bucket of fresh water.

Belle saw her dash the water into a metal pan that had been hanging beside the stove then slide the pan atop the fire. She moved to the corner of the room and, like the men, listened in stony silence to Belle's words.

She was only a shadow, still and silent, but something about her was familiar though Belle could not have said what it was. Her presence eased the anguish of the younger woman and Belle spoke more clearly now. While she had once been telling the men how she came to be in this state, she now felt as if she was telling more important things to this strangely assertive woman.

She had been handed down from the freight wagon at Lost Tree Spring and taken into the lair of the beast. He had immediately stripped her of her clothing and raped her. While she lay crying on the filthy mound of animal hides he called his bed, he had gone out and burned her clothes; even her satchel. Then the brutality began all over again.

Now the Native woman moved from her dark corner. "You have heard enough. You have seen her wounds. You know what he has done to her. That man killed my mother and the sister of my mother. He killed the couple who befriended my brother. He will hunt down this girl and kill her, too. You know he will. The tree cannot save her again. She is not safe here or anywhere while he lives. Go! Do what you will about him—nothing at all if you are afraid—but let me and your woman help the girl now."

"What *tree* saved her?" demanded one of the men.

"You know about the tree?" the puzzled Belle whispered. "Dora?"

"Go now," said the woman. "You will learn nothing more from her today."

The men—John Bragg, Merle Magruder, and Levi the Dutchman—took heavy coats from pegs beside the door and filed from the cabin.

Caroline Bragg helped Dora nurse the frightened Belle who slipped in and out of consciousness. They cleansed and salved her torn flesh, poulticed her bruises, and bathed her battered body with an attar of healing herbs.

Dora took a tiny tube from her bag and pondered the contents. The tube was made from the cleansed intestine of a ritually blessed, slaughtered, and then eaten, bird. Knotted tightly at each end, it was filled with a forest-green paste. In deep thought she returned the small object, unopened, to her bag.

Caroline Bragg watched from across the bed. Dora saw her watching and slowly shook her head. "She is too weak. It is strong poison. It sickens healthy women. This woman it will surely kill."

"But what if she is with child? *His* child?"

"In our culture she would be accepted as any other mother. In yours, I believe, she would be banished? Shunned? I cannot say. I do not know. Perhaps she is so weak his energy will not live inside her."

"Maybe. Now with Ben gone, Lettie could use some help out on her place. If this woman...if the child lives...where else could she go? Back to her family?" Caroline's words faded, her thoughts deepened and she stirred absently at the soup in the shallow bowl.

"Lettie will not be back," asserted Dora quietly.

304

"But...how do you know that?" asked the startled farmwife. "She's been missing only these few days and Ben dead but three."

"My dream," said Dora.

Belle's hand shot from beneath the cover and she clutched Dora's arm. "*I* saw Lettie. She was with me in the tree. We talked! She told me to stay there...to be safe."

"I know," shushed Dora. "Sleep. You must build your strength."

Caroline Bragg rose. "I'll go reheat this broth. Poor child is delirious. How would this little stranger—a mail-order bride from who knows where—know who our *Lettie* is?" Her worn cotton skirts barely whispered as she moved across the cabin floor to the new cooking stove in the far corner.

"*How*" *indeed,* thought Dora. Did *none* of these people see the resemblance despite the bruising and swelling of the once-beautiful face? She herself thought the sisters looked remarkably alike. But Belle was choosing to keep that relationship a secret for now. Was it shame, embarrassment? She didn't know; certainly wouldn't say. Then she chuckled; a low, throaty sound heard by the woman across the room.

Caroline turned to face her with one eyebrow raised in question.

Dora smiled at her. "In your culture this girl is my...I've forgotten how to say it...my stepping mother?"

"Oh my."

The three men rode in silence, each deep in thought. Merle Magruder knew who Belle was. It was he who signed the paper proffered by Owen Stark that would serve to draw the sister to this place. How could he know the man's only intention was to use the woman to destroy his own son? How could he have guessed the man was so vile? Unlike the Braggs who lived next farm to Black Bear, he hadn't believed the stories Ben and Dora had told the Charltons. He didn't believe that Stark was their father; that he had poisoned their mother and her unborn child; that he had sold Dora to the Indian hunters and Ben to the slavers. He had always believed it was all hogwash cooked up by the two to justify their living with, and living like, the Indians. In his mind, it took a lot to justify that.

He had meant well. He had hoped that a wife would mellow the angry neighbor. Instead, his obstinacy had helped desecrate a once-lovely young woman. Now it was up to him to make amends. He would do his best.

The shot startled him from his reverie. At first he thought it was a pine branch breaking in the cold. Then Levi pitched from his mount and the horse bolted. Bragg had dismounted, rifle in hand, and was seeking cover by the time the reality of the situation occurred to Magruder.

He dove behind a large deadfall and wondered why he wasn't dead. There had been time to fire another shot. Maybe Stark hadn't wanted to kill him. Did he think Magruder a friend? A tool, more like. Men like Stark didn't make friends. As if in answer his question a second slug tore into the dead tree just inches from his head. Stark was simply taking the time to aim very carefully.

Without rising above his cover he turned his head and found Bragg—not far away but behind a much smaller tree. He would be an easier mark than was Magruder. Magruder, hoping to give Bragg time to find a better cover, rose and fired a single shot then ducked again behind the log. As did Stark's second shot, his third came not quickly but with a frightening degree of accuracy.

Magruder again looked for Bragg but the man had done as Magruder had hoped he would do and was no longer in sight. It never occurred to Magruder that the man might run for home...or somewhere out of range of the deadly accurate big-bore rifle.

Magruder hugged the ground and slithered towards the butt-end of the tree. He knew his shots would have to come closer together. All this time he was spending moving around, Stark was taking aim on his hiding place. He sprang up, fired, and dropped again to the ground then rolled back to his original spot and, repeating the process, fired at the same time a slug tore into the tree where he had just been hiding.

This time though, Stark's shot was followed immediately by a lighter crack; then all was still. He waited, wondering, until Bragg's buffalo gun boomed through the woods. He reversed directions and returned to the butt-end of the log and was sighting his rifle in the direction of Stark's rustic shelter when Bragg called to him. He rose slowly, cautiously, and moved towards the hovel. Bragg stood over the body of Owen Stark.

Despite the frigid temperature, both men were sweating. They stood, staring at the corpse, panting with the realization that they, too, had come so very near to meeting death. Magruder crossed himself and breathed a prayer and somewhere in the back of his mind wondered about that gesture. He wasn't a Catholic but the moment needed a punctuation mark. That gesture seemed to be it.

Bragg grunted and picked up a large rock, heaved it at the side of the A-frame. It bounced off the shabby wall and rolled to his feet. This time he aimed his rifle at the wall, nodded to Magruder to cover his ears, then blew a hole through the wall. Grabbing a chunk of wood timber, he began to pull the wall to the ground. The men worked with a feverishness that was cathartic after the nightmare through which they had just wandered. They grunted and pulled and heaved and muscled the piddling shelter to the ground, tossing the dry timbers onto the body of Owen Stark.

At some point in the destruction, Bragg had gone back to where their comrade had fallen. After ascertaining that Levi was beyond human help, he whistled to the three horses and brought them to the cabin. Magruder was using his booted toe to sift through the meager belongings that had lain beneath the roof.

Bragg kicked disdainfully at the bloody chain affixed to a burned support pole. He sighed at the bloodstains on a large flat boulder partially buried in the floor. He glared at the unemptied thunder-mug that had rested in one corner. "What kind of animal doesn't even provide an outhouse?" he wondered.

Without words, the men searched the pocket of the dead man. Only an oft-folded piece of paper was within. Some of the names on the paper were crossed through, others were barely legible but Bragg was able to read the names of both Ben and Kani'tsa. The men brought pine boughs and dried needles and dumped armload after armload on the dead man. They used their horses to drag dead logs from the piney woods and heaved them atop the growing mound.

When they deemed the pyre large enough they scanned the horizon, the forest, the creek channel. Certain there were no witnesses, they used the paper to carry a flame from the man's small warming fire to the pine needles beneath the wood.

As they watched the blaze, Magruder again crossed himself.

"Second time ye done that, Merle," drawled his friend.

"I know. It just seems like we should say something. I don't feel like anyone was anymore all bad than the rest of us is all good. But I don't want to be prayin' for God to have mercy on his soul if he don't deserve mercy. So maybe I'm just prayin' God will have mercy on *our* souls."

"Well," said Bragg thoughtfully, "let's just pray that his soul gets exactly what it deserves."

FORTY

"*How* came you to be here?"

Belle smiled from her pillow. "I was just fixing to ask you the same question. Tell first, if you will, please. I am beyond tired."

Dora smiled. "It is the healing tea. It works better when one rests much.

"I knew your sister sent for you and you did not come. She worried for you. When your sister leaves the mine she does so by a trail that has long been sacred to our people. That trail has been blessed many times by our holy men so we feel her spirit when it is there. When she walks on that trail, her spirit soars because she is happy to be coming home, but this time her spirit was afraid. It came to me. It also visited my brother. I tried to call to him, to ask him to be patient, to wait for me. I rode at Striking Horse's back to come here more soon. Several times he must grip me because I am seeing Lettie and Ben and you and I cannot think to hang on to him. I saw Lettie's spirit go, but I have not seen my brother's spirit leave for his starwalk. My husband put me down at this door then he rode away to...how do you say it...errand. Perhaps he will find the spirit of my brother, perhaps...another. He will come here soon to bring me to our home and I will know. Now you must tell me of your...events."

"Mama would be so sad. She wanted me to marry a rich man who lived in Charleston but I could only think that I wanted to marry Lumpkin Charlton. I had seen an advertisement calling for a woman from Charleston. It said the beauty and charm of Charleston women was world renown and this man was willing to pay fare and passage to marry one. I and my friends had laughed at it many times even though we knew several women who had lost husbands and fathers and brothers in the war and were anxious to marry someone who could feed them. When the letter came from Lettie asking that I come here, I remembered that advertisement and I wrote to the man."

"What of your hope to marry Lumpkin Charlton?"

"How could I ever be happy if I were so selfish as to let a childhood crush prevent my helping my sister and her beloved? Of course, I let go my dream of marriage to Master Charlton. I could do no less.

"Only when I received the papers and the tickets at the train station did I learn the man wanting a bride was Owen Stark. I rode in dread all the way here. I hoped maybe, at the very least, I could find Mama's treasure for her. That could make the misery worthwhile. All the way, I prayed that Lettie would be at Black Bear to counsel me, but she was not.

"I spent one night there and kept my face hidden under my veil. Only Mister Magruder knew who I was. I begged him to help me get out of the contract but he said it was impossible—the contract was legal and binding. He kept me hidden the first day. It was on the second day that I was put on the wagon to go to my...husband.

"I went...to the place that used to be our home, Lettie's and mine. The rest is a blur. I had expected misery. I got Hell. He tied me to the wall posts and beat me unmercifully. Nothing in my entire life had prepared me for that. He nailed the gate shut from the outside when he crawled out to go somewhere then nailed it shut from the inside when he was inside. One morning he left without realizing the fire wasn't quite out. I managed to scrape one of the embers to the support where I was tied...."

"With your bare foot?" Caroline Bragg had come in from doing her chores and now, pale and trembling, pressed her back against the door, a hand to her mouth.

"Yes," nodded Belle. "My bare foot. I nursed that ember, blew on it, scraped pine needles on it, all things I'd seen Lettie do to our morning fires when we were little—I used to watch from the loft when she thought I was asleep. I knew he would surely beat me until I died if he found that ember and I so worried it wouldn't catch before he came back. But it did. It burned quite some time though before it burned deep enough into the wood that I could pull my ropes through."

"Oh, you poor child. How did you keep the heat from your hands and arms?"

"She didn't," said Dora, turning one of Belle's wrists so the woman could see the burns.

"I wanted to scream from the pain," whispered Belle, "but I just kept thinking of Lettie. Then, just at the moment the post gave way, I heard the horse returning. I couldn't get out so I grabbed a piece of wood. When...he put his head through the gate, I brought the wood down. I hit him three or four or more times then I dragged him inside and I crawled out and ran. I'd gone but a little piece when I heard his horse behind me.

"It was snowing and I had no clothes. I knew my feet were leaving a bloody trail. There was a tree in front of me and I thought to climb it. I ducked inside and it was warm and quiet. That's when Lettie came to me and told me to stay there. So I did. After awhile, the man rode away and I fell asleep.

"When I woke, it was night but the moon was out. Sometime in my daze I'd heard the freight wagons go up to the mines. I'd always listened hard for them when I was chained up and I knew they'd back in two or three days. Trouble of it was I didn't know night from day so didn't know how long I would have to wait. Somehow I remembered the way past our farm to Black Bear, so I left the tree and started running. There was no one about when I sneaked into the mule barn. I found some clothing, Magruder's I guess, and put them on then I ate some of the groats I found in a barrel.

"I slept until I heard horses approaching. I hid between the mules and that's where Magruder found me. He was with two other men. One was a miner who was looking for Lettie. The other was a man from Winthrop. I don't know who he was or why he was there.

"I tried to tell them what had happened. Magruder wouldn't let me tell. He said I would be an outcast in the town. People would call me a whore. He had the town-man and the miner sign a paper that said Magruder was the man I came out west to marry. That way, I would be saved from the shame. The miner and Magruder brought me here and the town-man went to warn the Charlton's that Stark was on the loose again. That moment was about the nadir of my whole life. I thought about Lumpkin Charlton and I wanted to die for sadness. I wish I could have told him all."

Dora was afraid to touch her patient. Every part of the woman had been beaten, battered, or burned. But she wanted to take her in her arms and comfort her—not just for the past but for the future. The girl would need a strong shoulder to cry on when she found that Magruder had withheld the knowledge that Ben was also sleeping at Black Bear the night that Belle spent under his roof.

FORTY-ONE

Jill carried her coffee mug across the room and stood before the huge fireplace. She remembered when she'd first entered the room and been so impressed by the massive stone hearth, and when she had married Lane eighteen months later right here on this spot. "I feel like we should all be sitting in the kitchen in the dark eating lasagna."

"You had lasagna on Thursday. What was wrong with my fried up chicken?" asked Frank.

Eight voices shouted, "Nothing!"

Jill looked around the room at her friends and family passing compliments to the cook. Her crew had been welcomed as family and the three were relaxing with their coffee and their hosts. After they had finished, if they ever finished, they would pile into the 'Burb with cameras and walking sticks and set out to explore Lost Tree Spring, variously called Rattlesnake Spring, Millie's place, or the hermit's hut.

Her father-in-law, Porter Bragg and his new wife Myrtlemay had driven up from Porter's hunting cabin—his Palace in the Pines, Myrtlemay called it. They had declined Jill's offer to ride up to the Spring, opting instead to stay and play with Tilson, Frank and Jennifer's year-old son.

Jennifer hurried in, bringing an enormous picnic basket. "Frank's going along. You know how he loves watching the sunrise from Slate Peak. Take two cars so he can come home instead of going to the Spring or he'd do that, too.

"Here's the leftover chicken and a few odds and ends. Dinner'll be at six, as usual, but it'll be something that will keep if you're late so don't rush.

"Oh, and I put a basket of late roses in the 'Burb. Leave them for those on the hill, if you will, please. I haven't been up there since May."

Jill slowed the Suburban across the swale that cut the dusty track leading to her mother's new project. She joked that it was an inverted speed bump but the road—rocky, rutted, and dusty—made speed bumps superfluous. The road climbed steeply from the Charlton ranch then dropped into this small drainage before climbing again to eventually level off at the old homestead her mother, Julia, had inherited.

"I think I could do with a map and a family tree," complained Tracker. "Tell me again where we are, where we're going, and just exactly why."

"Backwards or forwards?"

"Lane told us some of the more recent stuff when he was out there at the Leighton place. How is that related to this?"

"From the journals we've found, we think the story goes something like this. We're nearly there, though. Sure you don't want to wait till we see what's here?"

"AARRGHHHHH! Lane said you'd do this!"

"I'm not trying to be contrary! It's a long story and I want you to hear it all at once."

"We worked here earlier and we found nothing *but* bumpy roads so I know the place is at least fifteen minutes away. Tell fifteen minutes of the story! Please! Or we'll mutiny and put you out to walk."

"It's been walked many times by people much better than I, but okay already!

"Dominic LeGrau and Gabriela Eadrich married in Charleston, South Carolina and moved here as missionaries to the Native Americns. Lettie was born in San Francisco on the way here, Belle was born here a few years later. Lettie married a guy whose name was Ben Smith or Ben Adam, or something entirely different—we're confused about that. His mother was Native, his father, a Frenchman named Owen Stark so why wasn't he Ben Stark? Her parents were so annoyed that Lettie married a Native they took their other daughter and moved back east.

"Ben and Lettie lived on the homestead Mom is reconstructing. Ben was injured in a farming accident so Lettie went to work as a baker at the gold mines at Slate Creek, now called Chancellor, to support the two of them. She was hiking home after working one summer and was caught in an early blizzard. Ben braved that blizzard to try to find her but died when his cart and horse failed to negotiate one of those switchbacks we were on yesterday. They'd had no children.

"Shortly—we don't know how shortly or longly—before Ben died, Belle came out to help her sister care for him. And here's where the stories get mixed up. Legend in the valley has it that she married Merle Magruder. At about that same time, Owen Stark left the county but on his way past the depot he just happened to give or sell his deed to Lost Tree Spring, sometimes called Rattlesnake Spring, to Magruder. However," Jill paused, as much for effect as to hold her breath while she crossed a particularly rough patch in the road. "However, records and journals found at the depot indicate Belle, as a mail-order bride, married Owen Stark—Ben's father—first. I'd lean towards believing the journals, of course, but what if they were both right?"

"Wait! Stop! What does that mean?"

"Was Belle a bigamist? A widow? Like a lot of other things, we're still checking. Anyway, Belle married Merle Magruder, that's in the county records, but there is no record of a divorce from Stark that we can find.

She and Magruder had one child—Millie. My mother is descended from her. So, through Belle being the closest relative to Lettie, Mom inherited the homestead, and through Belle being the wife of Magruder, she was in line to inherit the depot...and the Spring if Stark did, indeed give the deed to Magruder. Either way, Belle was coerced into selling all. The woman whose family did the coercing left them to me out of remorse for her family's actions.

"We're basing this on journals and letters of Lettie, Belle and her daughter Millie, and Millie's Aunt Dora. We hope there are more journals, especially Lettie's. The ones we found were late ones, written at the gold mines. We think she'd have left most of her journals at home somewhere when she went off to cook. I'm hoping that's what Mom is so excited about, but they'd have been left over a hundred and fifty years ago so that's a big big hope."

"You never said anything about an *Aunt Dora* before!"

"Oh. The Indians named her Kanit'sa. She was Ben's sister. We're here. She can wait."

Her mother stood in front of the pile of weathered planks that had once been a barn. She squinted into the headlights. Jill put the rig in neutral and turned off the engine, coasting to a stop near the front of the rubble that had been a cabin.

She jumped to the ground. "I didn't mean to blind you with the headlights. I can't turn them off. They come on when the key turns on. It's a bother under these circumstances.

"Is Crystal still asleep? Shouldn't have slammed the door. It takes so long to get here I forget it's still early."

"Crystal is right here, dragging out shovels and spades. Your mother said you'd be here hours ago so I made lots of coffee. But now we've drunk it. All. Even Andy was here before you lot. I'm surprised you didn't pass him on his way to work."

"Good Sunday morning, Crystal. Morning, Mom." Jill gave her mother quick hug and a peck on the cheek. "We did pass Andy. He said you were rearing to go. Good grief! It's an hour before full-on daylight. How are we supposed to see to work?"

"Come into the trailer all of you. It'll be cramped but we can talk while fresh coffee brews." Julie herded her daughter and the other three archaeologists into the travel trailer she was sharing with her friend while they dismantled what was left of the old buildings.

"I was a bit disappointed when you didn't show up early Saturday morning but I understand your needing a day off now and then. We were poking around the creek Saturday afternoon and think we might have found something else of interest."

"Maybe we should draw straws to see who gets to be the first to reveal her surprise," Bill drawled from the makeshift couch.

"You have a surprise, too?"

Jill nodded. "We were giving the grand tour on Saturday and rode up to the Spring. Maybe it was the combined spirit of four archaeologists focusing on one spot that led us to it but we found what might have been a dam just up the creek from Great Grandma Millie's place. Wouldn't have made a deep lake but maybe enough of a pond to keep someone in water all summer. Do you remember Grandad saying anything about there being a dam there when he was growing up?"

Her mother thought a moment then shook her head. "He didn't talk much about those early years. About any years, really."

"No, Aunt Tiersie, neither.

"Anyway, we kept walking and found a big pit up in one of the rockslides—deep enough you could stand in it and not be seen by someone down at the shack. A good hiding place but for what we don't know. Gem found some wild squash plants growing in it. Must have been carried there by a bird or something.

"But that's enough about us. What have you two been getting into?"

"Cold water. It's probably a good thing you didn't come out yesterday. You'd have found us down at the creek just sitting on a rock."

"Sounds peaceful."

"It was, after the bear ate all of our chokecherries and moved on. But, while we were sitting there trying to look like a still-life we noticed one rock in particular looked like it had been specially chipped just to fit between several larger ones. After the bear left, and he really shredded that tree by the way, we pulled out the carved stone. We were right. It fit the opening like a cork. Inside was an icey cave. The creek ran through a little chamber and the water so cold it made a perfect cooler. I'm sure it would go a long way towards preserving supplies."

"Bear?" asked Jill.

"Crystal thought someone sent it to force us to just sit and look around. I'd believe it if it hadn't been such an impudent rascal. Waited till we'd picked a bucket full of fruit then just strolled up and started eating right out of the pail. We'd left it under the tree and gone over to sit on a warm rock and put our feet in the creek. When she'd eaten our berries she climbed up into the poor tree and broke it to smithereens. When she had her fill she dropped down, waddled about ten feet away and did that proverbial bear thing right there in front of us as if that was commentary!"

Jill, laughing at her mother's story, went over and hugged her. "And you without a camera or a cell phone. I'm glad you weren't carrying the bucket when she decided she wanted it. I'm also glad you didn't find a rattlesnake resting somewhere around that warm rock this late in the summer. The tree, I'm not so glad about but it'll grow back.

"Was there anything in the cooler?"

"No, Jill. It's been over a hundred years since someone lived here."

"I know, but I'm always hopeful. Wait a minute. If you found the cooler after you'd phoned Lane, what did you find that made you phone him in the first place?"

"I think it's a barrel, buried out on the opposite side of the barn from where you dug before. And it's full of stuff.

Jill and her crew studied the beginnings of a fresh pit dug beside the barn. Julia had scraped away the top layer of soil and exposed the tightly sealed barrel buried there. After freeing the lid and realizing she'd uncovered a cache of something or another, she'd carefully replaced the lid and phoned her son-in-law.

"We wanted to see how deep those uprights were buried but didn't want to dig right up next to them. We didn't want to scar them with our spades. So we picked the middle one, stepped out three paces, and started digging."

"Why?" Jill asked her mother. "I mean, why go out three paces? I'd think you could have dug to China and not known how far down that post went."

Julia looked puzzled for a moment. "I don't know. It seems silly now, but it made perfect sense at the time."

Jill laughed. "It's a good thing we don't have to justify every little decision we make, eh?"

"Or analyze it over much," agreed Julia. "Sometimes it's better to simply accept that there's a bit of mystery involved in most everything."

"Yep," threw in Tracker. "When I was a kid we always said, *The Devil made me do it.*"

"Tracker, how 'bout if you and Bill start setting out a square. I think two-meters this time, don't you? Gem, will you set up the mapping equipment? I'll get the paperwork started. I think we can safely use the same site number we used earlier. Mom, you and Crystal can help unload the gear unless you had other plans for your week."

Centimeter-by-centimeter the crew scraped away the layers of soil from around the wooden barrel. Each pail of dirt was filtered through a screen for anything

324

that may have been buried outside of the oaken cask. While some sides of the pit clearly showed where the original hole had been dug then back-filled around the container, the crew found nothing of interest around the barrel to record.

On the fourth day, a group that included Jill's crew, her mother and Crystal, her husband and his friend Andy, stood around the two-square-meter pit in the center of which rested the pitch-sealed barrel. The iron bands, rusted after so many years in the soil, were still intact; the wooden staves still snugly aligned.

"It was beyond the drip line of the roof," observed Lane to Andy. "Rain and snow-melt would have drained away from it so it might have stayed relatively dry. It appears to have been well coated with pitch, too, so the contents will probably be intact. I just hope we've not grown as old as that barrel before Jill decides to open it."

"I'm afraid to," said Jill, ignoring his teasing. "I want it to hold so much but I'm afraid there will be so little," she smiled.

"How little will be *too* little? Even a scrap would be something, and Julia has already said it's full."

Jill nodded and sighed then stepped into the pit near the barrel. She snapped a photo of the wooden lid, carefully lifted it off the barrel and passed it to Gem, then took a photo of the top layer of the contents.

"That's why Porter didn't come out this morning," Lane muttered. "She moves one thing than takes another picture. He couldn't stand the suspense."

"And he knows why I do it," Jill threw over her shoulder. "My notes might become fuzzy and my memory grow faulty. The photos help with both." She passed the camera to her mother then gently lifted the first item out of the cask.

The dried and curled scrap of leather was no longer than Jill's splayed fingers, thumb tip to pinkie. Jill would have simply passed it to one of her crew to be cataloged and wrapped for transport to her lab had not a tiny attachment caught her eye. She fondled it lovingly then tearfully looked up at her husband.

"Oh, Lane," she whispered. "It's one of Lettie's blue beads."

Lane stepped into the pit and wrapped her in his arms while she laughed and cried and marveled at their find.

"You knew she was here, you big softie."

"I was as certain as I could possibly be. I just didn't realize how the proof would effect me."

With that, she resumed her work, lifting out items, passing them to her crew, and taking photo after photo. As she was lifting out a patchwork quilt she'd heard the clink of glass-on-glass and carefully removed four gallon-size jars. The tops had been sealed with candle wax and the soft-sided books inside looked as if they'd been put there yesterday.

"We'll leave them sealed and wrap them in black plastic until we can get them to a lab that has facilities for preserving paper. We were scolded severely for reading the books we found at The Station before turning them in for preservation. We might have ruined them.

"I'd say there's not much we can do for this quilt, though. We can but try."

In the bottom of the barrel were the roots—carrots perhaps, and gnarly potatoes—surrounding a coffee can. Inside the can a roll of letters curled snuggly inside.

FORTY-TWO

Jill and Lane sat at the cozy kitchen table across from Julia and Crystal. Pierce Charleton brought in a pitcher of tea and his wife followed with a tray of tall glasses filled with ice cubes.

"Great grandpa Lumpkin would have enjoyed this day. He was the one who went up to Eden and packed up anything that wasn't nailed down—and some that was, truth be told. Went soon's he heard about Ben dying. Knew Lettie wouldn't be back. He was full of hope that he and Belle would live there one day and he didn't want some stranger wandering through fingering things. It's been stored in the granary ever since. Each generation has talked of moving it out and tearing down that building but no one wants to be the one to do it. We've all said it would be a shame to let the thing cave in on these few crates but still, we haven't the heart. Maybe the youngsters will do it. For us old folks it's still something of a shrine to those two who lived there.

"You take these crates home. There's not but three. I don't know what's in 'em and I'm not curious. The stuff means naught to me."

Jill wasn't quite sure she believed him. "We found some letters in a can buried out by the barn.

They're at the U-Dub being preserved but we have legible copies. Your great-grandfather Lumpkin and his father were mentioned several times."

"Oh, sure. Pappy loved those two like his own. Always said they both got raw deals from their real families. That's why they set so well together. Course, all I have is legend. Seems after that Belle woman came back she stayed over that side of the valley. Dumped poor Grandpa Lumpkin for that depot man.

"He never bore no grudge, though. Always said it wasn't her fault. Grandma Bessie never grumbled about the way it happened, either—said it was the only way she could have married Lumpkin. She knew she was second choice but she was content with that. And Lumpkin was always careful to treat her as if he'd wanted her from the beginning so they had a good long life together."

"What of Owen Stark?" asked Lane.

"Now, that's more of *your* family's legends. My family weren't none of 'em in on that but the way we've always heard it, three men—one of them your great-grandpa or more, plus a miner, and that depot man, Magruder—go after him and he kills the miner so the story goes. He's trying to do the same tother two and they's all afiring back and forth, but when they's a break in the firing the two of 'em belly-crawl up to his hidey-hole and find him dead. They cremate him then and there just to make sure he's dead. They gave out that Stark left the valley after selling his place to MaGruder so no one asked too many questions about his disappearin—glad to see him gone. Your grandpa Bragg doesn't tell what really happened till after Magruder dies.

"Trouble of it is, he swore neither of them killed Stark—swore the hole in the guy's head was no bigger than a pencil hole and they's both packing buffalo rifles. That'd be a good one for one of those tee-vee shows they call *Cold-Cases*, but I expect we'll never know for sure. Even after folks found out he was killed and hadn't just run off, no one was ever tried for his murder. Guess that's 'cause if you're powerful enough it's called an assassination, if you're bad enough it's called an execution. And no question about it—that one was a real pirate."

Jill smiled. "I wonder how old a case has to be before it moves from Cold Case to Legend.

"Can you tell us more of Belle?"

"Nope. Like I said, I don't believe she ever set foot in Eden. She stayed over tother side of the valley. Sure ran that town a pistol, though. Made Magruder into something better that he ever deserved to be but when he died she folded. Let those uppity Normans drive her out. Couldn't figure that."

"Maybe your Lumpkin was right," said Julia softly. Maybe she never wanted to be there in the first place."

FORTY-THREE

"It's a good thing winter's coming," chuckled Lane's father, Porter. Sheets of paper were stacked neatly on the table before him. A similar stack, though much thicker, rested before Jill. Porter's stack was an itemized list of the things Jill had sent to Professor Martin's archaeology lab. Jill's list had come in today's post and contained that same list with the addition of Martin's recommendations for the preservation technique and the conservation and storage of each item.

"You'll have all kinds of indoor time to sort through that stuff—especially if every item has to be preserved just so. Is this just the things from the barrel at Julia's place or have you included the things from Ben's boxes as well?"

"This list is only the things from the Charlton's granary, including the handwritten list Lumpkin compiled. The barrel contents were itemized and taken back to the lab with the crew," answered Jill absently.

"It says here, *Ben's Journals from undr matress – 5 count.* You really think that guy lay there in that cabin and wrote in his books all day then hid them in his bed? Why? Was he a prisoner? Was she a shrew so he didn't want her to know what he thought? I just don't buy that."

"We don't know yet, Porter. Maybe writing was cathartic; maybe just a way to pass the time. What was he going to do besides read? Certainly wouldn't be watching television. And I don't want to believe she was a nag. She worked out of doors all day. Maybe he thought she wouldn't be interested in what he had to say. From the brief peeks I sneaked I'd say he wrote a lot about religion and spirituality—the Indians theories compared to the Catholics philosophy compared to Lettie's Presbyterianism. There were sketches of farm machinery and cooking stoves. New things he wanted to build? I don't know. I flipped open one book to a page where he was talking about a treasure. I'm not sure if that was real treasure of some kind or reference again to the human spirit. Time will tell—I hope."

"What I hope is that these things and the ones we found in the barrel will tie into Belle's things that we found under the floor at The Station. And what about the Leighton place? If this was the sum total of his earthly possessions, why did he take you to that site? How long will this take anyway? When do you think you'll be finished?"

"Never," she answered softly. "There's no *finished* in archaeology. Each new answer brings up new questions; a new place to search. We can't go physically to the area in the time frame we're studying so there'll be a lot of unanswered questions."

"Even if we could go back to the same time and the same place you wouldn't have all the answers." Lane had come into the room carrying three mugs of hot coffee. He slid into a chair and continued.

"When I go to someone's home I see the pictures on the wall but I couldn't say why that one is there, this one is hanging here. Just as I couldn't say, Porter, why the best view you have of Liberty Bell Peak is from your chicken house though archaeologists might ask that in a couple of hundred years."

"No, don't tell us," Jill laughed, holding up her hand. "Some questions shouldn't have answers.

"Except for this little strap with one of Lettie's blue beads. It's really puzzling me. That burned pattern seems familiar and I'd like to do a little more research before I send it in. It looks like the bead was added later. That one ribbon is much shorter than the others by just the amount the knot would use, I think. But I can't get that sketch out of my mind."

"It's a flower."

"Don't start with me."

Lane laughed and repeated himself. "It's – a – flower. I'm sure of it. Look."

He took the small strip of leather that had been oiled and pressed out straight. The strip itself was only about three inches wide and roughly twice that long. From each corner hung a pair of narrow leather ties. He placed the strip on the metal lab table and turned the magnifier onto it. On a paper beside the strip he began to pencil a diagram.

"Will you bring me that clipboard I marked up down at the Leighton's place?"

Jill brought the clipboard and looked over his shoulder as he placed the clipboard beside the paper.

"Lookey here," he whispered in awe. "It's the same flower."

EPILOGUE

Belle saddled the big gelding and muttered at his agitation though she knew his mood was a reflection of her own. If she were planning a simple afternoon ride she'd take the smaller, sedate black. He had the gait, and disposition, of a rocking horse.

She really had no cause to be in such turmoil. Nothing she was planning was wrong. She was doing it this way to spare the feelings of her husband, Merle and of Lumpkin's wife, Bessie. The whole town would rock with gossip if she and Lumpkin were seen greeting in anything more than a simple nod should they chance to meet on one of the boardwalks that lined the dusty main street.

She mounted the horse, throwing her leg over his back to ride astride him rather than side-saddle as she'd been made to do at Mama's in that long long ago. She kept him tightly reined and pointed him towards the upper road, towards Papa's old homestead; towards the place she called Lettie's Meadow.

Once out of sight of the sweeping complex of barns and shops, she let the horse canter until he'd burned off some of his energy. She'd not ride all the way to the spring—the place where she'd lived as a child, and where her daughter and first grandchild now lived with Sven Todd. She hadn't been there since escaping from Owen Stark and she wasn't going to let the beautiful afternoon be spoiled by sight or thought of the place.

Before she reached the spring she would turn the horse onto a path that skirted the tiny farm on the south, then turn north along the western boundary and ride into Lettie's Meadow from above. She would find the idyll she'd shared with her sister without ever having to lay eyes on the place that held such terrifying memories—memories of events few people still alive knew about and those few loath to mention them.

Beloved Dora had reason enough to forget. She'd adored Lettie, her brother's wife. She was devastated by what her father had done to Belle and it was only by her hand that Belle now lived. The Indian woman cherished Millie for the niece she had become. But for all the deep feelings she held for those three LeGrau women, she would not betray the man she loved above all others. She would never speak of the errand her husband was on the day Owen Stark was shot and killed by an unknown marksman.

It was for Belle's daughter, Millie, that all of the others remained silent. Merle Magruder wouldn't risk loosing the love of the young woman who'd known and loved him as her father. Old man Charlton knew, of course. He'd been a good friend of John Bragg who'd burned the animal's lair. But the Charltons lived across the valley and seldom traveled as far west as Black Bear. Except for one, on this one day each year.

She'd first met him in Lettie's Meadow when Millie was still in nappies. On that day she'd been overcome by an intense loneliness and hoped that being in the meadow where she'd shared so many happy hours with her sister would ease that ache. She'd thrown some food into a tote-sack, taken the toddler up front on the saddle and told Merle she'd be back in a few days. She meandered into the meadow and found Lumpkin sleeping under the very tree she and Lettie had used as a backrest just before all Hell broke loose and Papa moved them back to Ohio.

Their conversation had been shy and halting as if each was embarrassed by the need to be near her sister. Instead of camping there, she'd ridden back home that night, afraid to be alone with him—afraid of her emotions, afraid of what he might feel.

She couldn't remember who, or indeed if either, had suggested they meet again. She only knew she looked forward to their now-annual meeting with anticipation and tenderness. She bathed in the old tin tub in the kitchen then washed her long, still beautiful, blond wispy hair. She washed and ironed the riding habit Millie had designed and sewn for her. And now she rode for the meadow as soon as the breakfast clean-up was finished.

She made no secret that she was going to Lettie's Meadow. Merle had gruffly offered once to ride with her but she insisted she needed the solitude. And it was truth. Her heart needed the silence of the ride, the gentle conversation and quiet laughter shared with a dear friend, and the contemplative ride back home in the evening. While there was no reason either spouse could not have shared the afternoon with Belle and Lumpkin, neither of the two friends was willing to give up that brief period of time in which there was only the sharing of memories and the acceptance of things they would not change.

Lumpkin Charlton was a man of business; a banker who's dealings with the gold syndicates took him to all parts of the world and she loved to hear about the unfamiliar places he visited. Exotic, she'd called them and he'd laughed. He discussed newly published books and spoke of small mementos of his journeys. Those books and items would arrive, as promised, on the next freight wagon—labeled as a gift from her cousin Elizabeth in Charleston. They'd been so forgetful as to hug only once. That was after the birth of his first child, a son he'd named Nathanial for the author they most enjoyed discussing.

Belle couldn't part with the books he sent so placed them on a corner shelf in the dining room and let others borrow them, always being careful to write the name of the borrower so to be sure of its return. Most of the trinkets she saved for Millie.

She had, some time back, began ordering a few items from the *Sears & Roebuck* catalog to sell from the dining room at the lodge. When Lander closed the general store she'd bought what little merchandise he had left. She lined the walls with the goods and had little reason to restock when she finally sold the last of an item.

Once she ordered a flat-brimmed hat like the plantation owners wore back at Mama's house. The style wasn't as popular now since that awful war had ended the way it did but she was sure it would look fine on her friend. He accepted it graciously, wore it proudly, and told everyone he'd won it in a poker game. Now her gifts were more sensible—limited to the things she carried in her saddlebags. Today it was small pork pies, fresh apple cake, and cold buttermilk.

The ride home was more depressing than the ride to Lettie's Meadow had been uplifting. She let the horse set his own pace towards the groats he knew would be waiting. She herself was not so anxious to be home. These brief encounters took her away from the chores and duties, the drudgery, which was her life with the man who had stolen her from her heart's desire. They were the rays of bright sunshine that underscored her drab existence.

The best part of going home would be the hour she spent in the barn, feeding and combing the animals—listening to the work team grind their oats with their heavy molars; to the cow huff and blow as she chased the last few kernels of grain into the corners of the manger; to the nickering of the gelding and the black as if they discussed their day. Only after they'd been turned into the near corral would she go inside.

She had put a venison roast in the oven before she left. It was much smaller than the ones she'd have cooked even just a year ago. There was just the two of them now and they ate their largest meal in the morning. There were potatoes left over from breakfast. It wouldn't take long to fry them up.

She thought it would be wonderful to walk into a warm kitchen with plates on the table, food in the oven, and a smiling companion awaiting her return. It would never be so. Merle would be sitting in his chair reading one of her books or whittling on a piece of pine branch. If he put anything on the table it would be the deck of cards with which he played endless games of patience whilst he waited for her to finish her chores then cook and serve his next meal.

She knew she was partly to blame for their cold co-existence. When she'd learned how he'd tricked her into marriage she refused to live any longer as wife to him. She would never expose him for the fraud that he was but she could not forgive him. So they'd lived like strangers for seventeen years now. He still maintained that he loved her—at the rare times they spoke of personal feelings—but she questioned even that.

She knew he understood all that she represented, all that she did for him. He knew what he would have to replace if she were no longer in his life. He loved her because her beauty evoked the envy of other men; because she cooked for him, cleaned for him, built his business for him—generally made his life easier and more pleasant. But was that not just a roundabout way of loving himself?

He had reared Millie as if she was his own flesh and blood and the girl adored him. For that, Belle would always be grateful. But gratitude could not generate happiness. She wasn't even sure it was happiness that she wanted. Neither was she content with the modicum of fame and power that had been hers during the blossoming of Black Bear and its surroundings. What she wanted, she reckoned, was a sign that her life had mattered; that the world would be just a little bit better for her having passed through it.

Would joy be too much to ask for? Perhaps a bit of conversation that didn't include mules? Today she had commented to Lumpkin about the *Aurora Borealis* of the past few nights and he had shared her awe. She had lamented a growing rodent problem and he had suggested a pet housecat. Then he went on to tell her about the feral cats that roamed the catacombs in Rome. He'd talked of Persia and the cats that had been bred to protect the beautiful rugs from the ravages of rats. She gasped at his description of the flattened muzzle and short ears that kept the sharp teeth of the rats from reaching the cat's face, of the thick long fur with a wooly undercoat and a long fluffy tail that ensured the rat's bite didn't reach the cat's body. She was horrified when he told her the cats were placed inside the rolled-up rugs before those rugs were loaded onto ships. How did they live? What happened to them when they arrived in port? He'd chuckled and told her most women were more interested in the rugs.

The freight wagon thundered to the stable doors and, without waiting to help change the tired mules for fresh ones, the driver jumped from his perch, grabbed a small crate and headed in Belle's direction. Lumpkin had been very secretive about the gift he said he was sending this time and, after the conversation about the rugs, she was sure it would be an exotic rug from that place he called Persia. The crate the driver carried, however, did not in any way fit her image of the crate that would hold a rolled-up rug.

"Better open this quick. 'Tain't makin' so much noise as 'twas when we left the docks." He dropped the crate in the kitchen and slipped past her, headed for the dining room and the dinner that always waited.

Befuddled, she stared at the crate and tried to get her mind off the idea of a rug. She went to the basement, returned with the crowbar and set to work opening the crate. She dropped the rod and jumped back with an uncharacteristic shriek. Embarrassed by her reaction, she laughed as the man came back to see what the commotion was about.

"I thought it was alive! Shame on that Betty girl for sending me such a realistic toy."

The driver looked at Belle with one raised eyebrow. "Best look agin. Then git'er sumpthin to drink."

That evening, Belle sat with the gray, long-haired kitten on her lap. Not strong yet, the cat was content to languish and purr between each round of fisticuffs with the yarn ball.

"What are you going to name that coyote bait—if she lives?" growled Merle.

"Her silvery gray coat is like an aura...like those shimmery lights from the north that dance through the night sky. So, for my cousin Elizabeth, I shall name her *Aurora Betty-Alice*. And I shall call her *Joy*."

About The Author

AMANDA MORGAN thinks she *should* have an affinity with regularly scheduled commercial television broadcasts because they and she were born about the same time. "We didn't interact, though," she points out. "My family didn't have electricity until I started first grade.

"I still find that watching television is one of my least favorite pastimes. We grew up entertaining ourselves—playing outside until (and often after) dark then reading or *wrasslin'* on a quilt spread on the pine board floor in front of the big pot-belly stove.

"When we grew too rowdy, Dad would slow us down by telling us about the time Aunt Millie got hurt doing just what we were doing, or Uncle Bill lost a tooth/broke an arm/blacked his eye because he . . . . Somehow, we didn't see his stories as admonitions or life lessons because there weren't any *you shouldn't*s or *you can't*s; these were just humorous anecdotes about his own childhood.

"We didn't know we were one of the town's *poor* families, though we knew there were people there who didn't get to do chores like we did and that there were some kids in school who wouldn't play with us. We knew we didn't have *money* but that was never made to equate to *poor* in our minds. Poor people lived in far away places like Africa and we thought we might go there when we grew up so we could help them.

"One day Dad came trudging up the dirt path after a long shift at the mill and pointed to a spot on the ground. *There's a dime,* he said. For kids who didn't get a dime even from the tooth-fairy, that was HUGE. We searched, we moved rocks, we pulled weeds. None of us could see a dime lying on the dusty patch of ground where we played. He finally came out, picked up a tote-sack that we had moved and shaken and moved again. He carried it to the car while explaining that the feed store paid ten cents for the return of their grain bags. Recycling. Way back then. Who knew?

"I once told Dad that my earliest memory was of the summer we lived in the chicken house. He chuckled and explained that we didn't really live *in* the chicken house. We simply stored our furniture in the chicken house. We lived outside."

Amanda's writing reflects the parable-like stories with which she was raised. If you are looking for words of wisdom, they'll be couched with a little bit of humor in the mysteries, the triumphs, and the tears. You won't find them by searching for *can'ts* or *shoulds*, and if you happen to miss them, that's okay. This is still a charming story—a story about strong women who refuse to think themselves a victim.

About The Illustrator

LYNNE WENICK is a multi-media artist who has spent most of her life in her home state of Washington. She loves music and is a much sought-after singer, guitarist, pianist, and violinist at functions that range from church services to bluegrass festivals. Retired from the hospitality business, she spends her time tending acreage she owns near Lake Roosevelt, managing the kitchens at several Bible camps, and sewing for her grandkids.

Lynne makes her home in the charming town of Odessa. "It isn't in the middle of nowhere but in the absolute center of everything. And the Lake Roosevelt area is truly God's country," she says. "I find the awesome, colorful, and diverse state of Washington an inspiration for my painting—an inspiration to just live life."

She could use some sanctuary … Somewhere to rest …

THE LIGHTS OF HOME
$15.95
6 x 9 Paperback
ISBN: 978-I-60290-134-6

FICTION / Christian / General
Publisher: OakTara at www.oaktara.com
www.amandamorganbooks.com

Archaeologist Jill Reade lives life in the fast-lane, racing from deadline to deadline. The only slow thing in her existence is her old dog, Trilby. When she receives a startling phone call from attorney Lane Bragg, she adds his request to her *like THAT's gonna happen* list. Alice Norman, he tells her, that strange woman she met at her grandfather's funeral, has died and left Jill a Bed & Breakfast in the middle of nowhere.

It's curiosity rather than the desire to run a public house that eventually drives Jill to go look at the place. Besides family legends she's heard of the area, it's very near the same National Forest on which her next project will be sited.

What she discovers in the small mountain community will cause her to question everything she holds dear...including her own independence.

"The LIGHTS OF HOME was great. It had the elements of historical fiction and mystery that I really like and a little bit of romance which is all I want!" – Joe M.

"You are quite the story teller!" – June A.

"Your book was GREAT!" – Louise B. (84 year-old Foodbank volunteer

She could use some sanctuary ... Somewhere to rest ...

A LIGHT OFF THE
STARBOARD BOW
Due out: Summer, 2013.

When pirates sink her ship and kill her husband, Lady Emmeline, daughter of a French Baron, wife to the son of a Viscount, is left to drown. Saved by a gnarly chunk of wood from the wrecked ship, she wakes in the hospital hut of a Catholic convent on one of the Abaco Islands in the Bahamas.

She has no money and no one to provide for her and her unborn child. Neither has she the foggiest idea of how one would go about supporting oneself and one's child under these circumstances. When she tries to borrow money for passage on a ship that could take her back to her father's barony she is warned that France is now in chaos, the aristocracy destroyed. She realizes that here her title is worthless; there, it could be a serious detriment.

Emmeline, raised as a Huguenot, finds that her survival might rest on how well she can work with the Catholic sisters, the Lutheran shopkeepers, the island natives, and maybe even the pirates.

Made in the USA
Charleston, SC
16 July 2012